THE
NEIGHBORS

THE
NEIGHBORS

ANIA AHLBORN

THOMAS & MERCER

Text copyright © 2012 Ania Ahlborn

Published by Thomas & Mercer
P.O. Box 400818
Las Vegas, NV 89140

ISBN-13: 9781612184456
ISBN-10: 1612184456

To my husband and best friend, Will.
Here's to me not poisoning your food,
and to you not killing me in my sleep.
Yet.

"It's a beautiful day in this neighborhood,
A beautiful day for a neighbor,
Would you be mine? Could you be mine?"
— *Mister Rogers' Neighborhood*

CHAPTER ONE

Andrew Morrison sat at a red light in his father's beat-up Chevy. Bopping his head to an old Pearl Jam CD, he shrugged off that morning's tension, put the past behind him, cranked up the stereo, and drove. *This is it*, he told himself. *This is freedom.*

Somewhere down the line, he had convinced himself that freedom didn't exist in Creekside, Kansas—that it couldn't. Hell, nothing could survive in that corner of the world except for an endless expanse of wheat and corn. But he had been wrong. As it turned out, liberty *did* exist, and he was mere minutes from his first taste.

Mickey Fitch…Drew could hardly believe it. To think that he'd be rooming with his childhood friend, living with the guy he'd looked up to for so long—a guy who had bailed him out of tight spots as a kid. Mickey was extending his hand to Drew after all these years, and Drew was determined to show his gratitude. He didn't have much cash, but he could spare twenty bucks; buy Mick dinner and make sure his friend knew he was thankful. After all, Mick was doing Drew a solid. He was letting Andrew move in on short notice, and with only a half month's rent. That in itself assured him: despite the time that had passed between them, they were still brothers in arms, and living together was going to be a great experience—the *best* experience.

He'd dreamed of this moment for so long, it felt nearly surreal to be knee-deep in it. Magnolia Lane was still a few intersections away, but Andrew was already there.

The light turned green and Drew stepped on the accelerator, rolling his rickety pickup through the interchange. He turned up his music, sucked in air, and belted out the chorus to "Even Flow" before laughing at himself. Lifting his right hand over his head, he nodded along to the rhythm, mouthing the words, not caring who saw. He had nothing to hide. The sky was bright, the breeze was warm, and the air smelled of honeysuckle and endless promise.

His eyes lit up when he turned onto Magnolia Lane, like Dorothy getting her first glimpse of a Technicolor Oz. Ahead of him: freshly laid tarmac, black and glittering in the sunshine; trees shaped like giant, leafy lollipops, perfectly pruned, not a single leaf out of place. He slowly rolled past a white picket fence— *a white picket fence!* A tiny Pekingese stuck its face through the whitewashed slats and barked, bouncing like a cartoon character with each yappy arf. Across the street, a woman in pink capris watered her flower garden. A few houses from hers, little kids screamed in glee as they jumped through an oscillating water sprinkler. They waved as Drew rolled past them, yelling out a unified *Hi!* when he waved back.

Glancing in the rearview mirror, he hardly recognized himself. He was grinning like an idiot. His chest felt full—like the Grinch, his heart had grown three sizes, threatening to break every one of his ribs.

His gaze snagged on the carefully painted curb numbers, bright white and reflective against the concrete. He pressed the brake a little too hard. The Chevy's tires gave off a half-second shriek—gone in an instant, but enough to momentarily mortify him.

"Shit," he whispered, shooting a look at his side-view mirror. The kids had paused in their antics, staring at the pickup that had come to a dead stop in the middle of their street.

Suddenly he realized just how out of place he was. His Chevy was a relic. It belonged in a junkyard far more than it did on the road. His windows were rolled down, his rock music turned up way too loud.

He jammed the volume knob against the stereo console, the music replaced by the kids' laughter and the occasional bark of that smash-faced dog. Easing his truck along the curb, he stared at the house just outside his window. It was gorgeous, a ginger-bread house pulled straight from a fairy tale. This one had a white picket fence as well, rosebushes bursting with bright red blooms. Matching hydrangeas, heavy with blossoms, dangled from pots that hung beneath the eaves of the porch. A wind chime shivered in the breeze, small rounds of capiz shell spar-kling in the sun. A hammock stretched across the right side of the patio.

Andrew exhaled a slow breath and reached for the door handle, stopping short when his attention paused on the house next door. He had been so dazzled by the residence in front of him that he hardly noticed the one directly beside it: a dwelling that, much like his truck, simply didn't belong. It was set back from the street more than the others, ashamed of itself. But it seemed inevitable—every neighborhood had a sore thumb. It was as though all of Magnolia Lane was filmed in brilliant color, but this sad little house existed in dreary monochrome. Its gut-ters sagged in a frown. The screen door hung at an awkward angle, like a waterlogged Band-Aid trying to hang on with all its might. There was no doubt that the next storm would tear it from its hinges, sending it tumbling down the street into someone's award-winning garden.

Drew couldn't help but feel sorry for it. Being an outsider was never easy.

He pushed the driver's door open to the cool early evening air, its metallic whine cutting through the murmur of a tranquil, tree-lined suburbia. This was a world apart from the street he grew up on. Less than five miles away, Cedar Street was desolate and lonely, snatched out of one of the seven circles of hell and thrown onto the flat Kansas landscape. The trees that existed there were sparse, exposing old houses to a relentless prairie wind. The ones that had survived the storms were husks of what they had once been: stripped of their branches, left dead in the ground by tornados that had done their damnedest to wipe that street off the map.

He inhaled the scent of lilacs and honeysuckle before grabbing a box from the bed of his truck, then began his trek toward the white picket gate. Balancing the box on his knee, he fumbled with the latch, blinking when he saw a silhouette move past the front window.

That was when he noticed the house number tacked next to the door.

Drew took a step back, placed the moving box down on the sidewalk, and fished the scrap piece of paper out of his back pocket. The number 668 didn't look right, and that's what the door of the fairy-tale house declared. He nearly laughed when he realized it, his stomach turning behind the faded cotton of his Nirvana T-shirt: this wasn't Mickey Fitch's house.

Mickey's was the sad monstrosity next door.

Disappointment bloomed into blighted hope. He had been stupid to think it would have been so easy. Nobody simply walked into paradise.

Drew narrowed his eyes, plucked his box off the ground, and marched down the sidewalk toward the sulking home next door. He had spent a good portion of his summers fixing up the house on Cedar Street—it, too, was a sad sight. If he could keep that old lean-to upright, he sure as hell could resurrect this place. All it needed was the straightening of gutters and a fresh coat of paint.

Magnolia Lane was handing Drew his own private metaphor: His life was a mess, and he was here to fix it.

Reaching the house, he pressed the box between the wall and his chest, balancing it on a raised knee before reaching for the bell. Before his finger hit the button, he reeled back, staring at the fat spider that sat beside the glowing button. It sat there, illuminated from behind, as if giving Andrew a final opportunity to forget the whole thing—to turn around and walk away. Shuddering at the thing, Drew knocked instead.

There was a long, dead silence. Was Mickey even home?

Then the front door swung open, and a death mask emerged from behind a tattered screen.

Mick peered through the screen door with a squint, as though he hadn't seen daylight in years. Dark circles under his eyes implied he hadn't slept for weeks, their shadows contrasting against his white shock of blond hair. He appeared older than Drew remembered, like he was aging at twice the natural speed. Kansas did that to some. It may have been the sun or the wind, the tornado sirens in the dead of night, or the hypnotic sway of wheat fields beneath an endless sky. This place pushed people to the brink of madness, assuring them that the wide-open landscape proved that the world was flat; the horizon held nothing.

This wasn't the bright-eyed kid Andrew had run to when Drew's dad had gone missing, when his mom had drunk herself into a stupor.

Drew had been preparing a wide smile for his old friend, but it wavered as he stared.

"Hey," he said, trying to appear as enthusiastic as he had felt a few minutes before. "Dude, this neighborhood is intense."

No response: Mickey remained motionless, staring out through the frayed screen door. Drew furrowed his eyebrows. The dead look in his old friend's eyes scared him.

Had he made a mistake? He swallowed against the lump in his throat, his pulse drumming in his ears. Mickey looked like he was deciding whether to let Andrew inside or tell him to hit the road.

Drew dared to pose the question, figured it was just a matter of time before it came bursting forth: "Are you OK? You look rough, man."

More silence.

He opened his mouth to speak again, to give Mickey some reason to go through with the deal and invite him in, but Mickey finally roused from his trance.

"Hey, man," he replied in a dry monotone. "Yeah, sorry." He motioned with a swoop of his arm for Andrew to enter, pushing the screen door open to let him inside.

Drew's heart sank. The inside of the house was as unfortunate as its exterior. An obvious path had been worn in the dirty carpet from the kitchen to the couch and then to somewhere down a hall, but beyond that, the house looked unused, coated in a layer of dust. Dingy curtains flanked the windows, one of the rods hanging low, as though someone had caught themselves on the drape to break a fall. Another window was covered by a bedsheet tacked to the wall by an army of staples, hundreds of them punched into the drywall in a crooked, glittering line. The smell wasn't as bad as it should have been—stale, with an undertone of dust and sweat, but otherwise innocuous.

Drew carefully placed his box down at his feet, allowing himself to fully take in the squalor. This was worse than Cedar Street. At least there, he had kept things under relative control. He spent weekends washing windows, painting the deck with leftover paint he found in the garage, anything to keep his grandparents' pride and joy from disintegrating in the wind. But *this*...this looked like Mickey had moved in and never lifted a finger.

Mickey had made a beeline for the couch as soon as Andrew had stepped inside. He mashed the buttons of a game controller, oblivious to the fact that Andrew was standing just beyond the front door, a box at his feet, waiting to be acknowledged by a guy he used to consider a close friend.

Andrew shoved aside the pang of apprehension that seized his heart. He could hear his mother slurring her words: *You need me, you know; you can't move out. Who will take care of you?* At least here he had some freedom—at least here he could improve himself rather than try to fix someone else.

"Um, should I just put this anywhere, or…" Andrew tapped the box with his sneaker. Rubbing the back of his neck, he continued to watch his new roommate from a distance.

"Mick?"

"Sure," Mickey said. *Put it anywhere.*

Drew closed his eyes, exhaling a muted laugh. This place was a pit. A hole in the ground would have been better. He didn't want to think about what the kitchen was like, let alone the bathroom—but this was the way these things went. First houses and first roommates were supposed to suck. This was the kind of stuff that made stories good for the telling.

He stepped away from the door, marched across the house to the window, and pulled the curtain back. A ray of early evening sun cut through the gloom, dust sparkling like diamonds in the daylight. Mickey paused his game, shielding his eyes as he peered at Drew's silhouette.

"So," Drew said, "you rent this place?"

Mickey was unresponsive, despite staring right at Andrew. Drew considered asking him what his problem was, but he decided to wait it out, watching Mickey squint against the sunset as if it was the first one he'd ever seen; a vampire rousing from a thousand-year sleep. After what felt like an hour of tense, contemplative silence, he watched Mick's face lighten. His expression shifted from dejection to something that almost resembled hope. When Mickey actually *smiled*, Drew's heart leapt out of his stomach and back into his chest.

"Yes, sir," Mickey finally replied.

"That's good. So you won't be opposed to some paint."

Mickey raised an eyebrow. "Seriously?"

"Um..." Drew looked around the place. "Seriously?" he echoed.

"Shit," Mickey mumbled, "you're not one of those germaphobes, are you?"

"You're not one of those people who show up on the Discovery Channel, right?"

Mickey shook his head, completely confused. "You mean like a zoologist?"

Drew bit back a laugh and shook his head. "Where's my room?" he asked.

And just like that, Drew had a new house, a new roommate, and a hell of a lot of work to do.

§

Creekside was but a blip on the map, yet over the years somehow Drew and Mickey had managed to lose touch. The last time they had seen one another as kids turned out to be the last time a nine-year-old Andrew had ridden his bike down the block to play Mickey's new Final Fantasy game after yet another fight with his mom.

Drew could hear screaming from inside the house.

He skidded to a stop just shy of the Fitches' driveway, two ambulances and a handful of cop cars blocking his way, as a pair of EMTs wheeled a sheet-covered gurney down the front steps and onto the walkway. Mick's mother burst out of the house. She ran for them before they could load the stretcher into the back of the ambulance, her face swollen with hysterical tears. Andrew's eyes widened as a police officer dashed across the lawn after her—just like in the movies his own mother didn't know he watched—but Mick's mom was a waif of a thing; she was quick, and the cop was slowed by his roundness and the pistol that hung heavy at his hip. Drew watched

Mrs. Fitch's hands fly out in front of her, her fingers clawing the sheet covering the gurney, screaming at the ambulance workers to *get away from him, get away!* One of the EMTs tried to fend her off, but she recoiled on her own from what was underneath.

As that sheet slid away, something heavy punched Drew straight in the chest, something that toed the line between queasiness and horror: that sensation of seeing something terrible but not being able to look away. What was once a head was now little more than a wad of pulp attached to somebody's neck. It was Mickey's dad—a man Drew had said hi to a hundred thousand times.

Mrs. Fitch screamed again, reeling away, her hands pressed to her face. Her torment shot straight through him, forcing an involuntary gasp out of his mouth. With his bike frame between his scrawny legs and his sneakers planted firmly on the ground, he could manage only to turn his head away from the scene, dizzy with dismay. His heart palpitated within the cage of his chest. Mrs. Fitch's cries sent chills tumbling down his spine despite the sun baking the back of his neck.

When he dared to look back, Mickey was in the open doorway of the house. His eyes were fixed on the ambulance, on the men who slammed the back doors shut, taking his dad away forever. Drew wanted to call out to him, to run over to him and ask his friend what had happened and whether Mick was going to be OK. Their eyes met from across the yard. Mickey's blanched expression curdled Andrew's blood.

And then Mick turned away and disappeared inside.

There were rumors about Mickey and his family after that. The neighborhood kids whispered about how Mickey's dad had gone crazy. The ladies at the supermarket would gather in the produce department on Sunday afternoons, using words like *drunk* and *abusive* and *no surprise*. Andrew had wanted to get the story firsthand, but Mick wouldn't talk to him. Mickey's dad was dead, and somehow, as if by magic, their friendship had died with him.

He was surprised how much he missed his friend after Mick moved away. He'd ride his bike to the empty house nobody wanted to buy, the For Sale sign staked into the Fitches' lawn sun-bleached and weatherworn. Drew would spend summer afternoons sitting on their wilted lawn, pulling yellow blades of grass out of the ground, spinning his bicycle tire, as though each revolution was one spin closer to Mickey showing back up.

Occasionally, he'd catch himself staring up at the ceiling when he couldn't sleep, wondering whether Mickey was alive or dead. After each inevitable fight with his mother, he thought back to the day he watched Mick lose his dad, wanting to make contact again. He ignored the impulse, convinced that if Mick wanted to get back in touch, he'd do so himself.

But that didn't stop him from searching for Mickey's name on Facebook, tugging on his bottom lip as he stared at his old friend's profile photo, which was nothing but an old Metallica record cover. He had written Mick countless messages, only to hit delete instead of send, always feeling stupid at how sentimental he sounded. He didn't want Mick to get the wrong idea, didn't want him to think that Drew was some whacked-out obsessive weirdo who couldn't let the past be the past. But when Andrew reached the point where he didn't have anywhere else to turn, Mick was always the one he'd reached out to.

And Mick was always the one who had saved him.

§

Drew spent most of the night unloading boxes from the back of his truck while Mick played video games, struggling with the screen door each time, trudging down a hall dark without a working light. Some help would have been nice, but he didn't want to complain. Mick had offered him a place to crash, and that was more than enough.

His bedroom was small but sufficient. The wallpaper was a hideous floral pattern, damaged by what must have been a water leak, but if all went according to plan, it wouldn't be long before he had those walls painted over, as well as covered in posters and corkboards and whatever else he could find. His favorite part of the room was the big window that overlooked the side yard and the perfect house next door. He could imagine living there while drifting to sleep, a house that would inevitably smell of cleanliness and home cooking.

Once the truck was empty, Drew stood in the center of his room and assessed his army of boxes. He hadn't thought to bring any furniture after the blowup back home. With no mattress, he settled in for the night atop a pile of his own clothes, thinking about his mother, about how she was sitting in that big house on Cedar Street all alone.

His dad's leaving hadn't been his fault—he knew that—and that was why he resented her that much more. She made him feel guilty with how helpless she'd become, her illness twisting her into something unrecognizable, something far removed from what she used to be. It wasn't his fault—but she wanted Andrew to be responsible.

Pushing a handful of clothes beneath his head to serve as a pillow, he promised himself that he had made the right decision. This was what he had to do to get on with his life, to get out from beneath her control. But even as he drifted to sleep, the guilt hung heavy in the back of his mind, swaying back and forth like a noose without a neck.

§

The sun made the insides of Andrew's eyelids glow red. When he finally peeled his eyes open, he winced, raising a hand against the glare. As he rolled onto his side, his lower back screamed against the movement.

There was something about waking up to the cheerlessness of an empty room, the bareness of blank walls, that made him feel helpless. He pressed the heels of his hands against his eyes. As soon as he set up his space, he'd feel better about the whole thing. He needed furniture. He needed to settle in. He needed to reestablish his relationship with Mickey. His intention of taking Mick out for a bite to eat had been pushed aside; he'd be appreciative later, after Mickey helped clean the place up.

He hadn't labeled any of the boxes he'd packed. It took him twenty minutes to find his toothbrush and a half-used tube of Colgate. Pushing a pair of earbuds into his ears, he let Bob Marley assure him that every little thing was going to be all right. Singing along beneath his breath, he trudged down the hall toward the bathroom. He'd used it the evening before but had kept his eyes half-closed, partly out of exhaustion, but mostly because he didn't want to see just how bad it was. But now, with the morning's light trickling through the window above the bathtub, the filth was undeniable—so staggering that even Bob couldn't sing his way around it.

Andrew stood in the doorway for a long while, staring at a sink covered in dried toothpaste and stray albino-like hairs. The mirror was unusable, sprayed with what looked to be toothpaste-laced backwash. There was no soap. There were no towels. The linoleum, half-covered by a dirty bath mat, was crusted in hair and grime. He pulled his headphones out of his ears and swallowed against the disgust crawling up his throat. Backing away with his toothbrush pressed to his chest like a cross in the hands of a frightened Catholic, he did an about-face and marched away.

§

A few minutes past eight in the morning, Harlow Ward watched a beat-up white pickup peel away from the curb next door. She smiled, shifting her weight from one red pump to another. With the truck out of view, she turned her attention to the pristine living room behind her, smoothed the full skirt of her dress, and regarded her husband with a bright smile.

"We have a new neighbor," she announced. "I'll make cookies."

§

Other than the Walmart across town, there wasn't much in the way of big retail in Creekside, so that was where Andrew went. Staring down a seemingly endless aisle of cleaning products, he knew exactly what he was looking for. He'd been going to the store for his mom since before he could drive. Grocery shopping came naturally, and buying cleaning supplies was even easier. His philosophy: buy the cleaner that had the brightest color, the one that looked like it would instantly kill you if you threw your head back and chugged. He was naturally drawn to the purples and blues, deciding on something called Kaboom, not because of anything on the label, but because of its name. He imagined Mickey's bathroom exploding beneath a violet mushroom cloud, giving him just enough time to bolt out of the house and tuck-and-roll onto the patchy front lawn. Or maybe it would cut through soap scum like a knife cuts through butter and leave Drew pleasantly surprised, like the smiling women on TV. *It's so easy!*

After tossing a few more household cleaners into his cart, including some Scrubbing Bubbles—because his inner child couldn't pass up cartoon-endorsed cleaners—he wheeled his way to the grocery section and considered his options. Anything requiring refrigeration meant he'd have to venture into the kitchen, and he was willing to bet that it was as nasty as the bathroom. So instead of getting his usual orange juice, he got a box of Capri Suns instead; and instead of getting cereal that required milk, he settled on some unrefrigerated pudding cups. If he wanted *real* food he'd have to go out for now, which was fine by him. The dining area at Casa de Mickey needed to be excavated from beneath its scrim of dust before it could be used in relative safety.

Dropping fifty-six bucks of his three hundred at the register, he drove back to his new home to scrub the toilet. There was something fundamentally wrong with taking a dump in a can that was dirtier than the inside of your own ass.

He parked along the curb and gathered his blue Walmart bags, dreading the task that awaited him inside. He paused midstride and turned his head toward that pristine house with the white picket fence. Drew bet their toilets sparkled the way clean things sparkled in Saturday morning cartoons. He bet the inside of that house smelled like cookies and fresh-cut grass, because those were the best smells in the world. His mom used to bake chocolate-chip cookies every weekend, a whole sheet just for him. That was before his dad disappeared. After Rick left, the only cookies they had came out of a bag. Drew wasn't sure, but he doubted the oven had been used since he was nine years old.

Inside the fairy-tale house, something shifted. He saw it for only a fraction of a second, but he was sure it was there. Someone had been watching him from behind the window curtains, staring at him while he stared right back, his arms weighed down by pudding and juice. Something crawled just beneath the surface of his skin, but he turned away. He was the one standing slack-jawed in the middle of the street, probably looking like a lunatic freshly moved out of the psycho ward and into the crappiest house in town.

In the driveway, Mickey's TransAm dripped oil onto the concrete. Drew had tried to give the guy the benefit of the doubt the night before, but after getting an eyeful of the bathroom, he was feeling a lot less chipper and a lot more judgmental. Mickey had always loved video games, so the idea of him being the type of guy to sleep all day and play MMORPGs all night wouldn't have surprised him. But the more time he spent inside that house, the more Andrew pictured Mick screaming into a headset, starting cyber-fights with kids half his age, smashing beer cans against his forehead like a modern-day Cro-Magnon.

These thoughts barraged his brain while he scrubbed grime out of the corners of the tub, scoured so hard that even Joan Crawford would have been impressed. He imagined Mickey stumbling into the bathroom, heady with sleep, his white hair wild like a blizzard, a wire hanger held tight in his grasp. *You think this is clean?* Wearing canary yellow gloves that reached halfway up his arms, Drew exhaled a laugh, inhaled chemical fumes, and was overtaken by a choking fit as he continued to scrub.

CHAPTER TWO

Red Ward looked good for his age; his wife, on the other hand, looked phenomenal. They were in their late fifties, but time had treated them well. Red was a fan of golf, and occasional yard work kept him in shape. Harlow had suggested he buy one of those fancy self-propelled mowers, but Red insisted on his old-fashioned reel mower. He claimed that he liked the workout, the way the exposed blades glinted in the sun and hissed against the grass. But Harlow knew better; Red endured the Kansas sun to keep out of her way.

Harlow had a svelte hourglass figure that girls half her age would have killed for. Unlike her husband, she hated nothing more than being caught out in the heat. She wore floppy-brimmed hats and enormous round-lensed sunglasses while pruning her roses in monogrammed gardening gloves. She'd have passed for Jackie O had it not been for that head of soft curls that rivaled those of Marilyn Monroe.

Although Harlow never did like that little tart. She had been ten when JFK ate a bullet in Dallas, remembering her mother's exact words the second the news hit the airwaves: "He was playing with the devil," Bridget Beaumont declared. "It's the only reason God would take a man like that out of this world. It's the only reason God ever takes *anyone* out."

Harlow was convinced that her mother had been right: JFK had been a sinner. He had asked for it.

She let the curtain slip from her fingers before turning from the window and glancing at her husband. Red sat in an over-stuffed leather recliner, his feet wrapped in a pair of slippers despite the Kansas heat.

"I like him," she said. "That truck is an eyesore, but he seems like a nice young man."

Red looked up from his newspaper, turned the page with a rustle.

Harlow turned back to the window, pushed the curtain aside again with a manicured nail, and watched the house next door, waiting for it to speak to her. And it did. Within seconds, the front door swung open and Andrew appeared, trudging across that corpse of a lawn to the trash can beside the driveway. He flung a trash bag into the container—those sunflower yellow gloves flashing in the sun—before marching back inside. As soon as he was out of sight, Harlow tapped a nail against the curve of her bottom lip.

"I should invite him over," she said, shifting her weight from one heeled shoe to another. "He'd like a home-cooked meal."

They all liked a home-cooked meal. Because it was true what they said: the quickest way to a man's heart was through his stomach, and Andrew looked hungry.

§

It was well after four o'clock when Mickey finally set foot out of his bedroom.

Drew had spent the entire morning scrubbing the bathroom as best he could, and thanks to his wealth of supplies, it very likely hadn't been as clean as it was in years. Sorting through boxes in his room, he paused, held his breath, and listened to Mick track down the hall. A door shut, followed by the distinct sound of Mickey taking a leak. When the door opened, he prepared himself for Mick's arrival, sure that his old friend would fill the space of his bedroom door. *Holy shit,* he'd say, wide-eyed like a kid on Christmas. *You have no idea how awesome that is— how awesome* you *are. That bathroom was disgusting. A wreck. I can't believe I ever let it get so bad.* That's when Drew would offer him a ghost of a smile and lie: it was nothing, no problem, no big deal.

But Mickey didn't appear.

His heavy footfalls made a beeline for the living room instead.

When he heard the front door slam and the engine of the black TransAm roar to life, Drew scrambled around the boxes that filled his room and peered out the window. Mick peeled out onto the street, then slammed the muscle car into first and flew up the road.

"You're welcome!" Drew yelled against the glass. When the sound of his words dissipated, the silence of the house felt heavy, oppressive.

He shoved himself away from his window and veered into the hall. He wasn't sure why he did it, why he stopped in front of Mickey's door, or why his hand naturally drifted toward the knob. But curiosity got the best of him. He wanted to piece together just what kind of a person Mickey had become. Drew pushed the door open just enough to stick his head inside.

The walls were covered in posters that boasted zombie-esque band members looking like they'd just dug themselves out of their own graves, with names like Mechanical Death and Post-War Suicide. There was a desk in the corner piled high with papers and cracked CD cases. A box of incense lay amid a pile of ash. A cheap acrylic lighter and a torn paper cup filled with change sat on an upturned milk crate beside the bed. Mickey's floor was invisible to the naked eye; clearly, he was untrained in the fine art of closet-keeping. The only thing that looked half-organized was a makeshift shelf Mick had constructed by screwing a two-by-four into the wall. An army of medieval-looking action figures were lined up there, still in their boxes, next to an impressive water bong that presided over the room. A twelve-gauge shotgun hung proudly over the shelf. Home defense. You never could be too careful.

Closing Mickey's door, Drew let his gaze pause on the door across the hall from his own. This one, he assumed, led to a third bedroom. But after trying the knob, he realized it wasn't the same kind as the others. It was the outdoor kind, lockable from both the outside as well as in.

A nagging seed of misgiving sprouted within his mind. Mickey was a bit weird, and he was severely lacking in the house-keeping department, but who put a lock like that on an interior door? It was like a big red button marked *Do Not Push*.

A moment ago Drew hadn't cared what was behind door number three, yet suddenly he had to know. He rattled the knob—locked—then gave the door a shove with his shoulder, but it didn't budge. He shot a glance down the hall, two thoughts simultaneously bumping against each other: first, that the key to the third hallway door was almost certainly somewhere on Mickey's desk; second, that Drew had forgotten to buy a replacement lightbulb for the burned-out one in the hallway.

He found himself staring into Mickey's room again, peering at the desk in the corner, carefully considering whether breaching the perimeter of Mick's bedroom was justified, or whether it just made him a nosy asshole.

Mickey's engine rumbled past the front window, and Drew froze. He had the urge to bolt back to his room, to pretend he'd never left his little space—as though standing in the hallway were some sort of crime. He pulled Mick's door closed and cleared his throat, trying to act casual as he started toward the living room.

Then Mickey filled the front doorway, and Drew immediately felt guilty—cradling a bag of McDonald's in one arm like a baby, Mickey offered his new roommate a crooked grin.

"Hey," he said, "thanks for cleaning the bathroom, man. It looks great. I really don't know how it got that bad."

Drew blinked.

"I got burgers," Mickey said. "Figured you'd want to eat."

"Um, yeah…totally."

"Cool," Mickey said, stepping across the living room and sinking into the couch. "You still game?"

A smile crept into the corners of Drew's mouth. As the two started into a round of Madden NFL he started to relax. This was the same Mickey Fitch whom Andrew had idolized in the past. Butterflies sprang to life inside his stomach when Mickey muttered a familiar battle cry: "Game on."

And suddenly, blissfully, Andrew was a kid again.

§

The day Andrew's dad didn't come home was the day Julianne Morrison stopped being his mom.

Julie was born and raised in Creekside, and while most people ran from the little Kansas town dead-center in the middle of the state, she had always loved it like a kid loved Disneyland—unconditionally; the happiest place on earth. She had grown up in the same house Andrew was raised in: a two-story ranch-style home with a charming wraparound porch and a bench swing that hung just beyond the back door. His grandfather, PopPop, had painted that porch a pretty pastel blue—Gamma's favorite color—and had built the swing out of bits of scrap wood when Julie was a little girl. He and Gamma would sit on it for hours during the summer, watching the sun dip beneath an ocean of farmland, lighting up the wheat like reeds of gold.

After both Gamma and PopPop passed, six-year-old Drew moved into that beautiful house with his parents. He hadn't wanted to at first, convinced it would be haunted. But they were happy there. The three of them would have movie nights every weekend; one Fourth of July, they played hide-and-seek in the wheat behind the house. Andrew had squatted between the tall reeds, waiting to be found. When he heard his parents getting close, he peeked between the flag-like leaves. He caught them kissing beneath a starry sky, the pop of distant fireworks echoing across the landscape.

But then things started to change. Rather than watching Saturday-morning cartoons with him the way they used to, his mom and dad drifted through rooms of the house like ghosts. They avoided one another, and when they did run into each other—usually around dinnertime—Drew would listen to them gnaw at each other while he silently ate his food. He wasn't sure what had happened, *still* didn't know how it had all fallen apart, but before he knew it, his mom would plop him on the couch with a bowl of popcorn, flip on the TV, and Andrew would spend movie nights alone.

Most mornings started out like all the rest, with his mom whipping up a batch of her specialty: apple pancakes with whipped sour cream. His dad had a job at a potato processing plant just a few miles shy of town. Every morning, after Rick finished his pancakes and downed his OJ, he'd ruffle Drew's hair as he passed the couch, and he'd leave for work without so much as a good-bye. Every morning, as soon as Drew heard his boots on the front steps, he would spring from the sofa and rush to the window to watch his dad pull the old Chevy out of the driveway. Back then, he wanted to be just like his pop—to work at a big factory and drive a cool truck. From his six-year-old kid perspective, those were the only two things you needed to be a man.

But the morning Andrew's father left for good, things were different. It was summertime, so he was still in his Transformer pajamas, watching cartoons on basic cable. There were no pan-cakes, no conversation between his mom and pop. When Drew asked his father about the old gym bag tossed over his shoulder, Rick had pulled him into a tight hug, ruffled his hair just like every other morning, and told him, "See you later, champ." But rather than climbing into the Chevy, his dad climbed into some-one else's truck instead. He was gone before Drew's mom stepped out of the kitchen to check on him.

"Get away from the window; turn on the TV," she told him. "*Scooby-Doo* is on."

"OK, Mom," Drew replied, squeaky-voiced, but he lingered at the window for longer than usual. Julie crossed the room, pull-ing the curtain closed on the still-parked Chevy just beyond the glass.

"How about we fill up your pool today?" she suggested, and that mysterious truck melted from Andrew's mind. Visions of sitting in his blue plastic pool blinded him with youthful bliss, and he raced up the stairs to his room to fish out his miniature Speedos and inflatable shark.

It was only when Drew found himself standing stark naked in his bedroom, trying to get a scrawny leg through the hole in his swim trunks, that he wondered whether he should have told her about the strange truck his dad had climbed into. But if he told her about the truck, he'd have to tell her about the lady driv-ing it, and that would ruin his day in the pool as quick as a tor-nado could ruin a Kansas town.

After that, the house decayed into a shadow of its former self. The whitewashed clapboards faded and peeled. The roof was ravaged by decades of wind, and the missing shingles never got replaced, because, his increasingly listless mother reasoned, the next storm would blow them right back off.

All that was left of Drew's father was Rick's pickup and his mother's sense of betrayal—betrayal that had festered into some-thing that Andrew could no longer handle. She wouldn't set foot outside her home: not to go to the grocery store, not to check the mail a few steps from the front porch stairs. Years before, she sometimes forced herself to walk along the wraparound porch and sit in her daddy's swing, but she could no longer even manage that. A few steps outside sent her into a panic, sure that the doors would lock and she'd never be able to get inside again. Andrew had been nine the first time he went to the grocery store alone, a shopping list stuffed into one pocket, a fistful of dollars stuffed into the other. He rode his bike more than three miles in a single direction in the blazing August sun, only to realize, far too late, that he had no way of getting those groceries back home. With plastic shopping bags heavy on his handlebars, he walked his bike all the way back to Cedar Street. When he finally arrived, the half gallon of milk had gone warm.

By the time Drew turned twelve, he found himself paying bills out of a dwindling bank account, forging his mother's name on checks so the city wouldn't turn off their water, electricity, gas. Julie had never worked—they had lived off Rick's salary. When his dad disappeared, the government checks started coming in. Drew would deposit them into an ATM before school each week, and would stop by the same machine after school to pull cash out. He had made the mistake of walking into the bank only once; the girl behind the counter had smirked at the kid trying to cash his mother's welfare check. The teller nearly refused to give it back to him, insisting that what he was doing was illegal, finally relenting when Andrew burst into a fit of panicked tears.

Somewhere in the middle of Andrew's fourteenth year, Julie stopped cooking. Suddenly, with the bills and the groceries and nearly constant takeout, welfare wasn't enough—and she wasn't helping the situation any, drinking through whatever was left of weekly checks. Random men would stop by the house each week, toting bags full of bargain-basement alcohol. One week, when there was nothing left in their cash reserve, Andrew couldn't pay the guy who showed up on their doorstep. Rather than letting him leave, Julie pulled him inside and led him upstairs. Drew sat on the couch with his hands over his ears, his face hidden against his knees. He started saving for his mother's booze after that, always careful to have enough cash so it would never happen again.

By the time Andrew graduated high school, he gave up any future plans and got himself a job. But the bills kept coming, kept growing. Julie kept drinking.

Everyone felt bad for poor Julie Morrison, but from where Drew was standing, he was the one who deserved Creekside's compassion. Between the job and the bills and finding his mom passed out drunk on the couch, he started to wonder just how fair life was.

And then he found out.

CHAPTER THREE

The next morning, Harlow Ward squinted past coils of steam as the new boy's pickup rolled down the street. Mickey's Pontiac was parked in the driveway—the kind of car the devil would drive if he walked the earth and lived in the heartland. She supposed that was appropriate; after all, Mickey Fitch was no saint.

She drained her cup of coffee, ran her thumb along the rim to remove the blotch of red lipstick, and crossed the dining room, her heels silent on the carpet. Dragging her fingers along the tabletop, she paused to admire her reflection in its polished surface, smiling at the woman who gazed back at her from below. Entering the kitchen with the distinctive click of high heels, she placed the still warm mug in the sink and gazed out the window onto a picturesque backyard. The hydrangeas were in full bloom, and the wooden trellis that clung to the side of the house was already heavy with rosebuds.

She leaned into her reflection in the glass, pursed her painted lips, and fluffed the easy curls that framed her face. She had an errand to run.

"I'll be back in a few minutes," she announced, straightening her pencil skirt with one hand as she balanced a plate of cookies in the other. She crossed the living room—the carpet so white, it was a wonder anyone had set foot on it at all. "I'm going next door."

"Should I go with you?" Red asked, but she offered him a knowing smile and approached his recliner in response. She stopped beside him, her fingers tracing a path from his ear to beneath his chin.

"Oh, Red," she said, "what in heaven's for? To help me take care of business?" She chuckled, then stepped out of the house.

§

Andrew never had a taste for thrift stores. They reminded him of just how bad off he and his mom were. But starting a new life meant new stuff, and he had no money for that any other way.

The place he'd found a mile from Mickey's place was a run-down secondhand junk shop that smelled of mothballs and unwashed clothes. There were two people working there, both sweet elderly women who would snap themselves in half with the least bit of effort. They followed him around like baby ducks, pointing out items that he had zero interest in. But he liked the attention, and they liked fawning over the "nice young man" visiting their store. After forty-five minutes of walking the over-stuffed aisles with them, Drew decided on a mattress, a bed frame with no headboard, a badly refinished chest of drawers, and a slightly cockeyed bookcase—all for sixty bucks.

Asking the women to help haul a mattress across a parking lot would result in two dead bodies in the bed of his truck, and digging a pair of graves for a couple of doting grandmas wasn't an efficient way to spend his afternoon. So, armed with the store's only dolly, Andrew struggled with his purchases alone. The mattress was the hardest part. He dragged it through the store and onto the sidewalk, then hoisted it upright just as the wind picked up, nearly tearing it out of his hands and into the street. The grandmas watched him through the window with their hands pressed to their mouths, waiting to see if he'd be lifted off his feet like a kite. They knocked to get Drew's attention, offering pantomimed advice. By the time the mattress was on the truck, he was exhausted, but it was only the beginning. The bookcase was next.

After half an hour of struggling in the hot prairie sun, Drew collapsed inside the cab of his truck and blasted the air as high as it would go. With the AC mercifully battering his face, he thought about how he'd have to wrestle all this crap out of the truck and into the house *without* a dolly, unless by some divine fate Casa de Mickey was equipped with such a utilitarian device.

He could breach the perimeter of that white picket fence and ask the neighbors. A house like that was destined to have a fully stocked garage. Maybe they'd invite him inside, if only for a minute. Or maybe he and Mr. Perfect Neighbor would unload his truck while the missus brought freshly squeezed lemonade out to them on a silver tray. Invigorated by the idea, he pulled the seat belt across his chest and pushed the Chevy into first.

A Sonic drive-in sign distracted him. His stomach rumbled. He'd just about kill for a strawberry shake, and nobody could tell him he hadn't earned it.

§

Harlow clicked up the cracked walkway of the house next door, grimacing at the dead lawn. It ruined the neighborhood like an ugly girl ruined a group photo. Most of the houses along Magnolia were charming—naturally, none so much as the Wards'—except for this wreck. Then again, it was her mother who had taught her that trick: standing next to the ugly girl in the picture made Harlow even prettier. That patchy lawn made hers look immaculate. Those sagging gutters made 668 Magnolia Lane look like an absolute dream.

She fluffed her hair, pulled a single Kleenex from her bag, balanced the plate of cookies on top of an open palm, and pressed the doorbell through the tissue with a grimace. *Ridiculous*, she thought. *How do UPS men not die of contamination?* She waited, pressed the bell again, and rolled her eyes when there was no reply. Everything was far more complicated on this side of the picket fence.

She walked along the edge of the house toward the backyard, the sad excuse of a lawn crunching beneath her feet. She nearly stumbled when one of her heels sank deep into the ground, grumbling beneath her breath when she had to lean against the dirty siding of the house to retrieve her shoe. Stopping in front of a window covered by a bedsheet, she pounded on the glass. She wanted to yell, wanted to scream at the top of her lungs, but she stood tight-lipped on the lawn instead, her teeth clenched behind her cherry-stained mouth. The bedsheet rustled. There was a crash—something falling to the floor—a flurry of clumsy footfalls, and finally a violent pull on that makeshift curtain by the occupant of the dark room inside. Wild-eyed, Mickey Fitch glared out the window; temporarily blinded by the sunlight, he looked ready to pulverize the joker who had decided to wake him, probably only a few hours after he'd hit the sack. He blanched when he saw who it was, and with hesitation he raised his hand to the window—a silent plea for a few seconds to react—before letting the curtain fall back into place.

Harlow snorted and did an about-face, mashing parched blades of grass beneath the soles of her shoes. She marched back to the front of the house and waited by the door.

§

Mickey pulled the door open and stared at the woman standing on his front doorstep. Despite being roused from his sleep only seconds before, he was fully alert, wide-eyed as his visitor pulled the screen door open and, uninvited, pushed her way inside.

It was hard to believe Harlow Ward existed in the present. Everything about her reminded him of that *Mad Men* show—her hair, her clothes; they were profoundly retro. For the decade he'd lived next door, he'd never seen her in anything casual. It was always high heels and makeup.

She clicked her way through the foyer, placed the plate of cookies on the coffee table, and marched herself back to where Mickey stood.

He opened his mouth to talk, and she slapped him hard across the face.

Mickey took an unsteady backward step, his hand pressed to his assaulted cheek. When he pulled his hand away, he saw blood.

Harlow casually adjusted her diamond ring, rotating it so that the stone pointed outward rather than toward the inside of her palm. His stomach twisted when she noticed him staring at her, offering up a hard smile.

"Those are for the new boy," she said, regarding the plate of cookies with an upward tilt of the chin. "Don't touch them. You're getting fat."

Mickey lowered his gaze. He hated when Harlow came over. The heat of his palm made the wound she'd just given him sting. Harlow turned away from him and stalked down the hall. He watched her pause in Andrew's doorway for a long while, assessing the unlabeled and unpacked cardboard boxes that were neatly lined up along the walls. He tensed when she started to head back into the living room, but stopped halfway down the hall. Her nostrils flared at the sharp scent that lingered just outside the bathroom. Pushing the bathroom door open, she stood there for a moment, then moved back into the living room. Mickey pressed a wet paper towel to his face from among the kitchen's disarray.

"Did he do that?" she asked.

"Yes," Mickey replied.

One-word answers were his way of complying, but Harlow wasn't satisfied. She strutted across the dirty carpet, her heels clacking against the kitchen's cheap linoleum, and caught him by his chin.

"When he gets back, you're going to be on your best behavior. Best friends. Like a dream."

Mickey nodded faintly before Harlow released her grip. She stepped back into the living room and circled the couch, assessing her plate of cookies.

"I should have used a bow," she mused, leaning down to adjust the gift tag on top of cellophane.

Welcome to the neighborhood! Most sincerely, Red and Harlow Ward.

§

Full of strawberry milk shake, Drew was regretting getting the large as he rambled back toward Magnolia. The shake sat sweet and heavy in the pit of his stomach, twisting his guts into a slow-growing ball of nausea that, as soon as he got to unloading the bed of the truck, would more than likely turn ugly. When he finally pulled up to that now familiar curb, he sat there for a while, his hands on his stomach, taking deep and steady breaths, as if patterned breathing would somehow make all that milk and ice cream disappear. With the AC on high, he squinted against the artificial wind. Movement from the corner of his eye caught his attention, and when he turned, he saw a figure standing on the perfectly preened lawn of the fairy-tale house next door.

The man was staring at him. When he met Drew's eye, the guy turned away and went back to pushing a bright red mower, but it was Andrew's turn to stare. Rather than wearing ratty shorts and a pair of old flip-flops, this guy looked just about ready to conduct an outdoor business meeting. Drew couldn't imagine how hot he must be in a pair of long slacks and dressy loafers that glinted in the sun.

The neighbor looked back over, and Drew instinctively ducked down.

His stomach flipped and soured. A second later he was shoving the driver's door open and bolting for the house.

After puking up a stream of still-cold pink, he unsteadily made his way back to the front yard. Sick or not, there was furniture to unload and boxes to unpack. He didn't feel like spending another night on a pile of his own clothes. Stepping back into the heat, he froze where he stood. Half of his furniture was on the sidewalk, as if on some sort of weird display. Mickey wrestled with the headboard.

"Hey," he said, spotting his housemate on the lawn, "figured you needed a hand."

Drew's first instinct was to smile, but that nagging kernel of wariness immediately followed. Andrew believed in first impressions, considered those first few moments as a window to who a person really was. Mick's most recent first impression hadn't been a great one; tired, sloppy, unaccommodating, he seemed like the last person to jump off the couch and lend a hand. But there he was, unloading Drew's stuff like he'd been paid to do it when he hadn't even been asked to help. Peering against the glare of the sun, Drew watched Mick work for a moment longer before dragging his feet across the lawn.

There was something about Mickey that felt off—a weird vibe he couldn't shake. Drew used to know a kid back in high school—Jeff Belkin. Jeff had been a real asshole, the kind of guy who could turn a simple conversation into the most unpleasant event of the day. Jeff had a coke problem. Nobody knew it at first, but after a while, it was obvious. Every time Jeff took a bump in the bathroom between class he'd turn into a fly at a picnic, constantly buzzing around people, wanting to talk, wanting to help:

what can I do, what can I do? Maybe Mickey had a drug problem, coke or speed or something. Maybe that was where the vibe was coming from—chemicals that were slowly frying Mick's brain.

Pausing beside the back tire, he raised an eyebrow at Mick.

"What happened?" he asked.

"What?" Mickey froze. He was a bundle of stops and starts, just like that Jeff guy.

Andrew motioned to Mick's cheek, a diagonal slash cross-sectioning his face.

"Oh." Mickey blinked, then furrowed his eyebrows. "Nothing," he said. "Just an accident."

"Some accident," Drew replied. "Looks like Norman Bates went after you in the shower."

"What?" Mickey shook his head. "Bates?"

"Norman Bates, man. From *Psycho.*"

Mickey stared at the house for a long while, then forced a smile.

"Oh yeah," he said. "Nah, it was just an accident. I haven't even seen *Psycho,* dude. I don't watch that old stuff."

"Are you serious?"

Mickey lifted his shoulders in a dismissive shrug. Drew wasn't sure why he was surprised. It was hard to watch the classics while picking off zombies in a first-person shooter.

"Come on," Mick urged. "It's hot. It'll go faster with two."

Back and forth they went, from the truck to Andrew's room. Mickey even helped move some of the cardboard boxes so they could squeeze the bookcase inside. On their last pass for the mattress, Drew noticed that their slacks-wearing neighbor had been joined by a woman who looked just as proper as he did. She stood in front of a rosebush, trimming stems with a fancy-looking pair of shears, wearing bright red heels in the grass. He couldn't make out her face beneath the floppy brim of her gardening hat.

It was disorienting to see them gardening in such proper attire. But Andrew was struck with a desire, a *need* to walk up to that picket fence and introduce himself. The woman noticed him looking. She lifted a gloved hand in silent greeting, a wide smile pulled across her lacquered lips. Drew looked down to his feet, struck by a familiar sense of awkwardness; it was the same unease he'd felt when he realized his truck didn't belong on Magnolia Lane, that *he* didn't belong in Oz.

"Those are the Wards," Mickey told him, hesitated, then continued. "They're all right."

They were more than all right. Because what kind of people gardened in business casual? *Perfect people*, he thought; people who wouldn't be caught dead on Cedar Street.

§

He and Mick just about killed themselves dragging that mattress down the hallway. Mickey went backward, slowing down when Drew yelped that he was about to trip over his own feet. He hovered while Drew organized his things, as if waiting to be told what to do. Finally unnerved by his roommate's sudden bout of assistance, Drew shook his head at him and shot Mick a look.

"I'll be all right," he assured him. "Really."

"You sure?" Mick asked, but relented when Andrew's eyebrow arched dubiously over one eye.

By the time Drew stepped out of his room, Mick was back on the couch, mashing buttons. Drew scratched the back of his neck, watching the game for half a minute before speaking up.

"Hey, do you have a screwdriver anywhere? I need to put the bed frame together."

Mickey paused his game, eyed his new roommate for a second, and tossed his game controller onto the couch cushion.

"Yeah, sure," he said. "Wait here."

Drew furrowed his eyebrows as Mickey wandered into the kitchen, disappearing through a door that led into a garage. He waited for a minute, rolled his eyes at how long it was taking, and sank onto the couch. Grabbing the controller, he was about to unpause Mick's game when the plate of cookies caught his attention. He leaned forward, plucked the little card from atop the cellophane. The flowing script declared the treat was from the Wards—those perfect next-door neighbors. It was flawless, the prettiest handwriting he'd ever seen, matching the woman who had written it to a T. His heart flipped when he put it together: she had been the shadow in the window the evening he pulled up, the night he thought their house was Mick's. She had seen him fiddle with their gate latch, had watched him realize his mistake and wander next door to the house that, no doubt, she hated. And instead of turning her nose up at the new neighbor who'd just moved into the crappiest house on the block, she stepped into her gleaming kitchen, grabbed a mixing bowl and a wooden spoon, and made cookies. For *him*.

Carefully pulling the cellophane away from the edge of the plate—a real plate, not a disposable one—Drew lifted a cookie to his nose, inhaling its sweetness before taking a bite. He fell back against the couch, his eyes shut, a chunk of chocolate melting on his tongue. They were amazing, as though she'd sprinkled magic into the mix.

He sat up when the kitchen door to the garage slammed shut. Mickey trudged into the living room, holding a Phillips-head screwdriver out for Andrew's approval.

"Have you tasted these?" Drew asked, getting to his feet. He took the screwdriver, Mrs. Ward's little card tucked into the palm of his hand.

"They're for you," Mickey said. "Forgot to tell you."

"They're incredible."

"Take them," Mickey said, waving a hand at the plate. "I'm on a diet."

A laugh burst from Andrew's throat. Mickey blinked at him, then retook his seat.

"Shit, you're being serious," Drew murmured. "Sorry, man. It's just that, you know, you don't look like you need it." It was a white lie—a tiny untruth to spare his friend's feelings.

Mickey responded by unpausing his game and shooting a guy in the chest with an assault rifle. Drew shoved the rest of his cookie into his mouth, grabbed the plate off the coffee table, and walked down the hall to his room.

§

The rest of Drew's day was spent unpacking. He had positioned the bed beside the window—when he was a kid, his bed had been positioned the very same way—so that the Wards' place was the first thing he saw when he woke up, and the last thing he saw when he fell asleep.

The walls still needed painting, but at least they were a clean slate. One was now home to that cockeyed bookcase, while the other accommodated his dresser. He stacked boxes along a wall he hoped would house a future purchase of a desk and a chair, though that would have to wait. Cash was tight, and his decision to leave home had included the hasty decision to abandon his job at the local grocery store. It had been a stupid thing to do, but it had felt right at the time. He wanted to start fresh, completely clean, and his grocery store job had been the very thing that had funded the life he was now running from. Bagging groceries and, later, ringing up clipped coupons had kept the Morrisons afloat for years. He didn't want to be reminded of that every time he clocked in for his shift. And, if his mother was miraculously cured of her agoraphobia, he didn't want her rolling a cart full of booze into his checkout lane.

After he'd spent nearly an entire day organizing, the strawberry shake debacle had been forgotten and his stomach twisted with hunger. It was either pudding cups or going out to eat, so he resolved to take a quick trip to the Taco Bell, pick up a couple of burritos, and call it a night.

He made a beeline down the hall, his truck keys in hand, but his plan was diverted by an unlikely sight. Mickey stood in the kitchen, the same pair of yellow rubber gloves Drew had worn pulled up to his elbows. His white-haired roomie stood hunched over the kitchen sink, scrubbing the stained porcelain with an expression of startling concentration.

Andrew stood at the mouth of the hallway, afraid to move, as if moving would scare Mickey and cause him to run. The smell of bleach soured the air, but the sweetness of Drew's satisfaction more than made up for it. He had hoped that scrubbing the bathroom would motivate Mick to get up and do the same; it appeared that he had been correct.

Mickey eventually noticed his housemate standing there, watching him with what must have been a stupid grin on his face. He stopped what he was doing—caught in the act—as though scrubbing the sink were some sort of crime. "Hey," he said.

"What're you doing?" Drew asked.

"Cleaning. The bathroom doesn't match the rest of the house now. So, you know…"

"Well…that's awesome." Hooking a thumb toward the front door, he gave Mick a questioning look. "I'm picking up food. You want a burrito?"

With those canary yellow gloves giving the big oaf a comical appeal, Mickey eventually nodded with a crooked smile.

"Sure," he said. "Thanks."

"I'll pick up an apron for you while I'm out," Drew teased. "It'll match your gloves."

Climbing into the cab of his truck, Drew paused in thought. Maybe this was going to work out. As odd a couple as they were, maybe he and Mickey would rekindle their friendship. Maybe it would be just like old times. Shoving the key into the ignition, he felt better about the future than he ever had before.

CHAPTER FOUR

The rumble of Mickey's TransAm roused Drew the next morning. Listening to the Pontiac scream down the road, he rolled onto his side and pressed his face into his pillow with a cotton-muffled groan. It felt early—way too early for Mickey to be up. He squinted across the room at the digital alarm clock he had brought from home, the numbers glowing like the cherry of a burning cigarette: a few minutes past eight.

"What the hell?" he murmured, the heels of his palms pressing into the sockets of his eyes. First the guy went full-fledged Donna Reed, and now he was up earlier than Drew. Next up: Mickey would return home with armloads of groceries and the insatiable desire to try his hand at Belgian waffles.

Half-asleep, he rolled out of bed, brushed his teeth while sitting on the toilet, and then hopped in the shower to wake up. By the time he was dressed, Mickey still hadn't come home, and Drew found himself standing in his room, staring out the window at the house next door. A shadow shifted behind glass. He squinted, trying to make out the figure that seemed to hover behind the curtains, wondering whether there was actually someone there, staring back at him, or if he was seeing the shadow of a swaying houseplant. The carefully cut lawn, the vigilantly pruned roses, the white picket fence standing proud against the big blue sky—it reminded him of the black-and-white sitcoms his mother used to watch; the ones where the men worked and the women patiently awaited their return, eager to ask about their day, ready to offer up a pair of slippers, dinner in the oven, raring to go. They were the type who held neighborhood barbecues and ran through wheat fields on the Fourth of July. These were people Andrew wished he knew.

He flipped open his wallet and fingered the corner of the card he'd found on top of the cookies the day before, then slid it back in place behind his driver's license. He thumbed through his dwindling stack of cash. With only one hundred forty-two dollars left, he was running dangerously low on funds. But he assured himself that everything would be fine. In their e-mails, Mick had assured him that money wasn't a big deal—Drew could pay his share of the rent when he got on his feet. The offer had struck him as overly generous, but he was thankful for it. And Drew was no freeloader; he'd pick up a job in the next few days. But until then, he needed paint.

The doorbell rang just as he grabbed his keys. He paused, the odd sensation of having to answer somebody else's door settling over him. Sure, he had been there for a couple days, but it still felt strange. It was a public admission of residence, assurance to whoever was on the other side of the door that yes, Andrew Morrison *did* live here now. The doorbell rang again. Drew squared his shoulders and walked down the hall, peeked through the peephole and blinked.

It was *her.*

Butterfly wings brushed the lining of his stomach. His belief in first impressions stood firm, and he definitely wanted to make a good one now.

Andrew cleared his throat, pulled open the door, and offered the woman from next door a confident smile.

"I missed you yesterday," she said. "Just wanted to be a good neighbor and welcome you home."

§

The first boy had taken less than a week. She hadn't liked him. He had been a slob just like Mickey, and it disturbed Harlow how at home he had seemed in that shithouse of a rental. His name had been Christopher Clark, and he hadn't had an inkling of ambition—no drive, no common sense in that empty skull. When Harlow had taken in the spectacle that had been Christopher Clark's bedroom, she had shaken her head in disgust. The boy had slept among trash, hadn't bothered to obtain any furniture; the entire room had the sharp stink of body odor.

But she pursued him anyway. He wasn't perfect, but dumb enough to not know any better, which gave her a sense of comfort. She intended on stepping up her game as time went on, but that first time on Magnolia, she had been nervous, and Christopher was easy.

But Christopher hadn't intrigued her. The act had felt empty, nothing but an exercise in testing the waters. His eagerness had made her sick, and that was what had ruined it in the end: that lack of reluctance. The hunt had been spoiled.

After Christopher, Harlow made more of an effort to find boys that sparked her interest. To her disappointment, finding upstanding specimens was more difficult than she had expected. For a time she had been so uninspired, she even let a few of them go. It wasn't worth the energy if the boy wasn't right.

But Andrew Morrison was different. She could already sense it. There was something raw about him, a vulnerability that was almost electric. The more she observed him, the more Andrew made her eyes sparkle with hope, from the sharp smell of a clean bathroom to a bright smile when he answered the door.

Andrew Morrison was perfect.

CHAPTER FIVE

ndrew watched Harlow Ward saunter down the cracked driveway, a frown pulling at the corners of his mouth, a sinking feeling heavy in the pit of his stomach. She had excused herself shortly after coming to Mickey's door, embarrassed by the mess she found inside.

Turning away from the window, he stopped in the doorway of his bedroom, his arms protectively crossed over his chest. He could only hope that Mrs. Ward's opinion of him hadn't been completely blown by something out of his control. Despite his best efforts, he had yet to tackle the living room and kitchen. He supposed if he'd led her to the bathroom, he could have reclaimed an iota of her respect.

Sure, he thought. *Mrs. Ward, please let me prove my worth by the sparkle of my tub.*

He realized, after a few minutes of brooding, that he was staring at something that didn't belong to him: the cookie plate. He had devoured most of those delicious treats in a single sitting, but a pair of them remained on patterned porcelain. It was a habit he had picked up as a kid—save the last few for later, because there was no telling when he'd have money for more cookies, more candy, more anything. Stepping forward, he lifted the plate from the top of his dresser, slid the remaining cookies onto a sheet of scrap paper, and ducked into the darkness of the hall.

After washing the plate in Mick's freshly scrubbed kitchen sink, he found himself standing in front of the Wards' picket fence. Regardless of what Mrs. Ward thought of him now, the plate had to be returned. It was all a matter of whether he'd be invited inside or asked to leave.

Nervous, he fiddled with the gate latch, imagining the plate slipping from his fingers and exploding into a thousand pieces at his feet. He clung to it, hugging it to his chest like Charlie had held fast to his golden ticket. It was Andrew's pass into the chocolate factory; he only hoped it was good for a few visits rather than only one. Climbing the front porch steps, he took a deep breath, reached out his free hand, and pressed the glowing doorbell button. His heart thudded in his chest. Like a kid on a first date, he was overwhelmed by the sudden urge to back out, but his feet were planted firmly—a conflict of mind and body.

Before he could talk his feet into moving, the front door swung wide. Mrs. Ward appeared surprised at the guest before her, her hand fluttering just beneath the hollow of her throat.

"Andrew," she said. "Hello again."

He watched her mouth waver between confidence and uncertainty. She hadn't been expecting him; very likely hoped that he wouldn't show up in this very manner—the grungy kid from the dirty house next door. That sinking feeling returned tenfold, threatening to pull him through the porch floor and six feet beneath the ground.

"I..." He hesitated, pulling the clean plate from against his chest and holding it out to her in offering. "...forgot to give this to you."

She blinked at the plate as if not recognizing it, and then her mouth bloomed into a beautiful smile.

ANIA AHLBORN

"You're so sweet," she said, accepting Andrew's offering of porcelain with a faint nod of her head. "Clean too?"

It was Drew's chance, his opportunity to tell her that what she had seen inside—the dust, the sadly dim interior—that hadn't been him. That was something he was going to change, was in the process of changing as they spoke. But before he could gather his wits and launch into an explanation, Mrs. Ward took a side step and motioned for Drew to come inside.

"Really?"

Mrs. Ward smiled at his enthusiasm.

"Of course," she said. "Come in."

Harlow led Andrew inside with a smile, a hand pressed against the center of his back to keep him moving as he gazed at pastel-colored walls and antique photo frames. The inside of the Wards' house matched its faultless exterior. He marveled at the fact that he had been right, it *did* smell like home cooking, and the delicate scent of cut grass drifted through the open windows. Sheer white curtains shivered in the breeze, drawing drifting shadows across a meticulously vacuumed carpet, as white and perfect as an undisturbed blanket of snow. The place was a museum, and while Andrew was overwhelmed, he also found himself enchanted by its freshness.

Placing the plate on the kitchen counter, Harlow turned to face Andrew with a warm smile. "Since I have you here, perhaps you could help me with something?" she asked.

Drew looked away from a rack of spices, each bottle carefully hand-labeled, and gave her a nod.

"I need a bookshelf moved," she told him. "Follow me."

Directing him to what looked like a home office, the gentle pressure of her hand was at the small of his back. It was the kind of room that looked like it came out of a magazine: deep mahogany-toned furniture, a green glass banker's lamp sitting next to a leather desk blotter. "There's the culprit," she said, motioning to a large bookshelf, a thing that looked to weigh a good two or three hundred pounds empty. "I'd move it myself, but the last time I tried to move furniture on my own I just about killed myself.

"Do you think you can manage it?" she asked. "I hope we don't have to take everything off it. That would just cause a messload of work, don't you think?"

Drew blinked at her impossible suggestion. The shelves were heavy with entire collections—Stephen King, Dean Koontz, a thick volume of Poe's complete works. And yet he found himself considering it, contemplating how he could make this hopeless task happen.

"You like horror?" he asked, casting a sidelong glance at the gorgeous woman beside him. Her classic look implied literary tastes running to the likes of Mark Twain, Emerson, and Thoreau; it was thrilling to think that she cozied up with the likes of *The Shining*, fantastic to imagine her curling up on the couch to indulge in old horror movies Andrew held dear: *Dracula, The Haunting, Night of the Living Dead.*

"It's more my husband than me," she said. "He's a bookworm. I would have asked that fellow you live with…what's his name?"

"Mickey."

"But since he wasn't home…" She paused, taking a moment to consider her words. "Honestly, I'm a bit relieved. I wasn't too keen on inviting him over without anyone home."

Andrew gave her a questioning look.

"Oh, you know how it is," she continued, offering the conversation a dismissive wave of the hand. "Word gets around, small town like this. You don't know?"

"Know what?"

Harlow cleared her throat, a manicured hand gingerly touching the back of her neck. "I really shouldn't have said anything," she said. "Anyway." Her smile returned. "Shall we?"

She stood beside Drew, scoping out the bookcase ahead of them while that tiny seed of suspicion about Mickey dug itself deep into the soft tissue of his brain.

"Mrs. Ward..."

"Harlow," she said. "Please."

Drew shifted his weight from one foot to the other. He considered mentioning the uncertainty he'd been feeling around Mickey. It seemed like, from what Harlow had just mentioned, he was right in having reservations. But he didn't want to seem petty; he didn't want her to think of him as a gossip, as someone who, like Mickey, should be kept at arm's length. Instead, he decided to focus on the task at hand.

"Harlow," he said, feeling both odd and exhilarated at being allowed to use her first name. "I really want to help." He met her gaze, his heart fluttering when their eyes locked. Had she been a brunette rather than a blonde, she would have looked like vintage Elizabeth Taylor. He imagined that her looks had intimidated thousands of boys—had made them weak in the knees but kept them at bay, because who could possibly be good enough for a girl like her? "But I think I might lose a limb if I try to move this thing myself."

Harlow offered the piece of furniture a perplexed look before exhaling a quiet laugh, as if just then realizing how impossible her request had been.

"I'm sorry." She chuckled with a shake of her head, loose curls sweeping across her cheeks. "I really am an idiot, aren't I?" She rested her hand on his arm, her smile lighting up her face. "Well, you're already here," she resolved. "I'll make you something to eat. What do you say? Eggs, hash browns, the works; I make the best breakfast in all of Kansas."

As if on cue, Drew's stomach let out a loud growl. He pictured himself sitting at a breakfast table, sunlight filtering in through crisp white curtains, sunshine glinting off a fresh pitcher of orange juice just like it would in the commercials.

"I really couldn't." It was the first thing to tumble out of his mouth—one of those things you kick yourself for saying but say it anyway. He was starving. After days of living off fast food, he'd have killed for a homemade meal. "Honestly, I haven't been here more than five minutes. There's no reason—"

"Nonsense," Harlow cut in. "It's the least I can do."

He shifted his weight uncomfortably, afraid to overstay his welcome. She noticed his uneasiness and shook her head with a glossy grin.

"What is it, afraid I'm going to bite?"

Stepping behind him, she placed both hands on his shoulders and gave him a steady push out of the room and toward the kitchen.

She hadn't exaggerated. She *did* make the best breakfast in all of Kansas. Drew gorged himself on crisp bacon and homemade bread. Even Harlow's eggs were just right—sunny-side up, bright orange yolks perfectly centered and runny, just the way Andrew liked them. Harlow sat across from him with a wistful smile. She kept his juice glass full and gave him a second helping of bacon without him needing to ask. Andrew gave her a satisfied grin as he ate, his cheeks stuffed with the best-tasting food he'd had in forever. By the time he was finished eating, he wasn't sure he'd be able to fit out the front door.

"Goodness," she said. "You *were* hungry. Had I known, I would have invited you over sooner."

Drew raised a bashful shoulder in a shrug, nearly apologetic of his appetite.

"The cookies were awesome too," he confessed. "Thanks for those."

"That roommate of yours didn't eat them all?" She raised an eyebrow in inquiry, but Drew shook his head no.

"Said he was on a diet." A moment passed between them—Andrew and Harlow staring at each other—before they both shared a laugh at Mickey's expense.

"Well," she said, rising from her seat, only to pluck Drew's breakfast plate from the table. "That's good to know. Now I won't hesitate to bake more."

Drew couldn't help himself. He beamed.

Walking him out to the front porch, Harlow offered him a thoughtful smile. "Come over anytime," she insisted. "My door is always open."

When she reached a hand out to brush a strand of hair from Andrew's forehead, he nearly recoiled at how strange it felt, nearly leaned into her touch with how much he craved the contact. He was sure that she had noticed him tense, but she didn't relent. Rather than pulling her hand away, she let her fingertips whisper against his skin. It was only when Andrew relaxed that she let her hand fall away.

"And, Andy," she said, stopping him as he descended the front porch steps. "Be careful, OK?" She nodded toward the wreck of a house next door, wordlessly implying Mickey with the tilt of her head.

Andy. His mom used to call him that—Sandy Andy, after a long day of playing out in the yard.

"I will," Drew promised.

When he unlatched the front gate and stepped onto the sidewalk, he couldn't help but to shoot a parting look over his shoulder. But Harlow was already gone, and Andrew already missed her.

§

Andrew needed to find a job. He was already low on money, and there was no way he'd be able to make next month's rent if he didn't get some cash coming in. The last thing he needed was for Mick to feel that Drew wasn't living up to his end of their bargain. Mickey would at least have a good reason to shoot disapproving glances Andrew's way.

Not like his mother. Even as he felt guilty for leaving her, he hated her for it. Leaving home was what kids were *supposed* to do—grow up, get out, start a life. The mortification he'd feel if he couldn't make rent, if he ended up having to go back home, would be enough to kill him.

He grabbed his keys off his mattress, took a Capri Sun for the road, and stepped out of the house and to the curb.

As the Chevy rambled down the road, Drew couldn't help but be struck by his shift in perception. Once upon a time, getting a job had meant keeping the lights on until he could escape Kansas completely. But now Andrew wanted nothing to do with leaving Kansas at all. His sole motivation was to find work and pay his rent, anything to keep himself on Magnolia Lane.

§

Sitting at a stoplight a few blocks from home, Mickey watched Andrew's pickup roll through a yellow light toward the center of town. He watched the Chevy grow smaller by the second before his eyes snapped to his rearview mirror. A silver Taurus was honking for him to move, the guy behind the wheel shaking his hands in muted frustration. His mouth moved soundlessly, silenced by the windshield, but Mickey could read his lips.

Slowly raising his right hand, he casually extended his middle finger and watched the guy's temper flare. He let the driver stew for a few more seconds, then stepped on the gas, smirking. Sometimes he wondered about his own set of scruples. He allowed Harlow Ward to do what she did without interfering, yet he couldn't climb out of his TransAm and pop a son of a bitch like the Taurus guy in the mouth.

"You're fucked up," he muttered beneath the roar of his V8. "You'll burn in hell for the shit you've done."

§

The music was an instrumental version of Billy Joel's "Only the Good Die Young." It was terrible, but Drew was a captive audience. He found himself tapping his sneaker on scuffed lino-leum, singing the lyrics under his breath. The door to the office at the back of the Thriftway finally swung open, and a guy in a pale yellow polo stepped in with a too enthusiastic hello.

"Hi there. Andrew, is it?"

Drew stood and extended his hand with a smile.

"Yes, sir," he said. "Andrew Morrison."

"Nice to meet you, guy. Please…" A motion to the chair Drew had just occupied. "Have a seat."

The pale yellow polo took a seat behind his desk, upon which a nameplate read, STEVEN CRYER, STORE MANAGER. Getting back into the grocery store business turned Drew's stomach—it felt like he was falling backward rather than moving on to bigger and bet-ter things—but this was his best shot at an immediate hire. He had experience—and no time to waste. Scoring a job here would allow him to look for something different between shifts.

"So, I hear you're looking to work for us."

"Yes, sir, if there's an opening."

"You've worked in grocery before," Cryer noted, looking over the handwritten job application Drew had filled out not a half hour earlier. "Says you were employed at Kroger just…" he paused, glanced up at Drew with a puzzled expression, "a few days ago?"

"Yes, sir, that's right."

"You were let go?" The look of suspicion on Cryer's face was a comical contrast to the smiling dollar sign mascot on the vinyl banner behind him. *Thrifty says: Shop at Thriftway! Best prices, guaranteed!*

"No, sir, I quit."

The suspicion immediately shifted to distrust. Drew could read the guy's mind: quitters never won, not even in the produce department.

"Looks like you were employed there for quite some time," Cryer noted, shifting in his seat. "Five years, which is impressive, so I did us both a favor and called in for a reference."

Drew's mouth went dry.

"Uh-huh," Cryer said. "Want to rethink your story?" With his desk chair groaning beneath him, Cryer leaned back and knitted his fingers together across his chest, as if he were convinced that managing a two-bit grocery store was the top of the food chain.

"I-I left," Drew stammered.

"You walked out. That's not the same as quitting," Cryer noted. "But here"—he tapped the résumé on his desk—"you say you *quit.*"

Drew stared down at his feet, baffled by how quickly this interview had gone to shit. He frowned, coming to the far-too-late realization that he shouldn't have lied. But it was too late for that now. He had been blinded by his need for work, by the charm of that morning's breakfast, by the fact that he'd rather live in a Dumpster than go back to where he'd come from. Cryer was about to tell him to get out of his office; he could feel it.

Suddenly, he heard his dad yelling from the kitchen. *Just say it. The truth will set you free.* Drew didn't know what truth Rick had been trying to get out of his mother that evening, but he knew the truth that would possibly save his chances here. Closing his eyes, he exhaled a defeated sigh.

"I really need this job," he murmured.

"I'm sure you do," Cryer quipped.

"My mother is an alcoholic," he confessed. "And she doesn't leave the house. Ever."

Cryer perked up, but Andrew hesitated. How could he tell this man—this *stranger*—about his mom? About the way she trembled if she didn't have her hourly drink; the way she melted into the couch with satisfaction when it finally hit her lips? Drew knew it was a disease, but he couldn't help be disgusted by her. How was he supposed to explain that to this self-satisfied grocery store manager and keep even a shred of his own dignity? Confessing her sins somehow turned *him* into a bad person. But it was his only shot at a job, and if he didn't get it, he'd wind up right back there on Cedar Street, miserable, watching her slowly drown herself.

"I haven't told this to anyone," he said, hoping that Cryer would lend him some mercy and wave off any further explanation. But the store manager looked far too intrigued to let it go. Drew swallowed against the lump in his throat, stared down at his hands, and dared to continue.

"I've been taking care of her since I was a kid, and just recently—last week, actually—I saw her walking down the street back toward our house."

Cryer leaned forward. "You said she never left the house," he countered.

"Exactly," Drew replied.

He'd been driving home from work when he spotted a woman hobbling along the side of the road with two paper bags. At first he suspected it was Mrs. Combs, a widow who lived alone on the outskirts of town. Every now and then, Mrs. Combs would wander into town on foot. Most of the time she'd get picked up by police; she had early-onset Alzheimer's and often forgot where she was. Drew had slowed his truck and leaned across the bench seat, rolling down the window to offer her a ride.

But it wasn't Mrs. Combs.

It was his mother.

He remembered the surge of joy that had speared his heart. *Holy shit*, he had thought. *She's outside. She's trying. She's really trying to get well again.*

He had pulled the truck over and jumped out of the cab, but a wall of nausea stopped him in his tracks. His mother refused to look at him, her face a mask of guilt. He didn't have to look inside those bags to know they weren't filled with groceries.

"The bags were full of booze," he told Cryer, his voice barely a mumble.

Cryer leaned back again, clearly relishing the tale.

Drew clenched his jaw, his rage bubbling up now as strongly as it had then. He had begged her to go out with him so many times—to hop into his truck so he could take her out for a burger, so they could go to a movie; he wanted her to see that the world still existed and she could still be a part of it. He had tried to help her beat her disease, had even suggested that they pick up and move somewhere new, start fresh. She had refused him every time. And yet she had temporarily beaten her agoraphobia—not to make her only child happy, not to make his life easier, not to make up for all the mistakes she had made, but to fill the empty liquor cabinet at home.

"So I packed up my stuff and I moved out," he said bitterly. "I didn't want to keep any part of my old life, especially not the part that supported her for the past five years, so I quit my job." He paused, corrected himself. "*Left* my job, I guess. I hadn't missed a day of work in like…" He shook his head, not able to remember the most recent unscheduled day he had taken off. "I don't know. A really long time. And I felt really bad about it, you know? The people there were great, and I should have put in my two weeks, but I just had to get out of there." He looked up, desperate for approval, for some glimmer of understanding. "Out of my house, I mean. And I didn't want her to find me, or send someone to find me, or, I don't know…" His words drifted off. He looked back down to his hands again.

"That's it?" Cryer asked after a painfully awkward few seconds.

"That's it," Drew told him. And just like that, he felt terrible.

He had raced back home after catching her along the side of the road, nearly mowing down their mailbox when he careened into the driveway. He stumbled out of the pickup like a drunk, careened up the porch steps, fumbled with his house keys. He dropped them once, then again, and finally flung himself inside, slamming the door behind him so hard and fast, all that was missing was the murderer, the ax, and the chase. With his back to the door, he saw the house he'd lived in his entire life through a new set of eyes. The house that his Gamma had lovingly decorated and his PopPop had kept up for so long was now little more than a living corpse. The sunny yellow color that had danced across the walls had faded to a sad brown. Nothing was clean. Nothing was new. There was no hope to be found, not in any of it.

The one thing that was truly different about that familiar landscape was that Julie Morrison wasn't in it. Instead, the self-proclaimed agoraphobe was dragging her feet along the road, two bags of booze heavy at her sides.

He had been betrayed. By his mother. His *mom*.

He stumbled forward, his vision blurred by tears, and did what he had only seen done in movies: he began to destroy the place. He dislodged the couch cushions and tossed them across the room, one of them clipping a small table full of knickknacks. Small ceramic figurines tinkled against the hardwood floor like rain, exploding on impact—all of his mother's precious trinkets, annihilated by a pang of hate. He grabbed the coffee table by its rim, overturning it with a sudden upward shove. Empty bottles flew up; glass tumblers spiraled through the air; a full ashtray spun like a Frisbee before crashing to the floor. When the table hit the ground, it fell with a cacophony of shattering glass, bottles exploding beneath its weight. The stink of alcohol wafted up from the floor. He backed away from the mess, knocking a lamp off a side table as he did, wiping at his eyes.

She had asked for it. She deserved it. But no matter which way he spun it or how he explained it, it boiled down to one thing: he had left her—an ill, mentally unstable woman; his own mother—alone. It didn't matter how much he had done for her or how hard he had tried, because in the end he hadn't tried hard enough. He had failed. And he had run. And nobody was going to give a shit about how he had given up college, how he had lost the only girl he'd ever loved, how he had spent Friday nights mopping up vomit rather than hanging out with the people who had once been his friends. Nobody cared about that because it didn't matter. Andrew was the bad guy. He was the one to blame.

Cryer sat silently for a long while, staring at Andrew as he replayed the drama that had become his life. A compassionate smile worked its way across the store manager's mouth.

"I appreciate your opening up," he said.

Drew blinked, that smile giving him hope. Maybe it *did* matter; maybe all that self-sacrifice was about to pay off, right here, right now.

"But given the fact that you didn't even put in notice..."

Drew shook his head. "What?"

"Well, you have to see this from my perspective," Cryer told him. "Admittedly, it doesn't look good."

"But I have experience," Drew protested, his voice cracking with emotion. He hated himself for how desperate he sounded. "There's no reason for me to leave *this* job. I *need* it."

"And I appreciate that," Cryer said. "I really do. But there's just nothing I can do."

Drew's stomach twisted. The back of his throat went sour. The nerves that had taken hold of his insides flared into anger; the guilt that Cryer had forced him to regurgitate roared into rage. He felt used. Cryer had known he was going to turn Drew down from the get-go, but he sat there anyway, allowing him to pour his heart out, and for what? Drew rose from his chair, trying to keep calm.

"I'm really sorry, Andrew," Cryer insisted, standing as well. "I know it's rough."

"Really?" The question tumbled from his lips before he could suppress it. He wanted to scream, to tell Cryer he was an asshole; he wanted to flip his desk the way he had flipped his mother's coffee table and tell him that nobody shopped at Thriftway anyway; he didn't need this job. But he *did*.

And then he remembered Harlow—her smiling face, the way the skirt of her dress swayed like a metronome when she walked, how her hair had glowed in the morning sun, the way she had brushed his hair aside as if assuring him that everything was fine, everything would be OK.

He exhaled a slow breath, glanced up at Cryer again.

"I'm sorry," he said, "you're right."

Cryer forced a smile, extending his hand across his desk. "Good luck," he said. "With everything."

Andrew shook the man's hand with a faint nod and took a step toward the door.

"Really," Cryer told him. "I mean it."

When Drew looked up at him again, Cryer really did look like he meant it. And somehow, that made up for how hard it had been for Andrew to make his confession. He hadn't told anybody what he had been dealing with. To see that it had affected a stranger, even in the tiniest of ways, made him think that maybe he wasn't in the wrong after all; that maybe, sometime soon, the weight of that guilt would lift from his shoulders, and he'd finally be free.

§

Creekside had a total of five grocery stores, so after the disaster at Thriftway, he visited the rest of them, minus the Kroger he used to work at less than a week before. He filled out three applications despite two of the managers telling him they weren't hiring, and scored another interview only to be told that they'd call him later. Drew tried to be optimistic, but that "later" felt like a "never."

His frustration started to mount.

He dropped into a couple of video game stores, a bike shop, three coffee places, and a Dairy Queen. Everyone shook their heads. Everyone gave him an apologetic smile, a shrug of the shoulders. It appeared that Creekside was far from immune from the Capitol disease. The economy had gone to shit, even in the heartland.

Despite the work he'd put into Mickey's house, he didn't want to go back there yet, didn't want to face the bitter reality that he was living in a dilapidated house—a blight on an otherwise perfect neighborhood. So he decided to get something to eat instead. But the urgency of his situation hit him full-on while sitting in line at a Burger King drive-through. After numerous fast-food runs, his funds were in the double digits. The seven dollars he handed to the guy at the window suddenly seemed an extravagant amount for a burger and some fries. He tried to enjoy his sandwich, but was hindered by his inability to stop thinking about how, if he kept going out to eat, he wouldn't last longer than a week.

Parked in front of the house, the aftertaste of french fries still on his tongue, Drew sat in his truck for a long while, staring blankly at the steering wheel. Suddenly overwhelmed by frustration, he grabbed the wheel, clenched his teeth, and tried to shake the damn thing free of the dash. It didn't budge, and eventually Drew simply slumped in his seat, his forehead pressed to the wheel. He had expected this to be easy. His current disillusionment only served as proof that he was an idiot. Because nothing was ever easy. Especially not this.

Throwing his door open, he paced the cracked sidewalk in front of the house, his fingers shoved through his hair. The locusts hummed in the trees, their incessant buzz somehow making the summer heat more brutal. Back and forth along that pavement, he tried to figure out what the hell he was going to do, somehow convinced that remaining outside would help him think. Turning his attention to Mick's house, he couldn't help but wonder if this was honestly better than living at home. Both places were suddenly neck-and-neck on Andrew's scale of disgust. If home was where the heart was, home was neither here nor there. If home was where you *wanted* to be, Drew's home was next door beneath the shade of a front porch; it was behind a white picket fence, not in front of a patchy, sunburned lawn.

His hands fell to his sides, leaving his hair in stressed-out disarray. He exhaled a sigh and stalked across the crunchy lawn.

Halfway to the house, he heard his name.

"Andy?"

He glanced over his shoulder at the pride of Magnolia Lane. Harlow stood in the front yard, her wide-brimmed sun hat and Jackie O glasses obscuring her face. One arm loaded with cut roses, the other extended over her head in a wave, she looked like a Hollywood starlet—the kind you'd see in a fancy spread about the next big actress: Harlow Ward, home from the studio, pruning her rosebushes and hiring local boys to move heavy furniture.

"You all right, honey?" Her voice chimed in the breeze like a songbird's chirp.

He didn't answer. How hadn't he seen her when he parked? She was damn near impossible to miss. It seemed as though she'd appeared out of thin air, but he hardly cared. She was exactly what he needed—a reminder that he had made the right decision, that moving here wasn't a mistake.

"You look upset," she said. "Is there something wrong?"

He determined then and there that Harlow wasn't real. She was a figment of his imagination, the personification of the perfect woman circa 1959. Most neighbors didn't bother to speak to each other anymore, but Harlow—he wouldn't have been surprised if she had been standing there with a sheet of her freshly baked cookies, those gardening gloves replaced by oven mitts. It was nice to know that someone cared enough to ask if he was OK; it was even nicer to know that the person doing the caring was Harlow, and he was the object of her affection.

"Everything's fine," he said.

"Oh good." She crouched down, tucked her flowers into an oversize basket, and straightened her hat before speaking again. "Come have lunch."

Drew cracked a smile. She was relentless. "I just ate," he confessed.

"Oh?" She slid her sunglasses down her nose, giving him a look. "Let me guess, McDonald's?"

He gave her a guilty look, then exhaled a helpless laugh when she shook her head at him with a sly grin of her own.

"Fine," she said. "Some other time, then."

She turned away only to pause a moment later, glancing back to him before stepping back to the picket fence between them. She plucked a rose from her basket and laid it across the length of the top rail. And then she turned again, disappearing inside without a word.

CHAPTER SIX

Red Ward had been working his afternoon shift at the Pizza Pit just a block from Kansas City College when Harlow Beaumont stepped into his life, and she caught his attention right along with everyone else's. Even flanked by her two foxy friends—a trio of Charlie's Angels if there ever was one—Harlow stole the spotlight. She entered the place the way Bridget Bardot stepped onto a movie set—sizzling as she walked, her long blonde hair blown back by an invisible wind machine. With Creedence Clearwater pouring from the Pizza Pit's speakers, she was a fantasy; a pair of bright orange hot pants paired with a white turtleneck; waves of liquid gold spilling over her shoulders, held in place by a white crocheted beret; legs for days.

Red had always been the silent type. He gathered empty plates and plastic cups off the table he had been busing when the girls stepped into the joint before moving to the table directly behind Harlow and her friends. Sneaking a glance at the books she'd placed on the table—theology, not a subject he would have guessed—he took stock of everything he could without being noticed—anything to get next to a girl like her. But Red's attention to detail didn't turn him into an international spy. One of the girls noticed him staring and turned up her nose, motioning to her friends with a nod of her head, then confronted the busboy who was taking a little too much interest in their group.

"Hey," she said with a mouth full of gum, its sugary pink scent drifting across the table, breaching the distance between them as she sat there, fluffing her bleached-blonde hair. She wasn't the kind of girl Red went for—loud, gaudy; Harlow's looks were far from tame, but there was a mystery to her, like she was hiding some big secret, and Red wanted to be the guy who figured out what that secret was.

"Hey, *you*," the bottle-blonde continued, peering Red's way.

He stopped what he was doing, which was little more than straightening the salt and pepper shakers, and offered Harlow's gum-snapping friend an innocent glance. *Who, me?*

"Yeah, you," she said. "I saw you looking over here, hotshot. You wanna take a picture?"

The girls giggled—all of them except for Harlow, who, rather than joining her friends in their needled chuckling, merely stared at Red with a half grin.

Red looked down nervously, continuing to straighten the table, trying to look busy and uninterested. But his heart was hammering against his ribs. Harlow was the prettiest girl he'd ever set eyes on. He wanted to talk to her, but courage was failing him.

"Did you see something you liked?" the girl continued. "Wanna get with me, huh?"

"Maybe he wants to come disco with us," the second Angel, a redhead, suggested. Her hair was a halo of fire, teased and curly. She leered at him when Red glanced her way, batting her green-eyeshadowed eyes at him.

"You want to come disco with us, baby?" the sunshine blonde asked. "Or are you too busy making pizza all night long? Wanna roll my dough?"

"Make love, not pizza," the fiery one quipped.

Again, they burst into laughter. The stunner between them cracked a knowing grin.

Red watched the girls eat from a distance, keeping away from them, not wanting to scare them away—though there was a fat chance of that happening with those two. When the loud ones rose from their table, rowdy and laughing, the quiet looker remained seated.

"What's the matter with you, 'Lo? Aren't you coming?" the blonde asked, shoving another wad of Bubble Yum into her mouth.

Harlow shook her head, offering them a shrug.

The girls blinked at one another before exhaling a communal groan.

"*Him?*" the blonde asked.

"Oh God," the redhead countered. "Spaz-city."

"He probably smells like pepperoni," the first joked.

"Yeah, his *sausage* does."

Another uproar of laughter. Harlow chuckled but didn't budge.

"Don't blame us when you get the clap from that dirty bird," the golden-haired one chided.

"He's a *busboy*," the redhead reminded her.

"I'll catch you later," Harlow told them.

"Whatever." The blonde sighed with a roll of her eyes, genuinely annoyed to be leaving the third Angel behind. "Just don't get preggo by the Italian Stallion."

"Yeah." The fiery one smirked. "Explain *that* to your pops. 'But, Daddy, he was a busboy,'" she teased, fluttering her lashes, her hand pressed to her chest.

"At least he's got a job," Harlow said.

Her friends finally relented, waving their hands dismissively and exiting in a cacophony of chatter. Harlow remained at the now empty table, one long leg crossed over the other, a pair of woven platform shoes lending an extra inch to her long legs.

His way clear, Red dared to approach her table. Harlow offered him a smile.

"Hey," she said. "Sorry about my friends. They're total airheads, you know." She shrugged again, excusing the others' lack of class.

"You want another Coke?" Red asked, motioning to her near-empty glass. "No charge."

"No charge?" Harlow raised an eyebrow. "Yeah, sure, I'll take another. What are you, the owner or something?"

"The owner of what? This place?" Red nearly blushed at the suggestion. He'd only be so lucky, owning his own business in a big city.

"Sure," she said, reaching for her purse. "Handing out free pop the way you are. You're either the owner or you've got a lot of soda money."

"Or I'm just buying a pretty girl a soda," he said, deciding to take the risk. "Something wrong with that?"

"I guess not."

"I get off my shift in ten minutes," he confided, sure that if he didn't make his move he'd never see this stunner again; and then he'd spend the rest of his life wondering *what if.*

"Do you?" Harlow smiled impishly at his confession, pulling a pack of Lucky Strikes from her bag. "You got a light?"

Red patted down his pockets, then motioned to the kitchen. "In my jacket…"

"Forget it," she muttered around the filter, digging through her purse for matches.

"Want to grab a drink?" he asked. "After my shift?"

Harlow gave him a look past her lashes, thick with mascara.

"Oh, I don't *drink*," she told him. "Daddy's a pastor."

"Yeah?" Red asked. "Is that why you're studying that stuff?" He nodded to her school books, and Harlow rolled her eyes.

"Yeah," she said. "Something like that."

"You think he's watching?"

"He's always watching."

"How's that?" Red asked, plucking her empty glass off the table.

"Through God's eyes, baby." She winked, lighting her smoke. "I imagine I'm going to be struck down any minute now."

§

The headlights of the TransAm cut through the darkness, casting weird shadows across the face of the house. Drew had nursed the day's wounds by watching talk shows and reality TV all afternoon when he should have been applying for work at gas stations and truck stops, but the bitter blow of countless nos had temporarily grounded him.

Mickey dragged himself through the door, and though he'd been gone the entire day, his appearance offered no clue where he had been. There was no uniform to suggest a day of work, no duffel bag or water bottle to suggest time spent at the gym.

"Hey," Drew greeted him from the couch.

Mick offered his roommate a nod of the head, attempted to force a smile, but his expression was unreadable.

"Where were you?" Drew asked.

"Out," Mickey replied.

"Just out?" Drew raised an eyebrow.

"Yeah, driving around," Mick said. "I'll be right back." Turning down the hall, he wandered to his room.

Drew pulled a face, squinting at the television.

Mickey resurfaced from his room a few minutes later, making a beeline for the fridge. He fished out two cans of beer, cracked one open while tossing the other at Drew. Taking a gulp midstride, Mick shuffled over to the couch and fell into his own personal divot.

Drew peered at the cold can of beer in his hands, then looked at his housemate, breaking the silence: "Can I get access to the network here? The password, I mean."

"The what?"

Drew leaned forward, snatching his cell phone off the coffee table. "The network," he repeated, pulling up the settings screen. "I've got, like, no service here. Can I log into the wi-fi?" He pointed the phone at Mickey, a network titled "my neighbors suck" highlighted on the screen. "That's you, I'm assuming."

Mickey gulped his beer and peered at the television before offering an unenthusiastic nod.

"Well, can I have the password? Unless you have a computer I can use."

"For what?"

"Job hunting," Drew confessed. "I went to, like, nine different places today and wanted to kill myself afterward. Nobody's hiring."

"Then how's the Internet going to help?"

Andrew lifted his shoulders in a shrug. "I have to keep looking, right? Unless you're about to bless me with a lifetime of free rent."

"What's wrong with the classifieds?" Mickey asked, throwing his head back to finish off his beer. Andrew stared at him in childlike fascination while Mick crushed the can in his hand.

"Seriously?" Drew asked.

It was Mickey's turn to scope his roomie out. "Seriously what?"

"You're going to make me go buy a newspaper?" Andrew shook his head, looking back to the TV.

They both sat silently for a long while. Drew chewed his bottom lip. Mick's refusal to let him access the network was a breach of etiquette; if there was a roommate code, this was certainly a violation of it.

A minute later, Mickey spoke up, as if sensing what Drew was thinking.

"I forgot it."

Andrew shook his head.

"The password," Mickey clarified. "I forgot it. I got hacked and I made it complicated, and I didn't write the goddamn thing down. Gotta call the cable company," he said. "It takes, like, an hour to talk to anyone."

Drew furrowed his eyebrows at his phone.

"I'll do it later," Mickey murmured.

"Don't worry about it," he said grudgingly, but he hoped that Mickey *would* worry about it.

They both went silent again, watching a Swiffer commercial as though it were entertainment gold.

"You know they can see that, right?"

Mickey glanced over to Drew.

"The network," Drew told him. "What you named it."

Mick offered the TV an intent look, and Drew felt that kernel of distrust wiggle at the pit of his stomach. Harlow had warned him, however vaguely, and the more time he spent with Mickey the more he was starting to believe that there was something to her advice. Perhaps that was why nobody had complained to the city about the state of Mick's house; maybe the people on Magnolia were scared of what he would do in response. Andrew watched his roommate out of the corner of his eye, trying to get a feel of what sort of danger Mickey could pose; what kind of criminal he could possibly be. But Drew couldn't very well ask him what his deal was. He'd have to wait it out, pick up on clues, piece it together himself. Or maybe he'd use it as another excuse to see Harlow; if Mick got too weird, he'd go to her for advice.

"You aren't worried that it'll piss them off?"

"Piss what off?"

"The Wards," Drew said. "Isn't it better to try to stay on good terms with the neighbors instead of, I don't know..." He shrugged. "Telling them they suck? What's wrong with them, anyway?"

Mickey glared at the TV, then exhaled a sigh and shot Drew a look.

"Nothing," he said. "Don't worry about it. Where'd you look, anyway?"

"What?"

"For work," Mick clarified.

"Oh, um...like everywhere? Grocery stores, DQ..." He rolled his eyes. "The job situation sucks."

Mickey said nothing.

"Where do you work, anyway?" he asked.

Mickey stood and gave Andrew a look—ironically, one of wariness. "I'm going to bed," he announced. "Lock up when you're done."

Before Andrew could push the subject, Mick dragged himself down the hall and disappeared behind his door.

Drew remained where he was for a long while, watching the flickering TV screen. He eventually turned off the TV, wandered to the front door, and threw the deadbolt in place, unable to help the incredulous smile that pulled at the corners of his mouth. It was funny, Mickey making sure that Drew locked up before bed—as though anyone would want to break into that dump; as though there was someone to fear on Magnolia other than the guy who lived in the creepy house with the crooked gutters.

Walking down the hall, he paused in front of the locked door directly across from his own—yet another reminder that Mickey was hiding something, that all was not well. Stepping inside his room, he closed his door behind him, his eyes set on the window across the way, on the glow of light coming from the house next door, on the single rose he'd placed on his windowsill, its stem stuck inside a plastic water bottle.

Wavering beside the door, he considered whether to lock himself in. He chewed his bottom lip, his memories of Mickey still redolent of childhood, of the good times they'd had. He wanted to believe his misgivings were little more than paranoia—his guilt for leaving his mother behind manifesting itself into uncertainty. Finally, he pushed himself away from the door, leaving it unlocked, sure that in due time his disquiet would pass.

§

Harlow pulled the palm of her hand across the top of the bed, smoothing wrinkles out of the comforter. While the house was pristine, this room was the one she cleaned the most; it was almost surgically sanitized. Nobody slept in that bed—at least not as often as she'd have liked—but she washed the sheets twice a week anyway, hopeful that her next guest would arrive soon. Nobody used the adjoining bathroom either, but she spent two hours a week scrubbing the sink, the toilet, the bathtub, until they sparkled like a cleaning product commercial. She vacuumed from the farthest corner of the bedroom back toward the door, leaving perfectly straight vacuum lines along the fibers of the carpet, imagining Andy doing the very same thing next door, determined to get that rat's nest clean.

Today she had attacked the task with newfound zest, and she smiled to herself as she pulled the bedroom door closed. She could hardly wait. This time, it was going to be perfect.

She waited until the lights went out next door, and then she waited two hours more. Slipping out of bed, she left Red snoring in their bedroom. Her slippers silent on the stairs, she crossed the house into her kitchen, slipped a key out of the pocket of her robe, and unlocked the basement door. A minute later, the locked hallway door in Mickey's house swung open, silent on its hinges, and Harlow stepped inside. She silently turned the knob of Drew's door, smiling as it swung wide, unlocked, opening in greeting as she crept inside. Drew rolled over in his sleep, his right arm jutting out over the edge of the mattress; no regard for monsters that may have lurked beneath the bed.

She stood over him for a long while, watching him dream. She was tempted to brush his hair from his forehead, yearned to touch his cheek, to let her robe slide from her shoulders before slipping into bed with him, naked beneath the sheets. She wanted to draw her lips across the shell of his ear, whisper that this was their little secret. *It's OK, sweetheart,* she'd tell him. *This is my way of showing you how much I love you.*

But it was too soon. She wanted him so badly, but it had to be perfect.

She eventually turned her attention to the dresser. Plucking up his wallet, Harlow drew a finger across the picture on his driver's license: Andrew R. Morrison, only twenty-three years old. Sliding it out of its plastic holder, she brought it to her lips, her gaze snagging on the small card behind it—the one she had tacked to a plate of cookies. Her heart leapt at the sight of it. He had kept it. She had been right; Andrew wasn't like the rest. Tucking his license back into place, she took a backward step toward the door, afraid that if she stayed any longer she wouldn't be able to help herself—she'd wake him up, she'd make him hers. She placed the wallet back on the dresser, then slid it to its edge, allowing it to fall to the floor. She lingered for a while longer, then finally stepped out of the room.

§

The door was the first thing Andrew noticed: it was wide open. The second was that his wallet, which he'd left on top of his dresser, was now on the floor, as though someone had rifled through it and accidentally dropped it on their way out. He blinked at it from the bed, and for a good long while he couldn't figure out what the hell he was seeing. Someone had been in his room; someone had messed with his stuff. Wallets didn't just magically slide across the tops of dressers. Doors didn't just open by themselves.

The sickening sensation of his privacy having been violated slithered over him. He shuddered, then threw the sheets aside, marching across his room to snatch the wallet off the floor. As he thumbed through its contents, he realized that nothing was missing. But his head still swam with betrayal. There was no doubt that someone had come into his room while he slept. That, piled on top of the locked door, the refusal to answer questions, the "forgotten" password: Drew suddenly felt like he was back home, surrounded by deception and lies.

"Son of a bitch."

Yanking the top drawer of his dresser open, he threw the wallet in amid his socks and underwear. Then he stomped down the hall, paused in front of Mickey's room, took a breath, and pounded on the door.

"Hey!" he yelled, his fist hammering against cheap wood. "I need to talk to you."

Mickey answered after a few seconds, groggy with sleep.

"The fuck, man?" He rubbed at one of his eyes, looking oddly childlike despite his wide shoulders. Mickey was put together like a bodybuilder, but Andrew refused to let his roomie's size deter him.

"Did you come into my room last night?"

Mickey looked confused, but Drew refused to buy into his feigned innocence. Harlow was right: Mick was bad news. Maybe that was how he got his cash: by ripping off his house-mates. Maybe he had been planning to take Drew's money as well, but was stopped short by some remnant of their childhood friendship.

"My door was open and my wallet was on the floor," Drew told him. "When I went to sleep, the door was closed and the wallet *wasn't* on the floor."

"Huh?" Mickey blinked back at him sleepily.

"You know, it's one thing to invite someone to live with you when the place is a sty," Drew told him. "It's another to come into someone's room and screw with their shit."

"Hey," Mickey said, raising a hand. "I didn't mess with your shit, man."

"Whatever," Drew muttered, then turned away, not sure what he had expected to accomplish—not entirely sure why he was so pissed. If the guy wanted to, he could snap Drew's neck without even trying, but Andrew's irritation refused to subside. He couldn't get the name of Mick's home network out of his head: *my neighbors suck*. It rubbed him the wrong way. He took it personally—an attack on the only individual in Creekside who seemed to give half a shit about what was going on in his life; the only person who had his best interests in mind.

"I bet you rob banks." It tumbled out of him involuntarily as he walked away. He winced as soon as it left his lips. It was below the belt, a result of his own feelings of inadequacy, of Mickey's disaffection.

"Rob banks?" Mickey exhaled a snort. "You think I'd be living in this shithole if I robbed banks? You're a real genius, huh? A real fucking Einstein."

Drew stopped in his tracks, eyeing the crappy carpet beneath his feet. He had half a dozen comebacks to Mickey's quip, but he held back, turning to face his former friend. "Look, I'm sorry," he said. "I just feel…" Drew hesitated, shook his head. "I don't know, like maybe you offered for me to move in here on a whim, but you never thought I'd actually show up."

Mickey stared at him for a long while, as though waiting for him to say something more. Drew was waiting for Mick to deny his theory, to shake his head and tell him that this feeling of his was ridiculous; of *course* he wanted Drew to move in. But Mickey stuck to the facts.

"Is anything missing from your room?" he asked.

"No," Drew muttered.

"Maybe that's because I didn't mess with your shit."

"Then who did?"

"I don't know." Mickey shrugged. "Maybe someone walked in through the front fucking door. It happens."

"I locked the door."

Mickey shrugged again.

"Are *you* missing anything?" Drew asked. "Have you checked?"

"I'm not missing anything," Mickey said flatly.

"So, despite the front door being locked, someone got inside, they rifled through my stuff, not yours, and they didn't take anything?"

"Maybe they didn't come into my room." Mickey stared at Drew, his eyes not once leaving his roommate's face. "Maybe they weren't after your shit. Ever think of that? Maybe they wanted something else. Or maybe it's just your imagination," Mickey added a moment later, "and you woke me up for nothing."

Drew turned away, ready to wander back to his room, but he was stopped short by the final nail in the conversational coffin.

"That's probably how you got here in the first place, right?" Mickey asked. "You overreacted?"

Mickey disappeared into his room. Drew felt like he was going to be sick—not only because he was terrible at confrontation, but because Mickey was right. Rather than approaching his mother with a demand for answers, Drew busted up the living room; he packed his shit; he abandoned her, just like his dad.

§

As a kid, Drew would take to the streets on his bike after arguments with his mom, and he'd usually end up at the Fitches' place. So it struck him as odd that after his argument with Mickey, Drew found himself cruising along what could have been every street in Creekside until he reached Cedar Street, his mother but a few hundred yards away. He parked along the dirt shoulder, far enough so that he wouldn't be noticed in case his mother was staring out any of the windows. The sky was growing dark with a thick roll of clouds. A storm was closing in from the west, and his old house always seemed to be hit first.

A twister had whipped along their street when he had been four or five. Distant sirens wailed, but Drew ran to the window instead of to the basement, where he'd been taught to go. A black cyclone, thick and slow, touched down and tore trees from the earth. With his nose pressed to the shuddering glass, he wondered what it would be like to run into that wind; wondered if he could catch it like a butterfly in a net, wondered if he could run through to the center without being plucked from the ground like Dorothy. *There's no place like home.*

Watching those clouds churning overhead now, he imagined the house on Cedar Street and everything in it being swallowed by the wind, speculating on how it would feel to lose his past, his mother, his entire identity.

"You'd cry like a baby," he told himself. "And now, if it happens, you'll never forgive yourself."

He spent more than an hour sitting along the dirt shoulder, deliberating whether to go inside. He could call the whole thing off with Mick right now and return to comfortable familiarity. At least here, on Cedar, he knew what was behind every door. But coming back meant giving in; it meant giving up Magnolia and returning to a life he couldn't handle anymore, living with a woman who was scared of her own shadow.

Drew looked away from his old house, his mouth sour with realization: He'd never look at his mother the same way again. Because he'd looked into the sun, and the sun had blinded him with its brilliance.

He still loved her. He always would. But Julie Morrison would have to learn to live without him. Because he couldn't do it anymore; he couldn't ignore all the things he deserved when they were right there, waiting for him on Magnolia Lane.

§

That night, a neighborhood dog had a barking fit. It wasn't the Pekingese. It sounded bigger, like a retriever, and the thing refused to let up, yowling like it was being skinned alive. Drew considered shoving his feet into his shoes and stalking across the street to bang on the owner's door; the entire neighborhood would surely thank him, because what kind of pet owner left a dog outside during a storm? But in the end he rolled over and pulled his pillow over his head to muffle the noise, and that was the way he slept.

Whether it had been a few minutes or a few hours, Drew's eyes shot open to a metallic bang outside. With the pillow secured over his head, he wasn't able to discern where it had come from; probably the wind knocking over someone's trash can. But it had sounded closer—almost directly in front of the house. If it *had* been a trash can, it had probably slammed into the side of his truck. The dog that had eventually settled down was in an uproar again, barking its head off from an undisclosed location. Groggy, Drew threw the pillow across his bed and pushed the window curtain aside, sleepily peering out onto the street.

His truck was parked along the curb, no trash can in sight. It was nights like these that Drew was thankful he didn't have a nice car. With his luck, a tornado would spear a tree branch through the front windshield of his brand-new ride before he could peel the temp tag from the back bumper.

Not seeing anything, he let the curtain slip from his fingers. He pulled the sheets over his head, burying himself again.

CHAPTER SEVEN

Andrew's alarm clock buzzed bright and early. His arm sprang out from beneath the sheets like a jack-in-the-box, and he slapped the snooze button without opening his eyes. He exhaled a groan into his pillow. He had expected graduating high school to miraculously change him into an adult, to make early mornings more bearable, but getting up had never gotten any easier. Drew was the same sleep-deprived kid in his early twenties that he had been as a freshman.

He dragged himself down the hall, paused in front of the bathroom, and glanced toward Mickey's door. He hadn't spoken to his housemate since their blowup the morning before. He regretted flipping out, but Mick's suggestion that someone had broken into the house was crazy.

He brushed his teeth, took a hot shower, and prepared himself for another day of filling out applications. Despite his better judgment, he was determined to visit Walmart—or as his mom lovingly called it, Wally World. Perhaps old Wally could give him the opportunity of a lifetime by allowing him to collect carts, or push a giant floor waxer up and down the aisles during the graveyard shift. Or, if he was *really* lucky, he'd be spending eight hours of his day cheerfully greeting old ladies at the door.

He stood in the center of his room, a tie hanging from around his neck, his cell phone in his hand, waiting patiently as the tiny computer tried to retrieve instructions on how to tie a Windsor knot on a single bar of reception. But it was impossible. Eventually tiring of the wait, Drew gave the necktie a firm yank and tossed it onto his bed. He grabbed his wallet, shoved it into the back pocket of his khakis, and marched down the hall to the front door.

Despite the storm the night before, the sun was hotter than ever. He squinted against the glare, crunching across the parched lawn, keys jingling in his hand. He climbed in and shoved the key in the ignition; the engine turned over, sputtered, and died.

Andrew furrowed his eyebrows. The Chevy was an old piece of crap, but it had always been reliable. He tried again, but it was the same story. After a third try, Drew exhaled an exasperated laugh, his hands falling to his lap in defeat.

"Awesome," he said, full volume so the truck was sure to hear him. "That's awesome. Seriously."

He popped the hood and trudged around front to peer at an engine he didn't know a damn thing about. It was little details, like learning how to fix a car, that he had missed after his father had failed to return. He knew how to change a tire, and he'd learned how to change the oil off a website, but it was textbook knowledge. It wasn't ingrained in him the way it would have been if his dad had taught him those things.

Tangling his fingers in his hair, he took a deep breath and counted to ten. This was his *dad's* fault, his *dad's* shitty truck. Taking off to God only knows where, he had left Drew with little more than a handful of memories and a pickup that now sat dead in the street. But Andrew supposed that was only appropriate. His father had left him stranded just like this heap of scrap metal.

He shot a glance toward Mickey's TransAm, wondering whether Mick had learned to work on cars with his father before he had died. Standing in the shade of his popped hood, Drew remembered seeing Mick's dad in their driveway every now and again, the legs of his oil-stained jeans sticking out from beneath a Ford station wagon. There was no doubt that Mickey had learned how to be a mechanic the way a boy was supposed to. And that was great, seeing as how Andrew had gone and screwed up their rapport by banging on Mick's door the morning before. Crossing his arms over the lip of the open engine compartment, he rested his head against his forearms, wondering what the hell he was going to do.

"Son?"

Drew looked up with a jolt, surprised to see a man standing just a yard away. He had never seen Harlow's husband up close before, couldn't remember whether he'd ever caught the guy's name. But he was unmistakably Harlow's: perfect teeth like off a toothpaste commercial, loafers glinting in the sun. Guy Smiley personified.

"Looks like you're having some trouble," the man said with a smile. "You're Andrew, I take it?"

"Yes, sir."

"Harlow's told me about you. She said you were kind enough to come over and help her out." He extended his hand toward Drew. "Red."

Drew took the guy's hand in greeting, shook it.

"Redmond," he clarified. "Though nobody ever called me that save for my mother, and she only called me that when she was good and steamed."

Drew couldn't help the grin that spread across his face as Red turned his attention to the truck. The Wards just kept getting better and better. Harlow was perfection, and Red...well, Red had Ward right in his name: Ward for Ward Cleaver, the perfect TV dad.

"First time you've had problems?" he asked.

Drew nodded. "Yeah, she's never broken down on me before."

"How long have you had her?"

"Since I was six."

Red gave him a curious glance.

"She used to be my dad's. He left and I got the truck."

Red raised an eyebrow and looked back to the engine.

"Consolation prize," Drew confessed.

"That was nice of him," Red murmured.

As the man tinkered beneath the hood, Andrew took a few steps forward to look himself.

"You know anything about cars?" Red asked.

For a split second Drew was about to lie. Not being able to fix his own truck—well, that was embarrassing. Automobiles were supposed to be a common denominator among men: cars and football, both of which excluded Andrew Morrison from all of man-dom.

"I don't," he confessed, "other than changing the oil, really."

"Try to turn her over for me," Red suggested.

Drew climbed behind the wheel and gave the key another twist. The engine sputtered. Red waved a hand at him from behind the hood.

"You've got fuel, right?" Red asked, Drew rejoining him next to the front bumper.

"Half a tank; filled up a few days ago."

Reaching into his pocket, Red drew out a small Swiss Army knife. He flipped through the various tools, came to one that functioned as a screwdriver, and began to unscrew the distributor cap.

"What about your spark plugs?"

"Those should have been changed out a few months ago," Drew said. "I paid for it."

Red shook his head. "Just because you paid for it doesn't mean it was done, son. If you want something done right, you have to do it yourself."

With one screw down and one to go, Drew watched Red carefully remove the cap, exposing the distributor.

"Well, there's your problem," he announced. "See this?" He held up a small part for Drew's inspection. "That's your distributor rotor."

Drew cleared his throat as Red waited for some sort of response, and despite the lightbulb Drew wished had appeared over his head, there was no sudden realization, no true understanding of what the small part between Red's fingers meant.

"OK?" Drew said.

"It's come loose," Red told him, "which is why your truck won't start. No rotor, no spark, no go."

"Is that normal?" Drew asked. "For it to come off like that?"

Red pressed the rotor back onto its stalk. "I wouldn't say it's common, but it's not unheard of."

"Huh."

Drew watched Red press the rotor into place.

"Should have asked your roommate," Red suggested, nodding toward Mickey's sleeping Pontiac. "He probably knows cars."

Drew rolled his eyes before he could stop himself.

Red gave the kid beside him a knowing look. "I had a roommate once; worst decision I ever made. Seems like it's always the same old story."

"Mrs. Ward mentioned something about Mickey," Drew admitted, shifting his weight from one foot to the other. "Something about his history; she didn't say what it was."

Red nodded, apparently familiar with Harlow's reservations about their neighbor. But he didn't waste time on gossip, motioning for Drew to try the engine once more.

"Go ahead, give it a shot."

Andrew walked around the front of the truck and climbed into the cab. Pushing the clutch to the floor, he gave the key a turn. The engine sputtered once, then roared to life.

"Hell yeah." He laughed, smacking the steering wheel with satisfaction.

Red appeared in the driver's window, smiling at Drew's approval.

"Well, there she goes," he said. "Lots to do?"

"Job hunting."

"That's no fun. What kind of work are you looking for?"

"Anything," Drew admitted. "I'll take whatever I can find."

Red looked impressed, his expression drifting toward contemplation a second later.

"I've got a lot of odd jobs around the house," he said after a moment. "Harlow's a handful, and any renovation takes three times as long with that woman. She's a perfectionist."

Drew grinned. He knew she was. She wore that personality trait like a badge of honor on her dress lapel.

"I like you," Red confessed. "I like your work ethic. And you can't get a job better than the one next door. What do you say?"

Andrew blinked. It was too good to be true. He was hit by a wave of relief. Now he'd been saved not once, but twice—and both in the same morning. Working at that perfect little house, fixing a kitchen faucet or, hell, even retiling an entire bathroom—it was leaps and bounds above scrubbing dirty toilets at a fast-food joint.

"Are you serious?"

"Absolutely," Red said. "Harlow seems to like you as well, so why not?"

"As long as you don't need me to work on your car," Drew said. "Because, honestly…" He lifted his hands from the steering wheel, shaking his head. Red laughed.

"We'll start tomorrow morning," Red told him. "Eight o'clock." He extended his hand.

"Awesome, yeah," Drew replied, shaking just a little too eagerly, not even bothering to ask what Red was going to pay him. The idea of working for Harlow was so alluring that at that moment, money was the last thing on his mind. "Really, thank you. This is great."

Red waved at Drew as if to say it was nothing. "Nonsense; thank *you*," he told him. "See you tomorrow." And then he turned and walked away.

§

From behind the curtain, Harlow smiled.

CHAPTER EIGHT

A few blocks north of Magnolia, Drew found himself standing in the dirt parking lot of the local farmers' market. The market was in full swing despite the storm the night before, regardless of the fact that it would more than likely roll in again. The place was dotted with little booths and hand-painted signs: strawberries, three dollars a pint; freshly baked loaves of bread, two for five dollars. A little girl and her mother sold lemonade while others hawked their watermelons and organically grown zucchini.

Overwhelmed with gratitude, Drew was determined to give the Wards a proper thank-you for all that they'd done. Sitting in his just-fixed pickup, he was no longer unemployed, and while he barely had enough cash to scrape by, he owed a debt, and he planned on paying it.

An older woman occupied the booth closest to him. Her carefully painted sign assured anyone who was looking for a unique gift that yes, she had cellophane and would arrange the purchase into an attractive gift basket, perfect for that special someone. Drew didn't know the Wards very well, but a fruit basket was a classic gift. Anytime someone greeted a new neighbor on television, they presented a big basket full of fresh produce. He thought he remembered the ritual signifying bounty, or that the recipient would never know hunger. Whatever the meaning, he was sure Harlow would appreciate the retro touch.

"Do I buy the basket first and come back to have it arranged?" Drew asked the woman behind the precarious wall of wicker. She sat on a collapsible fishing chair, her hands busy with two aluminum knitting needles looping through the air like twin conductor's staffs. She nodded at him with a smile.

"For someone special?" she asked.

He picked up on her tone. Someone special, in her eyes, should have been a pretty young lady in a free-flowing summer dress—a beautiful girl with an easy smile and hair that rode upon the wind. Once upon a time, that girl had been Emily, but Emily was gone. And while Harlow may have not been Andrew's age, she was still beautiful, still pure and elegant and utterly sophisticated. Drew offered the woman a smile.

"For a neighbor," he answered. He flushed when he realized he had almost said "a friend."

"Sweet child," she said. "Neighbors are important too. Just don't forget Robert Frost."

"Sorry?"

"Frost, dear," the woman repeated. "The poet. Don't tell me you haven't read him."

He knew the name, and he was sure he'd read an obligatory poem or two in his senior English class, but nothing specific came to mind.

The woman rose from her chair, put her knitting aside, and picked out a basket from the pile.

"Good fences make good neighbors, dear. But a pretty basket never hurt anyone."

She handed the basket over with a smile. Drew reached into his back pocket for his wallet, but she waved the notion away.

"Pay later," she told him with a wink.

Drew blinked at her refusal. "Are you sure?"

"Well, are you going to run off with my basket without coming back?" she asked with a teasing smile. "You wouldn't deny an old woman a few minutes of your time on your way out, now, would you?"

"Of course not," he told her, taking the basket from her hands. He couldn't help shaking his head as he walked away from her booth. Since he'd moved onto Magnolia, everything had turned to gold.

By the time Drew had walked around the entire market, he had collected a bouquet of fruit, complete with a grapefruit as big as his head. There was a pint of freshly picked strawberries, a couple of oranges, and a giant slice of Saran-wrapped watermelon. He plucked up a pineapple as well, recalling that it was a symbol of hospitality, and filled the remaining nooks and crannies with plump cherries. Unable to resist temptation, he popped one of them into his mouth, tasting summer. He spit the pit onto the ground before heading back toward the baskets, remembering his Gamma's warning: *Don't swallow the seed, or a tree will sprout inside your stomach and roots will shoot out your toes.*

He set the heavy load onto the old woman's table, and she put her knitting aside once again and got to her feet. She was a lot like Drew's Gamma before she had passed away—shrinking down toward the ground while Andrew grew up toward the sky. *It makes it easier to reach for the stars,* she had told him. *So reach while you're young.* He missed her; the way she used to balance him on top of her feet and dance with him on the wraparound porch. PopPop knew how to play the guitar, and he'd play old country songs while Drew and his Gamma danced, his mom and dad dancing and laughing together just a few steps away.

He watched the older woman work in silence, arranging the produce with a contemplative expression, stacking and draping, making sure it looked like Drew had picked it out of a glossy-paged magazine. A pink ribbon was the finishing touch.

"For friendship," she told him. "May it go well for you, my dear."

She offered him the basket with a fond glint in her eye. He paid her, thanked her, and nearly skipped back to his truck.

Once on Magnolia, with the basket precariously balanced on his knee, Drew struggled with the Wards' front gate, fiddling with the latch. Moving up the walkway, he took deep pulls of air that smelled of fresh-cut grass, thrilled to be on the other side of the picket fence yet again. A momentary breeze carried the perfume of Harlow's roses across the yard, while breezy licks of jazz danced out an open window. A pair of fresh white curtains billowed outward into the afternoon sun. It was absurd in its perfection; another world—one that Andrew would be allowed to experience on a daily basis starting bright and early tomorrow morning.

He pressed the glowing doorbell button and heard it ding above an accompanying piano. But the footsteps he expected didn't come. He pushed the doorbell again, but still, nothing. Taking a few steps to the side, he peeked in through the long window beside the door. The place looked empty. His anticipation dwindled, a tinge of disappointment coloring his good spirits.

Just as he was about to give up, Harlow called from the sidewalk.

"Andy, honey…" He turned, and there she was, appearing out of thin air. "Good heavens, darlin'." She paused, placing a hand to her chest as she blinked at the comically oversize fruit basket in Andrew's arms. "What's *that*?"

Drew grinned as she made her way up to the front door, holding the basket out to her.

"I just thought, since Red was nice enough to offer me a job…"

Harlow's surprise melted into what looked like genuine enchantment, and for a split second she was the most beautiful girl he'd ever seen: the way her hair shone in the sun like gold,

ANIA AHLBORN

the way her bright red lips pulled back with exhaled laughter—just like his mother, once upon a time.

"For me?" Her lashes fluttered almost flirtatiously.

He nodded, and she shook her head as though it were the nicest gesture she'd ever known.

"My goodness, you're the sweetest thing in all the world, do you know that? The *sweetest* thing."

Drew felt his face flush as she leaned in to kiss his cheek. She smelled like sweet vanilla. He pictured her pushing that basket of fruit from his arms and onto the ground, oranges rolling down the front steps and onto the lawn. She'd shove him against the wall next to the door, her mouth against his, her knee coming up on his hip, the entire neighborhood peeking through their blinds at Mrs. Ward and the boy next door.

Startled, he took a step away from her. *What the hell was that?* His heart thumped against his ribs. His initial thought was that Harlow was seducing him, but that was ridiculous. She hadn't done anything at all, save for giving him a peck on the cheek. He stood staring at her as she plucked the basket from his hands and stepped around him, her high heels clicking against the porch. Pushing open the front door, she offered him a look over her shoulder.

"Come in," she told him.

The door had been unlocked.

Andrew hesitated, that flash of fantasy making him uncomfortable in his own skin. There was something wrong with him. Harlow was gorgeous, *hot*, even, but she was old enough to be his mom. Hell, that was one of the things that drew him to her—the fact that a long time ago, before the world fell apart, his mother was a lot like Harlow. And yet, there he was, imagining things that made him feel like a total creep.

But he couldn't refuse her invitation to go inside. That would have been rude—a complete contradiction to the gift basket she held in her arms. Taking a steadying breath, he followed her into the house.

84

§

Mickey cracked open the screen door as he watched Harlow click up the sidewalk. He saw Drew offer her a giant basket, a ridiculous pink ribbon fluttering in the breeze. He clenched his jaw as Harlow leaned into him. When Drew followed her inside, he almost called out: *No! Stop! Don't!*

Something tightened in his chest, like a tourniquet around his heart.

"So you just randomly decide to grow a conscience now?" he asked himself, disgusted. "You let her bring him here, and now you have morals?"

He grimaced, let the screen door slam closed behind him, and turned to look at a fresh plate of cookies on the coffee table.

Harlow's perfume still lingered in the air.

§

Mickey had been in his early twenties when he came out of a Narcotics Anonymous meeting to find a strange woman leaning against a slick black Cadillac, looking like the president's wife. Her hair shone beneath the streetlight like spun gold. Her lacquered lips looked as though they'd been coated in ruby-colored glass. The porcelain finish of her skin glowed ethereal in the moonlight, and her curves...they invoked images of classy pinup girls posing with fighter jets and power tools. With his hands deep in the pockets of his jeans and the hood of his sweatshirt pulled over his head, he couldn't help glancing her way, and she smiled widely enough to show off her perfect teeth. She gave off the scent of money like a pheromone. Some poor junkie's overprotective mother, he thought.

He hesitated when she flagged him down. She told him she was waiting for a "friend," that she hadn't expected to run into a dashing young man such as Mickey when she had set out for the community center that night. He smelled vanilla when she leaned into him a little too close, her lips brushing his cheek as she invited him to a late dinner.

He would have been a fool to decline.

Mickey didn't know she was married, and even if he had, he wouldn't have cared. Despite her age—at least forty was his best guess—the woman was hotter than fire: everything from the way she talked to the way she batted her eyelashes, her chin tipped downward just so—it was an instant turn-on. Just having dodged possession charges, he was in the shittiest spot in his life. Banging a woman like this, married or not, was a welcome distraction.

The night was predictable. Dinner. A few too many drinks— Mickey stuck to beer while she ordered exotic cocktails. She laughed a little too loudly, flirting like a girl half her age. Sex in the back of her sleek black Cadillac had been phenomenal. She had been wild, bloodying his back with her nails, bucking beneath him like she hadn't been properly laid in years. For half a second, Mickey could have sworn he was in love.

A week later, she was parked in the same spot outside the Creekside Community Center, waiting for him. They repeated the process, this time trading the backseat of the Caddy for a roadside motel just off the freeway. She dragged her fingers up and down his chest as he stared up at the cracks in the ceiling.

And then things started getting weird. She started calling him even though he hadn't given her his number. She started asking questions: *What are you doing? Where are you? When can I see you? Why haven't you called?* Suddenly their torrid affair was turning sour. Harlow Ward wanted more than Mickey was willing to give, and that was strange, because he could sense that she *knew* she was pushing him beyond his comfort zone. He wanted to tell her that it was over between them, that he didn't want anything to do with her, that it was just a fling, get over it, get fucking over it, lady, get a life. But for whatever reason, he couldn't bring himself to do it. He didn't like confrontation. He was ill equipped for dealing with life.

Stressed out, Mickey folded beneath the strain of her advances. He found himself at his dealer, Shawn Tennant's house. Unable to cope, he shoved bills into the hand of a man he had sworn he'd never allow himself to see again.

The next afternoon, Harlow left a message on Mickey's voice mail: he would either meet her for dinner that evening, or he'd regret it for the rest of his life.

Mickey declined the invitation; the woman was a goddamn nutcase.

A day later, Mickey's cell buzzed inside his pocket. "Your little friend?" her unexpected voice told him when he answered. "He's dead, which is a real shame, since the cops are going to pin it on you as soon as they get here. You'd better beat them over here."

He didn't think—didn't stop to question *why* the cops would finger him for the crime, didn't consider that she could have been bluffing. He didn't question these things because the number on his caller ID hadn't been Harlow's.

It had been Shawn Tennant's.

He hadn't driven as carefully as he did that night in all his life. He drove beneath the speed limit, slowed on every yellow light rather than blowing through them like he usually did. Every fiber of his being told him to floor it, to break the land-speed record and get to Shawn's as fast as he could, but logic screamed no. Harlow was giving him a chance to fix this, and the last thing Mick wanted to see was the flash of red and blue in his rearview mirror.

The scene was brutal, bad enough to have Mickey stumbling away from it, nearly tripping over his own feet. There was blood everywhere. The walls. The carpet. The ceiling. Had it not been for the pulp that used to be Shawn in the center of the room, it would have almost been beautiful—a Jackson Pollock in thick scarlet paint. Mickey turned to run but crashed chest-to-chest with the woman he'd been avoiding for weeks. Harlow gave him a stiff-armed shove into the room, and if she hadn't had a way of pinning Shawn's murder on Mickey before, she had one now: Mickey's sneakers skidded on the carpet. He staggered backward, his arms flying out behind him like a pair of featherless wings. The wad of flesh that used to be Shawn caved beneath Mickey's weight as his palms sank wrist-deep in human remains.

"Oh, dear!" Harlow singsonged, raising her hand to her mouth in faux surprise. "*That's* going to stain."

Mickey scrambled to get to his feet, his throat closing up, threatening to suffocate him. But the harder he tried to get up the more he slid around, spreading Shawn's entrails across the floor like finger paint. He exhaled a scream—one that sounded far away and detached, as though somewhere in that room, somewhere away from that gore, Mickey was watching himself roll around in blood.

"You're a murderer," Harlow announced, canting her head to the side, doglike, watching him struggle, watching him gasp for air. "And you know what's even worse?" she asked. "Not only did you kill him, but you stole all his drugs too. And from what I see in Mr. Tennant's ledger, you were his very last customer."

Mickey blinked up at her, unable to process what was happening.

"I'm not a police detective by any means," she said, "but my husband *does* watch a lot of *CSI*. I'm pretty sure your name being the last name in that book marks you as suspect number one."

He shook his head at her, speechless, waiting for her to let him in on the joke. This was some sort of trick, like that Criss Angel guy who walked the streets of Vegas blowing people's minds. He began to scramble again—but rather than trying to escape the mess, he was leaning into it, moving his arms in wide swoops to try to put Shawn Tennant together again. *Humpty Dumpty*, he screamed inside his head. *Humpty fucking Dumpty*. Because if he gathered the parts, if he scrunched them up together, he'd be able to ride out this nightmarish trip.

Shawn must have laced his coke with LSD. *What an asshole*, he thought.

"Mickey," she said flatly, apparently tired of watching him slide around like a kid at an ice-skating rink. "Stop moving."

He didn't.

"Stop moving," she snapped. "Or the cops will find you right along with your friend here."

Mickey's hands slipped beneath him. He fell flat on his chest, his T-shirt sopping up Shawn's blood. The metallic scent—like warm iron—wafted across the floor and assaulted his lungs, assuring him that nobody had laced his drugs, that there was no smoke and mirrors here. He was sober. Awake. This was real.

"*Mickey*. Darling." She offered him a smile. "I'll kill you. I promise."

He twitched, his eyes glazing over in alarm. Numbed with shock, he could think only one thing: her high heels matched the color of his hands, and his hands matched the color of Shawn's insides.

Mickey Fitch spent that evening weeping—sniveling between dry heaves while scooping up human remains with his bare hands. Harlow sat across from the scene in one of Shawn's armchairs, one leg crossed over the other. When Mickey finished his assignment, Harlow stepped to the edge of the bloodstain that had overwhelmed the carpet, leaned in, and held a tightly wrapped bag of white powder out to him—his payment. Delirious with fear, Mickey reached out to take it, wrapping his bloody fingers around the plastic, only to pull back a second too late. Harlow's smile was brilliant. She gazed at the fresh fingerprints on Shawn's stash, Shawn's blood marking Mickey as his killer.

"Oh, Mickey." She sighed. "You're so stupid. I love it."

As it turned out, nobody cared if a guy like Shawn Tennant got axed, be it murder or otherwise. Mickey had pulled up the carpet in his drug dealer's apartment—the final step in that particular cleanup—while Harlow tossed things into a couple of crappy old duffel bags. In the case of a vanished drug dealer, all it took was a few missing items to get the cops to drop the case.

It scared Mickey how easily the crime was covered up.

After that, Mickey moved into the house next to Harlow's. He hadn't wanted to, but she hadn't given him a choice, and Mick wasn't ready to go to jail.

That was when a series of short-term roommates began to filter through the house, all of them stragglers—kids trying to get away from their parents, kids who *wanted* to disappear. They were always fresh from a fight—slammed doors and screamed words, accusations and tears. Rent was cheap at Mickey's place. It was a beacon of hope, a ray of good fortune that nobody could pass up. And Harlow was the cherry on top. She fed them, listened to their stories, comforted them.

And from what Mick had put together, Red didn't seem to mind. There was no way he didn't know what Harlow was, and yet he stuck with her, napping on the porch hammock and mowing the lawn, as though he never heard the screams.

Now, sitting in a dirty house twelve years later, Mickey pressed a hand over his mouth while his knee jackhammered up and down. He hated this part, hated being involved, hated knowing that he was part of the madness.

He would have never invited Andrew to move in, not of his own free will. But that was the bitch of it: Mickey's free will was gone. He didn't have any privacy, couldn't do anything without

Harlow knowing about it. She knew every nuance of his life, because she had *become* Mickey Fitch. When Andrew had contacted him on Facebook, he had been contacting Harlow Ward. When Harlow boasted about exchanging e-mails with Mickey's childhood friend, he crossed his fingers and prayed that she'd mess up, that she'd say something in one of her e-mails that didn't make sense and Drew would back off, weirded out.

But Andrew didn't have a clue.

Andrew had just been a kid the last time Mickey had seen him, but there was something about him, a profound sadness masked in hope. Mick had picked up on the same thing in Drew years ago, and it was what made him reach out to the neighborhood kid with nobody to hang out with. Harlow had picked up on it too. Drew had reached out to Mickey, and Harlow had caught his hand instead.

Chewing on the pad of his thumb, he considered what he could do to keep what was going to happen from happening. But he knew it was no good.

Stay out of it, he told himself. *Disconnect.*

Because he knew it was either him or Andrew, and Mickey wasn't ready to die.

CHAPTER NINE

The afternoon sun shone through the windows. A vase of daffodils winked at Andrew from the center of Harlow's breakfast table. She had settled into chopping the fruit he had brought, insisting on making a perfect summer salad. "It's to die for," she told him with a wink. She flitted about the kitchen, more like a bubbly schoolgirl than the refined woman she was supposed to be. She hummed while she chopped, expertly dicing while Sinatra crooned.

Drew watched her hips sway, the blade of a butcher knife catching the morning light. His nerves prickled as she danced, anxiety uncoiling itself beneath the cage of his ribs. The more he watched her, the more those disorienting thoughts crept back. He was tempted to reach out, to catch her hand and pull her close.

He winced at the bristle of anxiety stirring just beneath his skin. If Harlow suspected, she'd run him off. She'd tell him never to come back.

He looked away from her, chewing his bottom lip as he stared out the window toward Mickey's place, trying to construct excuses for why he had to leave. But before he could formulate a plan, she placed a bowl of chopped fruit in front of him with a smile.

"*Bon appétit*," she told him, placing a dainty spoon on the gingham place mat next to his salad.

Drew smiled in thanks, hoping it didn't look as awkward as it felt. Seeing her strictly as a mother figure would have been far easier if Harlow didn't insist on dressing to the nines; if she didn't traipse around in pumps that made her calves look so damn appealing. Magnolia Lane was lined with dream homes, but he had yet to spot a woman to rival Harlow's looks. He had seen a few neighbors walking up and down the street since he'd moved in—one had been pushing a stroller, another had been walking her dog. Both of them had been unremarkable: ponytails and sweats, not full-skirted dresses and Audrey Hepburn shades.

Taking a seat across from him, Harlow placed a small bowl of fruit salad in front of herself and took a bite. "My mother used to make this for me when I was a little girl," she explained. "She wasn't much of a cook, but she could do fruit."

"My mom doesn't cook either," he confessed. Mothers felt like a safe subject.

"No?" Harlow arched an eyebrow.

He shook his head in reply.

"She used to, but she got sick."

"Sick?" Harlow's expression went dark with concern. "Oh, Andy, I'm sorry."

Drew lifted a single shoulder in a halfhearted shrug. "It's OK," he told her. "She's been like that forever. Ever since my dad—" Drew blinked at a distant noise—the muffled hum of a garage door rolling up. Harlow lifted her chin, listening to the sound of Red's engine purring as it pulled up to the house.

"Sounds like Red is home," she announced.

Drew lowered his eyes, waiting for Red to walk in, to sense that something was off—men were supposed to be able to pick up on that sort of thing; like a sixth sense, they were supposed to know when the neighborhood kid was ogling their sweet, innocent wife. Drew swallowed a mouthful of fruit as Harlow wiped her hands on a dishtowel, waiting for her husband to come in—Donna Reed, anticipating her beloved's return. Red stepped into the house through the kitchen door. Drew half-expected him to bellow out, *Honey, I'm home!*

"Andrew," he greeted with a clueless smile. "I thought we weren't starting until tomorrow."

He was sure his guilt was obvious. Sitting at the table, his hand in a viselike grip around the spoon, he waited for Red to pick up on Drew's mental transgression.

"Honey, look what Andy brought us," Harlow gushed, motioning to the basket with the sticky knife blade. "Sweetest boy."

"For the job," Drew clarified. "Just to say thanks."

"Well, that's really nice of you, Andy, but you don't have to buy us things."

Harlow shook her head as if to say that she agreed. Drew offered the room a hesitant smile as Red met him at the kitchen table, taking a seat across from him.

"You may think you do because we don't know each other too well just yet," Red told him. "But that'll change. You'll learn things about us, and we'll learn things about you. For example, did you grow up in Creekside?"

Drew nodded. "My grandparents bought a house on Cedar before my mother was born. She inherited the house, and I grew up in it just like she did."

"Your mother lives in town?" Red asked, sounding surprised. He shot a glance at his wife.

Again, Drew nodded, his eyes fixed on his hands, suddenly more uncomfortable with the topic than with his own wanton thoughts.

"What does she think of your new place?" he asked, dubious. "A bit of a hole, wouldn't you say?"

"*Red.*" Drew looked up to catch Harlow batting her lashes at her husband. "Don't be rude."

"No, it's OK," Drew replied. "It's true. It's crap."

It was pathetic in comparison to where he sat now—like a rich man asking a bum how he was enjoying his cardboard box on the corner of a busy street.

"She hasn't seen it," he confessed. "We didn't part on the best of terms." Another shrug, another pause. "But if she did, she probably wouldn't see much wrong with it. Our house on Cedar is just as bad."

Harlow joined them at the table with a frown. She reached for Drew's hand—he tensed, and she removed it, a flicker of hurt punctuating the blue of her eyes.

"She doesn't take care of the place so, you know, it isn't like she'd raise hell over a dead lawn or a dirty kitchen."

"Dead lawn," Red mumbled, distaste obvious in his tone. "I have to tell you, I've never liked that house." He glanced at Harlow and scoffed. "Lowers property values, just like I said."

"And what do you propose we do, sweetheart? Burn the place to the ground? A burnt corpse of a house next door instead; would that be better?"

"It would be more satisfying. And maybe that Mickey fellow would move."

Harlow cleared her throat, rose from the table, and went back to her chopping, leaving Andrew to assume that Mickey was a touchy subject. But after a moment, she picked up the conversation again.

"He used to be a drug dealer," she said, tight-lipped, placing the knife down on the cutting board. "I didn't want to bring this up, Andy, but I really don't know if living in that house is the best idea. You know how those drug people are—they try to drag you into that seedy world right along with them. I wouldn't be surprised if that house was full of whatever it is he's selling."

Drew's mind immediately spiraled to the locked hallway door.

"And you know what will happen if the police show up?" she asked.

Of course he did. They wouldn't just bust Mickey. Drew would be escorted away in steel bracelets as well.

"Let's not get overexcited," Red interjected. "First off, we don't know how long ago that was. He may have been clean for years."

But Mickey didn't seem clean. Drew *wanted* to believe that Mick was a slob by nature, but the truth of it was, he was probably too busy getting high to give a shit about the way the place looked. Drew's stomach tightened at the thought of it, remembering the early morning when Mickey had left the house. Maybe he had left to meet his supplier. Maybe that was why he had gone through his wallet while Andrew was asleep; he was looking for money. But none of it had been missing. Maybe Mick was struggling with his own set of scruples, because they used to be buddies—almost best friends.

Drew suddenly felt sick.

"Once a pothead, always a pothead," Harlow insisted.

Had Drew not been mentally freaking out, he would have laughed at Harlow's comment. He was reminded of *Reefer Madness*: *Women cry for it; men die for it!* Dope addicts—what a nightmare! He pictured Harlow peering through the window at Mickey's house, her eyes wide with horror while Mick smoked a joint in the driveway, waiting for him to keel over and die of a cannabis overdose.

"Andy?" Red leaned in to catch the kid's attention.

"Yeah?"

"What do you think?" he asked. "Is there something funny going on that we should know about?"

Sure there was. Mickey was weird. He lived in filth. He slept all day. He didn't have a job. That was what made Drew uncomfortable:

because people without jobs couldn't afford houses, and they couldn't afford to buy piles of video games or to pay for the Internet, whether they knew their password or not. There were plenty of red flags—certainly enough for him to make assumptions.

Yet despite it all, Drew held back. He knew that the Wards didn't like Mickey, and he was sure that Mick had his own bone to pick with the Wards—but Mickey was his friend. If he ratted him out, there was no telling what Red might do. Mickey would probably get arrested; the house would go into foreclosure. Hell, Drew definitely wouldn't be able to stay there anymore, and where would that leave him? Back home?

"I don't think so," Drew lied. "I mean, I haven't really been paying attention." He shrugged. "He sleeps a lot."

"Of course he does," Harlow quipped, her face twisting with distaste.

"Well, if you do see something strange, you let us know," Red told him. "We need to stick together."

"Like good neighbors should," Harlow added.

Drew pressed his lips together in a tight line as he looked from Harlow to Red and back again. He wanted to protect Mickey, and yet he couldn't help but wonder how it would benefit him if he told the Wards the truth. If Mick's house ended up repossessed, that would leave Andrew homeless. It would be the perfect excuse to ask Harlow and Red for a place to stay, at least temporarily. But the thought of tricking them into more hospitality, the thought of using Mickey for Drew's own gain—he wasn't *that* desperate for acceptance; he wasn't *that* dazzled by life behind the white picket fence.

"Yeah," Drew finally replied, "absolutely." He swallowed against the lump in his throat. If it came down to it, it was either Mickey or the Wards—and unfortunately, for his roommate, Mick didn't quite have the charm.

§

Harlow's mother, Bridget Beaumont, had been dead for nearly forty years. She'd caught a flat along Highway 64 on her way to Little Rock to visit a friend. The man who stopped to help looked nice enough—a cowboy wearing shiny new boots and a Stetson. He tipped his hat, gave her a polite *ma'am*, and bashed her knees in with the tire iron he found in her trunk. The police found her along the side of the road, her skirt a dozen yards from her bloodied body.

Reggie Beaumont lied to his daughter that night, explaining that her mother had gotten into a car accident—a slip of the foot rocketed her into a tree, a freak accident—it meant that Jesus wanted her in heaven. But Harlow knew he was lying; that was, after all, what Reggie Beaumont did.

She read about it in the paper a few days later: Oklahoma City socialite, wife to the illustrious Pastor Beaumont, dead at thirty-three. Raped. Murdered. Found just outside Plumerville, Arkansas, God rest her soul.

Fifteen-year-old Harlow had her first date three months later. Reggie blamed it on Bridget's death, the way Harlow had suddenly gone wild. The pretty tulle dresses were replaced by miniskirts and platform shoes; glitter and curls were traded in for lipstick and a teasing comb. Reggie took a step away from his angel, his hands held in front of him in defeat. She was a girl, and there was only so much a father could do. He would pray for her. Jesus would show her the way.

Danny Wilson took Harlow to see *The Exorcist* after buying her a cheeseburger and vanilla shake, then brought her back to his apartment to show off his baseball trophies, proud of the ugly resin statues that lined the shelf above his desk. She listened to him rattle on about how great the district game had been in '72, how he had been the one to throw the winning pitch. The crowd had held its breath, bursting into a cheer as the umpire roared, *You're out!* Danny talked and talked, and she listened like a good date was supposed to, staring at one of his trophies, trying to decipher the tiny pitcher's expressionless face. She glanced back at Danny, four years her elder, as he put on a Johnny Cash record and slithered up next to her, a slick smile pulled across his mouth. She felt her calves brush the edge of his mattress as Johnny strummed his guitar, her heart pattering beneath her blouse.

Harlow knew Danny was this kind of boy. He was smiles and sunshine on the outside, but something dark lurked beneath his grin. It was why she'd gone out with him in the first place. She wanted to see what it was like for a boy to want her, to see what it felt like to tease him and walk away. When Danny pushed her down onto the mattress, Harlow imagined that he was a lot like the man who killed her momma: wooing younger girls with smooth talk, with food and scary flicks. And finally there was the trip back to the guy's place, the rock and roll and dirty thoughts, the carnal need to take advantage, to possess and destroy.

Harlow's chest heaved as he worked the buttons of her blouse free. Dizzy with a sudden bout of anxiety, she tried to catch her breath when he pushed her skirt up around her hips.

With Johnny jiving over Harlow's protests, Danny pushed her wrists into the sheets when she tried to push him away. She saw the glint in his eye—a look that confirmed Danny meant to go through with it; after all, he hadn't spent money on dinner and a movie to get nothing in return. She closed her eyes, picturing her mother fighting the guy who had killed her, kicking and screaming until he had to shut her up forever. Her father's sweaty, lascivious face flashed across the thin veil of her eyelids; his hair plastered across his forehead, the tip of his vulgar tongue dragging across his bottom lip.

Vertigo bloomed behind her eyelids. Her wrists hurt beneath Danny's grip. She was suddenly in her mother's shoes, knowing that the worst was yet to come.

Lying on Danny's bed, Harlow forced herself to relax, just as she had been taught.

"Atta girl," Danny mumbled against her ear, his mouth sloppy with spit. He released one of her hands and reached beneath her skirt, hooking his fingers along the waistband of her underwear. That was the moment—during Danny's blink of preoccupation—that Harlow's mistake became too much to bear. She should have never gone out with him. She should have never come back to his apartment. She had been stupid, *so stupid*. Her arm shot outward. She grabbed a baseball trophy from the shelf beside his bed.

A dry yelp fluttered past Danny's lips. He rolled off her, his hands pressed to his forehead, blood pouring over his face like a fast-leaking faucet. Harlow watched him blink furiously as she scrambled to her feet, the statue still held fast in her grip. He sat up, staring wide-eyed at his gore-smeared palms. As soon as he looked up to give her an incredulous look, she reeled back and hit him again. Danny howled, throwing himself at her, but she sidestepped him without much trouble. His eyes were squeezed shut against the sting of blood. She lifted the figure above her head, ready to hit him again, pausing only to consider how red the blood looked in the light of his room—almost movie-magic scarlet, as if this were nothing but a scene in a film. Danny's cry shattered that illusion as the statue cracked against his ear. His blood-sticky hands flew away from his face, holding them out in self-defense. He was trying to say something—trying to plead for his life—but no words would come out. She hit him again.

Hit him a fourth time.

Hit him in the same spot just above his ear over and over until he started shaking like he'd stuck his finger in an electrical socket. His seizure caught her off guard and she jumped back, giving him room to thrash, not wanting to bloody her new shoes despite backsplatter covering her blouse and skirt. He whipped around for nearly a minute before going still, a lake of gore blooming around his head like a Japanese sun.

She stood over him for what could have been hours, Johnny Cash dwelling on the misery that had swallowed his life, singing Danny Wilson a eulogy before his own mother knew he was dead.

Realizing what she had done, she pressed a hand over her mouth; she smeared the fine red mist that had settled along the girlish curves of her face. Her eyes were wide with denial. She hadn't killed him, couldn't have possibly…he was so much bigger than her; that statue had been so small; she was just a girl, just a silly stupid girl.

But a small spark of vindication burned within the storm of Harlow's shock. The longer she stared at him, the more her fear bent toward satisfaction. Danny Wilson was going to rape her, just like the man along the highway had raped her mother—just like her saint of a father had raped *her* for all those years. For all she knew, after Danny was through taking advantage of her, he would have bashed her head in with the very same trophy himself, if only to keep her mouth shut. She was the pastor's daughter, after all. If news of what he'd done had gotten out…she was *sure* he would have killed her. He wouldn't have had a choice. It had been self-defense. It wasn't her fault she was three steps ahead of him.

Squaring her shoulders, Harlow grimaced at the body at her feet. She didn't know much about Danny, but she knew enough to be sure that he was a rotten, dirty sinner. She had done God's work here.

"Thanks for the date, Danny," she murmured, her eyes narrowed at the dead boy on the floor.

She got home late, sneaking up the stairs to her bedroom while her father watched *The $10,000 Pyramid*, Dick Clark's grinning face welcoming her home. She didn't make a sound as she crept up the stairs in a pair of Danny's jeans, one of his shirts hanging limply from her shoulders, his trophy tucked safely into her purse. She stuffed her ruined blouse and skirt into the corner of her closet. She'd burn them tomorrow.

A day later, Danny Wilson's name flashed across the TV screen. Harlow sat at the edge of the couch, her fingers curled against her bottom lip, waiting to see her photo blink onto the screen. But the police announced that they currently didn't have any leads. Harlow squinted at the screen from behind her father's TV chair, her arms crossed protectively across her chest. If her story had been written on the pages of the Good Book her father preached from, he would have stood in front of his congregation and called it a miracle—an innocent girl with blood on her hands, redeemed by the glory of God.

Jesus saves.

The news flashed an image of paramedics rolling a gurney out of Danny Wilson's apartment, his collapsed skull veiled by the white sheet they had pulled over his body.

"My Lord," Reggie murmured.

Harlow spoke up from behind his chair. "The Lord has nothing to do with it. He was probably bad."

Just like the man who had left Bridget Beaumont on the side of a rural highway. Just like her own daddy, who'd eventually get his too.

§

Andrew had been in love once, and the girl of his dreams was the complete opposite of Red's. While Harlow strutted around the university campus with her hair blowing in the wind, Drew's fantasy was a quiet girl who sat at the back of the class, hiding behind her long brown hair, doodling aimlessly in the margins of her notebook.

Though their fame had faded twenty years prior, Emily's favorite band was A-ha; she loved Christopher Walken movies and wanted to be an artist. Her dream was just like everyone else's: she wanted to get out of Creekside, move to a place like LA or New York. She wanted to *be* somebody, because everybody was a nobody in a town like theirs.

Drew fell in love with Emily the first day of his freshman year. Walking into his biology class, he spotted her hunched at a desk. Andrew got there late and was stuck directly in front of the teacher's desk; a hulking football coach who, by some unfortunate miracle, got talked into teaching biology to a bunch of brainless kids.

Despite his feelings for her, Andrew sat back and watched Emily float through the halls of Creekside High for more than two years. They hung around the same circles, had the same friends, worked together as techs on the same school productions. During the summer between his sophomore and junior years, he even sat next to her in a mutual friend's basement while eating Doritos, drinking Mountain Dew, and rolling thirty-sided dice, neck-deep in a weekly role-playing session—an activity that assured them geek status upon their return to school in the fall.

A week after classes started up again, Andrew walked up to Emily while she stuffed books into her locker, pressed his palm against the locker next to hers—trying to play it cool—and asked her out. Ducking her head with a bashful smile, she tucked her hair behind her ears and lifted her shoulders up in a shrug.

"Sure," she said, "if you want."

Drew did want.

She walked away from him without another word, but she had said enough. Andrew's life had been transformed.

They were the typical high school couple. They fought. They got jealous. In the two years they were together, they broke up half a dozen times, only to reconcile over rented movies and mutually adored CDs. They'd spend hours in darkened rooms, Drew's hands beneath her shirt, Emily's fingers working the top button of his jeans. They had their own song. *There's something about you, girl...that makes me sweat.* During their last semester, they were inseparable.

But what solidified their relationship was the pregnancy scare. Emily wept in a panic on Andrew's bed, announcing a missed period between gasps of air. It was at that very moment that Drew made the decision: he would accept the consequences of their actions. He would sacrifice everything for this girl.

It turned out to be nothing, which at first felt like a blessing, but quickly transformed into a curse. A baby would have saved him from the other woman in Andrew's life—the one who would ultimately tear them apart.

Emily was serious about getting out of Creekside, and Drew was the first to know when the Art Institute of Chicago accepted her. He tried to be happy for her, tried to pretend that he was excited, but it wasn't easy. He wanted to leave as much as she did, but knew he never would.

Standing on the sidewalk next to her old Ford Festiva outside of Emily's house, she turned to look at him, her eyes bloodshot. She had pleaded with him to come with her, to be irresponsible for once and do what he wanted. But in the end, Andrew watched her drive away, down the block and out of his life.

They had promised to keep in touch, but long-distance relationships were tough; despite their never officially breaking up, Emily started to write less and less. Every night, just before he drifted to sleep, Drew pictured her falling for a brooding artist with more talent than he knew what to do with—more talent than Andrew would ever possess. He knew that, inevitably, they'd drift apart like buoys in the ocean; only he was anchored, and she was free. After a few weeks, his incessant thoughts of her being with another guy began to fade, buried beneath daily frustrations, beneath exhaustion and defeat. But there was one consideration he couldn't shake: the fact that despite how much it had hurt, he couldn't blame her for leaving.

He let her go because he loved her.

He wouldn't have come back either.

CHAPTER TEN

A ndrew's first assignment was to work on the yard, despite its already preened perfection. He had expected to work inside, but he wasn't about to complain. Work was work, and he was happy to do anything Red asked of him. Red explained that the grass had to be cut twice a week with the push mower, exposed blades and all, because it created the cleanest, closest cut.

"Those fancy mowers," he said, "they tear the grass instead of cut it. The lawn is a living, breathing entity, Andy. That's like a barber tearing out your hair instead of using scissors."

Drew stood next to him in the compulsively organized garage, trying to put all the details to memory. This was Drew's chance to make yet another first impression, and he wanted the work he did for the Wards to be as flawless as they were.

Then there were Harlow's roses. Red started to explain these, but Harlow overheard and stole Andrew away. She escorted him to her prize rosebush, taking a branch delicately between her gloved fingers.

"You have to be gentle," she told him, standing a little too close. Explaining the delicacies of cutting the branch at just the right angle, she showed him how to do it for more than forty-five minutes, pruning an entire bush on her own to make sure Andrew understood the technique—showing him just how skilled she was with her hands; yet another observation that made him uncomfortable in his own skin.

He pushed the mower up and down the square lawn, row by row, while Red listened to Led Zeppelin and relaxed in the hammock, keeping an eye on his grass between newspaper articles. It was weird—Red didn't strike him as a classic rock kind of guy. It made him think that there was more edge to Red than met the eye; secrets, like maybe he used to drop acid and went to Woodstock. When he'd first heard those riffs drift from inside the Wards' house, his heart clenched into a fist.

Drew's own father had been a Zeppelin fan. Andrew had grown up listening to "Kashmir" and "Stairway to Heaven." His mom had spun Rick's old records for nearly a year after he left. Anytime Led Zeppelin came on the radio, Drew would switch the station. He didn't like reminiscing on the fact that his father had cared so little about him that he up and disappeared; not even a single visit afterward, not a single phone call or Christmas card.

Hearing that music slither out the window and coil around him within the safe haven of the Wards' picket fence made him grit his teeth. It felt like a phantom assault, like his dad was rising from the ether to assure him there was no escaping his past—Andrew would forever be a product of his environment: a broken, angry, fucked-up kid, because both Rick and Julie made it so.

Drew pushed the mower onward, the white rubber of his sneakers turning a brighter shade of green with each step. He considered asking Red to switch the music to something else, but eventually came to a conclusion: if there was ever a chance to turn a bad association into a good one, this was it.

After he finished with the first half of the lawn, Drew raked the clippings the way he'd been shown, trying to get as many of them into a black garbage bag as he could before moving to the opposite side of the walk.

"Good job, Andy," Red said from the porch.

Up and down, row by row. Drew laughed to himself as he wiped sweat from his forehead with the back of his hand. *Wax on, wax off, Daniel-san*. Red wasn't much of a likeness for Pat Morita, but Drew was sure he could pull it off; this was an invaluable lesson in lawn care, an exercise that would protect him from the goons of Cobra Kai.

As soon as he moved to the roses, he felt Harlow's eyes on his back. Shooting a look toward the house as casually as he could, he noticed her standing in the open window. He lifted a hand in a wave, confirming that everything was OK.

Despite the small size of the Wards' front yard, it took him nearly four hours to complete his given tasks, taking extra time to make sure his work was up to spec. By the time he was finished, the blazing heat, combined with his concentrated effort, had him ready to collapse. Having expected to work inside, he hadn't thought to slap on any sunblock; now his skin felt like it was on fire, hot to the touch, sizzling with sting. And yet, despite his sunburn and the throbbing in his lower back, he felt a sense of satisfaction as he settled into a chair at Harlow's breakfast table, gulping down a tall glass of sweet tea, the condensation cold against the palm of his hand. He lifted his damp palm to his forehead, cooling the redness that was surely there.

"I really can't believe you did that," Harlow told him with a shake of her head, but her momentary look of disapproval melted into amusement as she sat across from him. "You look like a lobster," she teased.

Drew cracked a smile and gave her a helpless shrug.

"You did a great job," she said, leaning forward to place her hand on top of his.

Her touch was innocent enough, but it renewed Andrew's anxiety. It was the way she drew her thumb across the top of his hand—back and forth, like Emily used to do. It rekindled his sense of loneliness, reminded him of how much he missed that kind of contact.

After Em had left, Drew had had a few opportunities to get together with other girls. He had jumped at a couple of those chances, but his heart hadn't been in it, and after a few romps in their beds, he called it a day. None of them had compared to Emily. None of them had captured his imagination the way she had.

He fixed his attention on the varnished tabletop, not wanting to look at Harlow while simultaneously not wanting to pull away from her touch. But something had to give, and he eventually slid his hand out from beneath her own, scratching at the side of his neck. He hoped that Harlow wouldn't notice his retreat, hoped that he'd done enough to make it look natural rather than awkward. But Drew was starting to realize that nothing was easy with Harlow. She had a sixth sense about things, picking up on every facial expression, every shift of weight, every itch that didn't need scratching.

"Are you OK?" she asked, a ghost of a frown pulling her mouth down at the corners.

Drew let his gaze meet hers. Fortunately, she didn't look upset, just concerned.

He nodded, forcing a smile. Seeing her as anything but the charming woman next door made him feel dirty, like he didn't belong in the holy place that was the Wards' home. It made him feel like a sinner, as if he were lying somehow, as though he should step back from the sanctuary of their home before he destroyed it with unclean thoughts, with unwarranted desires.

"I'm fine," Drew told her. "Just tired."

"Do you feel sick?" she asked, her look of concern ever-present. "I hope you haven't given yourself sunstroke."

Andrew shook his head, giving her another tight-lipped smile.

"Well, I sincerely hope not," she said, "because I've planned dinner for the three of us tonight."

"Dinner?" He was exhausted from the day, and from trying to corral his indecent thoughts, and the thought of collapsing onto his bed was so appealing, but hunger would most certainly rouse him from whatever coma he slipped into, and the idea of having Taco Bell for the umpteenth time turned his stomach.

"I won't take no for an answer," she told him. "I've already bought enough for three." Harlow rose from the table, pressing a cool palm against his cheek. "Go home, take a shower, have a nap. And then come back at seven."

"OK," Drew relented, feeling like he was accepting more than a dinner invitation, like he was consenting to the growth of thoughts he wanted to escape. It was almost as though Harlow was doing it on purpose: inviting him over more and more often, leaving cookies, appearing out of nowhere just as soon as he needed some reassurance that his decision to move had been the right one. He had to assume that her sixth sense alerted her to the fact that he was uncomfortable, that something was bothering him just beneath the surface, and yet, if it had, she was choosing to ignore it.

Exhaling a breath, Andrew rose from his seat and gave her a parting smile.

"I'll see you then," he told her, moving out of the kitchen and toward the front door.

As he shut the picket gate behind him, he told himself that it was nothing; these thoughts would dissipate. He was love-struck by what Harlow represented—family, happiness, wholesomeness, and compassion—not by Harlow herself.

But the flower he kept on his windowsill suggested otherwise. The handwritten card tucked behind his license told another story.

There was something about Harlow the woman, not Harlow the substitute mom, that Drew just couldn't shake.

§

Exhausted by a long day in the sun, Drew was spent; but Mickey sensed something else when Drew returned home—an uncomfortable energy. He told himself to ignore it—to ride it out just as he had ridden out the ones before.

But as soon as Drew stepped through the door—uneasy and dragging his feet—Mickey was struck by a sense of responsibility. This was his buddy, his childhood friend. This wasn't some stranger off the street that Mick could erase from his memory.

Andrew still had a chance, and Mickey was the only one who could warn him.

"Tired?" he asked.

Drew stopped in the hall, regarding Mickey with a curious look. "Yeah," he responded after a second of hesitation. "Long day." Then he turned toward his room.

"Hey, you want to go get dinner or something?" Mick asked. Christ, how weird that felt to say. He had always been a man of few words; forcing himself to make small talk made his skin crawl. Until tests had proven otherwise, his own mother had thought him to be autistic, but Mickey Fitch simply didn't like to speak. It made him feel vulnerable. The more words that came out of his mouth, the more his lack of education was exposed. But this was too important to go unchecked. If he kept his silence, his roommate would soon be an ex-roommate, just like the others. And Mickey wasn't OK with that.

Andrew looked about as uncomfortable as Mickey felt. Paralyzed, he stood in the mouth of the hallway like a spooked animal in a hunter's sights. Mickey suddenly wanted to laugh, wanted to tell Drew that if he was freaked out now, wait until he got a load of what he was going to tell him over a plate of nachos at the local greasy spoon.

"Um…" Drew cocked his head to the side, offered him a baffled look. "I'm actually going next door."

Mickey's chest tightened. "I thought you said you're tired," he protested. "Screw it; we'll get a pizza. Watch a flick."

Drew gave him a faint smile.

"Hey," Mick said, a lightbulb going off above his head. "We can watch *Psycho*. You know, with that Norman guy? I've been meaning to watch it since you brought it up, man..." But his enthusiasm was short-lived. Drew shook his head, declining the invitation.

"I already said I'd go to the Wards'," he confessed. "I'm too tired for a movie anyway."

"That's kind of what I want to talk to you about. I don't think it's a great idea for you to be hanging out over there. I mean, did old man Ward give you a job or something?"

"Or something," Drew replied. There was more edge in his tone than Mick had expected.

"Look, man." He raised his hands to his chest, assuring Drew he meant no harm. "I'm just saying, you know?"

"Yeah?"

"I've lived here for a while..."

"How long?"

"Like ten years...but that isn't the point."

"What is?"

"The point is that, you know, after living somewhere for a long time you start to, well, *notice* things."

"You mean like network names?" Andrew countered. "'My neighbors suck'?"

"Look, I'm just saying that not everything is as it seems or..." He paused, rerunning his words to check they sounded right. "Yeah."

"So they're hiding something," Drew concluded.

"Dude, *yes*." Mickey exhaled a relieved breath.

"Like what? Do you think that maybe they're, I don't know, drug dealers?"

Mickey's relief was replaced with wariness.

"Judging by your expression, I'll take it that the Wards are right?"

"Whatever, man."

"So you've never dealt drugs?"

Mickey hesitated for half a second.

Drew shook his head. "That's great," he muttered. "Fucking awesome—I'm living with a felon. Thanks for the heads-up."

"Hey—"

"Now every time I see a squad car cruise down the street I'll reflexively shit myself."

"That was a long time ago," was all Mickey managed to say, but Drew wasn't interested. He shook his head and waved off whatever details Mick wanted to share, making it clear that he didn't care.

"Hey, whatever...you didn't tell me before, so don't tell me now," Drew said, turning his back on his housemate. "I have to take a shower."

"Andrew...you need to listen to me," Mickey insisted, but the only response he received was the sound of the bathroom door closing, the click of a lock. Drawing a hand down the length of his face, Mick turned away and stared across the living room. "Shit," he muttered. This was worse than he thought.

Harlow was taking her time to nurture him, weaving an invisible web. Andrew actually *cared* about her. He was already trapped, and Harlow was hovering just above his head, her red mouth pulled into a malevolent grin, poised to strike. Straight for the heart.

§

Sitting at a dining table waxed to a mirror finish, Andrew smiled as Harlow placed a pot roast in the center of the table. The house smelled better than any restaurant Drew had ever been to, Bobby Darin's buttery vocals making a perfect scene even more charming. Harlow stepped away from the table, taking it in with an artistic eye. She placed her hands on her skirted hips, a frilly apron still tied around her svelte waist. After a moment of consideration, she made a motion as though remembering something, untying her apron as she turned back toward the kitchen.

Red gave Drew a smile from across the table, already sipping a glass of wine. His attire struck Andrew as a bit strange—a stiffly starched shirt paired with a deep-crimson tie. Who wore a tie to a dinner in their own house? Nobody that Drew knew, unless it was Christmas or Thanksgiving, and even then, the ties were less than serious—ties featuring the Grinch and succulent cartoon turkeys, ties that had flashing LED lights and played stupid songs. This wasn't a special occasion, at least not that he was aware of, and yet there was Red, buttoned up, his tie standing out like a warning flag against his white shirt.

Andrew returned the smile, though it was a bit of a puzzled one. But before he had time to dwell on Red's choice of dinner attire, Harlow stepped back into the dining room with a basket of fresh-baked bread.

"I always forget something," she said with little laugh, stepping around the table to her seat. She paused beside her chair as if waiting for something, her gaze locked upon her husband. Red didn't seem to notice, and eventually Harlow quietly cleared her throat and took her seat.

"Well, *bon appétit*, everyone," she said, plucking up a bowl of roasted baby potatoes, holding them out so that Drew could serve himself.

"This is amazing," Andrew told her, and really, *amazing* was the only word he could come up with to appropriately express what was set out before him. This was the quintessential family dinner—the kind of dinner Drew had watched on television throughout his adolescence but knew he'd never have again.

He had made an attempt at such a meal when he had been seventeen, reading through his mom's old cookbooks, making giant grocery lists and fighting the crowds on Christmas Eve. He nearly pulled it off, having draped his Gamma's old kitchen table with a white tablecloth. Not brave enough to attempt making a cake himself, he'd picked one up at the market and decorated it with cranberries and mint leaves. He spent all day in the kitchen, Christmas carols filling the house, the tree shimmering with multicolored lights. He had nearly invited Emily but decided against it; his mom never liked anyone inside the house other than them. His chest swelled with pride when he stepped back and observed the meal he had created for himself and his mother. It was beautiful.

Leading his mom into the kitchen, he held his hands over her eyes. When he revealed what he'd prepared, she stared at it for a long while, dumbfounded. And then she turned and ran upstairs, weeping. Drew tried to get her to come back, but she refused. She didn't want Christmas dinner, not without Rick there. Christmas was a family affair, and the Morrisons had no family to speak of.

Drew ate dinner alone that night. He hadn't tried another dinner since.

"So, Andy..." Red said.

Drew looked up from his plate, a large silver spoon held in his right hand. He stuck the spoon back into the bowl of parsleyed potatoes still in Harlow's hands.

"What's your plan?" he asked.

Harlow blinked a few times, as though against the sudden stab of a loose eyelash. Drew caught the waver in her expression: a quick blink from charmed to agitated. But it was gone as quickly as it had appeared.

"My plan?" Drew asked.

Harlow placed the potatoes next to Red. She didn't hold them out for him the way she had for Drew.

"Your plan," Red repeated himself. "For the future."

"Oh." Drew looked down to his plate. Harlow was busy dishing out his portion of pot roast, spooning sauce and carrots over his slice. Andrew couldn't help but notice her blouse. It was looser than what she normally wore, and when she leaned toward him just so, he could see the outline of her bra. He was suddenly struck by the fact that he had no idea how old she was, and her body wasn't giving away any secrets. From the little he could see, she'd be at home in a bikini, lounging in the sun on the front yard lawn.

"Andy?"

Drew blinked. Red was still waiting, probably looking to be impressed by his answer; something in the vicinity of getting out of Kansas, going to college, studying to be a brain surgeon or an astronaut.

"Honestly?" Drew hesitated, carefully stabbing a baby potato through its center, just waiting for it to slip out from beneath his fork tines and shoot across the room, destroying this vision of perfection. "I don't really have a plan; at least not right now."

Harlow cut into her pot roast, placing a tiny bite into her mouth.

"You haven't thought about it? Isn't that a bit…" Red searched for the right word.

"Weird?" Drew helped him out. "Yeah." He nodded. "It's weird."

"So then, why no plans? Surely when you graduated from high school you had a goal in mind."

"I didn't," he admitted. "When I graduated high school I was working at the Kroger on Main. I had been for years."

"That's a nice store," Harlow interjected. "Wonderful floral department."

"But what would you *like* to be?" Red pressed.

Drew lifted his shoulders in a shrug. "You don't really dream about the things you can become if you know you can't become them. I mean, I guess you could, but it doesn't seem all that realistic."

It was a strange conversation to have—one he hadn't had with anyone up until now. Nobody had ever bothered to ask him what he wanted to be when he grew up, at least not after his Gamma and PopPop had passed away. It seemed as though his grandparents had been the only ones to fantasize about what their grandson would grow up to achieve.

"What's holding you back?" Red asked.

"I already had two jobs," Drew said. "The grocery store, and then there was my mom." The confession felt different here than it had at the Thriftway, more natural. It didn't turn his stomach the way it had there. As strange as it was, Andrew actually *wanted* to tell the Wards about his past.

"I don't follow," Red said. "Your mom?"

"She's agoraphobic."

Red shook his head, still not getting it.

"Agoraphobia is a fear of crowds," Harlow clarified, lifting her wineglass to her lips.

"It's worse than that," Drew said.

"Oh?" Harlow frowned in concern.

"There's a wheat field behind our house," he told them. "She won't go out there either. She doesn't leave the house."

The three of them went silent for a moment; Harlow drinking her wine, Red chewing on his pot roast, Drew struggling to stab another potato without incident.

"And she's an alcoholic," Drew added.

Harlow pressed a hand to her chest. Red peered at his plate as if dissatisfied with the quality of his meal. After a long moment, Harlow spoke with confidence.

"That's terrible, Andy," she said. "But I sincerely hope you know that none of that is your fault."

Andrew nodded slowly.

"The fact that you were brave enough to leave that situation..." She shook her head, reaching out to squeeze his hand. "She couldn't have asked for a better son, Andy. I can't imagine what you went through."

"That's some sort of disorder?" Red asked.

"It's an anxiety disorder, yeah," Drew admitted. "After my dad left, it kind of…ate her up."

Red frowned from across the table while Harlow gave Drew's hand a final squeeze, releasing it and going back to her meal. She smiled warmly, apparently pleased by Drew's opening up. Seeing that empathy in her eyes made him feel a thousand times lighter. The guilt of leaving his mother behind had been weighing heavy on his conscience, but the understanding that Harlow was radiating, the tenderness that veiled her expression, it woke the butterflies in his gut.

"If your mother is disabled, shouldn't you still be at home?" Red asked.

Harlow choked on a bit of potato, lifting a wineglass to her lips.

"You said your father left," Red reminded him. "So, if she can't leave the house, and she's alone…"

Those butterflies dropped dead, one by one.

"Red," Harlow cut in sharply. "You're being rude."

"How am I being rude?" he challenged.

Andrew tensed. His stomach twisted against the food he'd just eaten, refusing to digest another bite.

"Are you meaning to suggest that Andy should be limited by someone else's problems?" Harlow asked, her eyes flashing at her husband.

"We're talking about his mother," Red said. "That's hardly 'someone else.'"

Harlow snorted at his answer, looking away from him. "Didn't you leave *your* family behind, Redmond?" she asked. "I recall something like that happening, don't you?"

Red's face went taut.

"I could have done worse," Red shot back. "Some people do." Harlow blanched.

"I…" Drew spoke up, desperate to save the situation. "No, Red, you're right. I *should* be there."

Before he could continue on his path of self-deprecation, Harlow cut in again.

"You deserved better, so you left. And good for you, honey," she said with gusto. "You can't let the world hold you back. You're too smart for that. Too young."

But Red's interrogation had left Drew shaken. It was the last thing he had expected. Red was typically so friendly, so approachable. It was as though someone had flipped a switch. Eerily, it was reminiscent of what had happened back home. One day, everything was perfect. The next, his parents were fighting over everything—and their disagreements had started just like this: out of nowhere and nothing.

But it hadn't been nothing; it had been a woman in a truck Andrew hadn't seen before—his dad crawling into the passenger's seat with that duffel bag heavy on his shoulder. It had been his mother pulling Andrew away from the window, instructing him to watch cartoons as if it was just another day. But she had known all along that it hadn't been. It had been the first day of the rest of their fractured lives.

Perhaps this was like that. Red knew. He had caught Andrew looking at his wife, and maybe he had noticed the way Harlow smiled when Drew was around. The invitations to come over were growing by the day. Tonight it was dinner. Tomorrow? He could only guess.

Drew swallowed against the tension, his eyes cast downward, his guilt having returned tenfold.

What kind of a son turned his back on his mother in her worst moment? What kind of a neighbor coveted his neighbor's wife?

"I'm a bad person," he admitted. As he heard it out in the open, his entire body tingled with the confession.

§

Those four little words made Harlow want to cry. They made her want to tear at her hair and wail. Because Drew's confession was her own, one that had been tormenting her for most of her life—from the first night her father had slipped into her bedroom and slid into bed next to her, making her promise she'd never tell her mom; from the night she had left Danny Wilson dead in his apartment. Hearing Andrew declare his own feelings of inferiority turned her inside out like nothing she had ever felt. Sitting at that dining room table, she wanted to reach out to him, wanted to pull him close and press him to her so fiercely that the strength of her embrace would make him disappear. She wanted to absorb him, to make him a part of her that could never be lost or taken away.

Her heart thudded in her ears as she stared at him—nothing but an ordinary boy who turned out to be extraordinary. His guilt made him beautiful. His vulnerability made her buzz with desire. Suddenly, she found herself reevaluating her plan. Andrew Morrison wasn't just another passer-through.

Andrew Morrison was *the one*.

Harlow's gaze drifted across the table to her husband. Red had his head down, chewing his food with a vexed look across his face. And suddenly she hated him with all her being, hated him for making Andrew feel guilty, hated him for trying to scare her darling away.

Again, silence. The ticking of the grandfather clock filled the spaces between their words. Harlow sat stick-straight, so tense it was a wonder she wasn't trembling. Red dropped his fork and folded his hands together, pressing them over his mouth as if in prayer. Harlow waited for him to excuse himself from the table after his bad manners had been made so clear, but it appeared that Red was determined to keep his post. She looked back to Andrew, the boy beside her looking defeated and disturbed. Leaning toward him, she dipped a hand beneath the table, resting it on his knee.

"You're *not* a bad person," she whispered. "Don't ever say that again."

Failing to elicit a response, Harlow leaned back, her hands folded in her lap.

"Look at the work you did today," she said, full-volume now. "You did an amazing job, Andy, better than Red could ever do. Better than any of the other boys."

She caught herself a second too late, snapping her mouth shut. Her nerves were getting to her. She waited for him to ask *what other boys*, but he didn't, and she exhaled the breath that had caught in her throat. *Stupid*, she thought to herself. Red was looking at her from across the table, one eyebrow raised in an arch of bitter amusement. It wasn't like her to make such a sloppy mistake, but it was just like Red to catch it.

She had blown her cover. Red was already suspicious, but now there would be no denying that something was different this time.

Regaining her composure, she plucked up her wineglass and took a nerve-steadying drink.

After another long moment, Drew exhaled a sigh and shook his head before sitting up in his chair. "I'm sorry; I'm a lousy dinner guest. I should probably go."

"You've had a long day," Harlow agreed.

Folding his napkin into quarters, Drew placed it next to his plate and slowly slid his chair away from the table. Harlow rose as well.

"Thanks for inviting me," Drew said, and his uneasiness broke her heart.

She reached out to him again, but Andrew stepped around the table before her fingers made contact with his arm. Watching him move across the dining room, she swallowed her nerves as Drew stopped next to Red's chair and extended a hand.

Red remained seated.

He didn't make eye contact with the boy standing next to him.

He didn't take Andrew's hand.

Drew swallowed, quietly cleared his throat, and turned away.

Just as Drew was about to step onto the front porch, Harlow stepped into the foyer and placed a hand on his shoulder. He turned, offering her a weak smile, and before she could stop herself, she pulled him into a tight embrace. "Don't pay attention to him. You're a good person," Harlow whispered, rubbing his back in reassurance. "A wonderful person. The most wonderful person I've ever met."

§

Harlow watched Drew walk down the darkened sidewalk before marching into the kitchen. Red was placing dishes in the washer.

"You moron," she snapped at him.

He stood up straight, a dirty dish held in his right hand.

"'Shouldn't you be home with your mother?'" Harlow snorted. "What are you trying to do, make him cry?"

He shook his head, pulled the under-sink cabinet door open, and fished out a bottle of dish detergent.

"If he comes over here to tell us he can't work for us anymore…"

"And why would he do that?" Red asked.

"Because he's gone back to his mother like *you* told him to," Harlow said. "Because he doesn't want to work for someone who makes him feel like shit. I swear to God, Red…"

"That isn't going to happen."

"…I'll wait until you're fast asleep, and I will kill you," Harlow said flatly. "I'll slit your throat from ear to ear like a brand-new smile."

"Really?" Red asked, unfazed. "Or maybe you can fall in love with him," he said. "Maybe you can do that right in front of me. That would probably kill me too."

Harlow stared at her husband for a long while.

"You're crazy. *Love*." She spit the word out, trying to make it sound as foul and ridiculous as possible. "He's just another boy."

Red laughed with a shake of the head, closing the dishwasher door.

"You've always been a good liar," he said. "But never to me."

He began to walk away, leaving Harlow beside the sink, but he stopped in front of the entryway, looking back to her, a look of genuine hurt dancing across his face.

"This wasn't the deal we made," he reminded her. "You promised this would never happen."

"I don't know what you're talking about," Harlow said, her hands balled into fists at her sides.

"No?" he asked. "That's why he's still alive? Because of your disinterest?" He smirked. "So kill *me*," he demanded, balling his hand up into a fist before striking himself in the chest, directly above his heart. "Give *me* some of that passion."

"You'd like that, wouldn't you?" she asked, turning her back to him.

Once upon a time, he had been the boy who had stolen her heart. He had been her Andrew. But after so many years, Red had gotten boring. He didn't excite her, and he wasn't excited by anything she did. He used to worry about her getting caught, but even that had subsided. Once, Red had understood that Harlow did what she did to squelch her overwhelming sense of worthlessness. That she did what she did to mourn the loss of her innocence, to grieve the loss of her mother. He had been so sympathetic, loved her too much to be horrified, and he had stayed.

And yet, somehow, they had grown apart. Red no longer cared about what Harlow had to do to be whole. He cared only about what was for dinner. Over time, Harlow had transformed from the girl of his dreams to the happy housewife, and she hated him for that.

"Come on," he said, motioning for her to come with him. She knew what that meant. He wanted to go upstairs, wanted to "make up" and forget the whole thing. "Prove it to me," he told her.

Prove that Andy didn't mean anything. Prove that she didn't want anyone but Red.

Harlow looked down to her feet, her toes sore from being squeezed into her shoes for so long. Placing a hand on the counter, she bent her leg, catching one of her shoes by its bright red heel. She repeated the process once more, eventually standing on the cool kitchen floor in her bare feet. Tipping her chin upward, she stared across the room at her husband, her jaw clenching as she considered her options.

Finally, she cleared her throat and replied. "No."

She watched Red's hope dwindle, then disappear completely as her answer sank in.

§

Their first date was typical: they went for dinner and drinks, watched *Apocalypse Now*—Red loved it, while Harlow couldn't have been more bored—and ended up at Red's place a few minutes past ten. He lived in a crappy little apartment. It wasn't difficult to see that the pizza place was Red's only source of income. But despite his lack of funds, he had splurged on a fancy joint for dinner—giant T-bone steaks with baked potatoes and dessert; he'd paid for the movie and popcorn, and he couldn't have looked happier with the expense.

Regardless of his footing the bill, Harlow was sure it would be the same story as soon as they got to his place. He'd pour a few cocktails, put on a bad record he thought got girls in the mood, and then he'd proceed to bed her. And that was exactly what Harlow wanted, because despite the fact that the things her daddy had done to her once terrified her, she now found that wink of fear an irresistible high. It was just a matter of talking Red into it. Some boys needed to be smooth-talked into tying down their date, but Red was smitten by her; he wouldn't need much convincing.

Just as she expected, Red headed toward the stereo as soon as they were inside. He put on some Rolling Stones, then walked over to his kitchenette and pulled a half-empty bottle of gin from an overhead cabinet. Harlow hated this part—telling them what she wanted. It was so graceless, but all the guys before Red had shrugged and fallen into the act without so much as a complaint. She'd fight them first, trying to get away as they held her down. Once that part was over, all they had to do was whisper into her ear, *Don't tell your mother.*

Meeting him in the kitchen, she cornered him between the wall and the refrigerator. With her mouth on his neck, she slid her hands down his chest, freeing the buttons of his shirt, working her way down to his belt. She'd taken him by surprise; he precariously held a glass of gin in one hand, the other wrapped around the handle of the refrigerator as if hanging on for dear life. He was older than Harlow by a couple of years, but he radiated an odd sense of virtue, so wide-eyed and love-struck during their date that Harlow had nearly asked whether he was a virgin, but she resisted the temptation, not wanting to scare him off.

Plucking the glass of gin from his grasp, she bit her bottom lip and unbuckled his belt as Red breathed heavily, seemingly shocked that this was all happening so fast. And that was when Harlow took the opportunity to make her request.

Red refused.

He blinked as her fingers danced across his chest, her mouth against his ear, then shook his head, disbelieving, as though he didn't know what to make of the girl he had brought home. As soon as Harlow saw that look, she flushed with embarrassment and snatched up her bag, ready to flee, but Red stopped her. He blocked the door, refusing to step aside when she tried to push him out of the way. He caught her wrists, and that was when she burst into tears.

That night, Harlow told him everything. She told him about her father sneaking into her bedroom, about how her mother had been raped and killed. She even told him about Danny Wilson, so tired of keeping that secret buried. She was sick, crazy; maybe Red would turn her in and put her out of her misery.

He didn't.

Red had been stunned, but rather than calling the police, he wrapped his arms around her and let her cry. And then he leaned in and whispered, "He was going to hurt you. You're not a bad person."

And as if by magic, the hard shell of Harlow's guilt cracked apart and fell away.

They fell asleep on his bed, all of her secrets spilled between them. When she woke up the next morning and saw that he was still there, she knew she had to have him forever. He was the only person in the world who understood her. He was the only person who could make her whole again.

Harlow and Red were married in a private ceremony two months later.

Reggie Beaumont wasn't in attendance.

He died in an unexplained house fire a week before their union.

CHAPTER ELEVEN

D rew couldn't sleep. He lay on his mattress, staring out the window at the Wards' house, trying to place the ache that had crawled into his heart. It was still early and the Wards' lights burned bright. He could just make out the outline of furniture through the sheer white curtains. The muffled sounds of Mickey watching TV slithered beneath his bedroom door—lots of shooting and explosions and screaming, as though those sounds were coming from the house next door and not the television in the living room.

Rolling over, Andrew put the fairy-tale house to his back. It was all he'd seen, all he'd thought about for the last few days. He had replaced his old life with a white picket fence, with pretty curtains and home-cooked meals. But now, after what had happened with Red over a plate of pot roast, he couldn't deny what he'd left behind. Stepping out of a black-and-white world and into a Technicolor fantasy was easy; leaving the brilliant colors of the rainbow behind to return to a monochromatic life—that was next to impossible. But Dorothy had been able to do it, and maybe she was right: Maybe there really was no place like home.

After a few minutes of staring at the wall, he sat up, crept across the bed, and grabbed his cell phone from atop his dresser. The room lit up in cold blue as he scrolled through his contacts, stopping on an entry that simply read "Home."

Glancing out the window again, he hesitated, almost felt like he was betraying Harlow in some unspoken way. He had allowed her to creep into the corners of his heart, filling the spaces his own mother had left empty and dark. And yet he still missed his mom. Despite her abundance of shortcomings, he wanted to hear her voice.

Pulling in a steadying breath, he connected the call. He was ready to hang up after five rings, but just as he pulled the phone away from his ear, Julie Morrison's voice drifted toward him from the other end of the line. "Hello?...Drew, is that you?" she said, as if she'd been waiting for his call.

He couldn't help but smile.

"Hey," he said. "Yeah, it's me."

"Drew...I know you're angry with me," she said. "I've been selfish. It's really..." she paused. "Well, it's unforgivable. I'm ashamed of myself."

Andrew hesitated.

"I'm glad you called," she pushed on into the silence. "I think I've dialed your phone a thousand times since you left." His bottom lip quivered when she exhaled a weak laugh. "I always hung up before punching in the last number. Silly," she murmured. "But I've missed you."

It was all Andrew needed to hear. Suddenly, it was as though their blowup never happened. She told him she was proud of him for being out on his own, that she was happy for him, and that maybe, if she could manage it, she'd be able to visit his new home sometime soon. "I want to see what your life is like now, an independent young man..."

Listening to her marvel over how he had gotten a job at the Wards', how he had bought all his furniture at a secondhand store, he could almost see his mom, young and vibrant with her hair done up in curls, wearing her favorite red dress with the white polka dots—the dress she used to wear nearly every Sunday when they went to church. That dress reminded him of the way she sang, louder than anyone else, squeezing his little hand in hers as she bellowed out hymns. Being quiet throughout the entire sermon would win him a trip to the candy shop, where he'd buy a big sack of cherry sours, ones that matched the color of her dress.

Somehow, her being happy for him erased all her wrongs. Drew's bitterness melted away, and all that was left was a loving mom; not as perfect as Harlow, but at least she was his.

§

Arriving at the Wards' place bright and early the next day, Drew just about bounced as he walked, a big smile plastered across his face.

Red noticed the shift in his mood right away, and a pang of annoyance coiled inside his chest. He had hoped that the awkwardness of dinner the night before would have kept that boy from coming back. Red had a limit, and Andy had crossed that boundary, whether he knew it or not.

"Good morning," Drew greeted him.

"Morning," Red muttered. He wasn't in the mood to talk. Instead of chatting, he gathered supplies for Andrew's next task. He noticed the boy eyeing his glossy black Cadillac, the Kansas plates reading *YESLORD* in tall block letters. Harlow had special-ordered it from the state MVD. It matched her mother's license plate from Oklahoma—a tribute to the late Bridget Beaumont. When Red turned from his workbench to face his employee, he noticed him squinting at the plate a little too thoughtfully for Red's taste. The kid blinked when Red tapped the tip of his screwdriver against a can of white paint. With Drew zoned out the way he was, it was the perfect opportunity to lay down the law, to tell him to keep his eyes to himself. Red had seen him looking down his wife's blouse the night before. But instead, Red decided to play it cool, motioning for Andrew to follow him around the side of the house.

Walking to the side yard with the kid behind him, Red contemplated what Harlow would do if he grabbed Drew by his ears and snapped his neck. Red could just as easily pay Mickey a visit too; shoot that white-haired idiot with the gun he knew Harlow kept in her purse and leave him there for her to find. She'd run to Mickey for help with Drew's body, most likely in a fit of genuine tears—but Mickey would be dead, and the bitch would have to bury her darling Andy with her own two hands.

But Red wasn't like his wife. He was merely an observer, watching Harlow hunt, claiming that it was the only thing that kept her sane. After their first date and her confession, she had begged him to help her, begged him to save her from herself. And for a while she convinced Red that his love had cured her; it had kept her hands clean for more than two decades.

Red turned to Drew, pointed out which window trim needed to be repainted white, but Drew was far from focused. Irritated, Red wagged a paintbrush in front of Andrew's face.

"Did you get all that?" he asked, motioning to the window trim. "You have to tape off the glass before you paint," he reminded him, then paused, brow furrowed. "You look distracted. Are you sure you're up for this?"

Drew took the paintbrush from Red and shook his head with a smile. "I'm fine," he assured. "Just thinking. I've got it. Tape off the glass."

Red looked unsure, but he stepped away anyway, leaving Andrew in the yard with a bucket of white paint at his feet.

§

Harlow was inside, chopping vegetables for a lunch salad. She watched Red carefully as he explained the job to Drew beyond the window. That man was on probation as far as she was concerned.

When she noticed Red's aggravation as he stepped away from Andrew, the muscles of her jaw clenched. Stepping away from the kitchen counter, her heels clicking against the floor, she stood at the mouth of the living room, waiting for the screen door to slap against the jamb. She clutched a wet tomato in her left hand, a large butcher knife in her right, peering at her husband when he came inside.

"Salad?" Red asked, feigning casualness, acting as though the previous evening's discourse hadn't happened. It was just like him to sweep things he didn't want to deal with under the rug. He was a mouse, too scared to do a damn thing, just like he was too scared to let her go after one measly date. She had had an excuse to fall for him—he had sincerely cared—but Red could have just as easily thrown his hands up and looked for another girl.

But he hadn't. Harlow was convinced: without her, that man wouldn't have a shred of self-confidence. He *liked* what she did, *liked* having such a dark secret. It made him feel powerful, and that power came without an iota of personal effort.

"I *saw* you," she said in an angry hiss. "What did you do?"

"I'm going out," Red said, deliberately ignoring his wife's question. "Pick up a few supplies." He knew it would rile her, but he was too irritated to care. Maybe she'd break down and beg him to tell her what was going on; maybe, for once, she'd act like she cared about him and what he did, if only to keep her precious Andrew within reach.

Harlow pointed the knife at her husband with a scowl. "You go back out there and tell him I'm making lunch."

"He's a big boy," Red told her. "I think he should go home for lunch."

Harlow's expression went livid.

"You *think*?" she snapped. "I don't have you around to *think*."

"Well, maybe I'm tired of not thinking," Red said. "Maybe I've had it."

"You've had it?"

"I'm not helping you with this." He motioned to the side of the house; Andrew was there somewhere, painting trim that had been repainted a dozen times over by Harlow's boys.

She blinked at him, shaking her head, the morning sun glinting off the blade of the knife in her hand.

"Excuse me? With *this*?"

"With anything," Red corrected, but as soon as he said it, his skin went tingly with nerves. He waited for her to laugh, and she did, right on cue.

"You refuse to help me with anything?" Her eyes turned to the ceiling, that bitter chuckle poisoning the atmosphere around them. "You mean you refuse to unload the dishwasher ever again? Because God knows I have to ask you to do *that* forty times a day."

"Jesus," he murmured. "Don't start, OK?"

"Don't start?" She snorted. "Don't start what, the laundry? Because I can't remember the last time you helped me with *that* task, either. But hey…" She held her hands up, the tomato in one, the knife in the other. "What was I thinking, asking my husband to help with household chores? Am I nuts? I must be, Red. I must be, since you're not going to help me with *anything*."

Red squeezed the bridge of his nose, wincing at the headache that was stirring just beneath the surface of his skull. She was like a vampire; the mere sound of Harlow's voice was sapping his energy.

"Jesus Christ, just stop. He didn't say a damn thing," he told her. "He was zoned out."

Harlow blinked, suddenly looking like a woman who'd just been given terrible news.

"Zoned out?" she asked. "You mean like on drugs? Oh my God…"

"Not like on drugs," Red muttered. "Like zoned out, in la-la land. He was thinking about something else. I asked him; he said it was nothing, so it's nothing."

"Right," she quipped. "Because you turning into a psycho during dinner last night was nothing."

"I'm going," Red told her, hooking a thumb toward the front door. "Do you need anything?"

Harlow exhaled a frustrated sigh, shooting daggers at him. But Red wasn't in the mood. He lifted his shoulders and said, "Fine," before turning to go.

"Eggs," she spit out. "And butter. Unsalted."

He pulled the keys to the Cadillac from his pocket.

"Oh, and we need toilet paper."

Red stopped at the front door, his eyes closed. He stood there for a long while, contemplating telling her to go to the store herself, but he decided to suck it up instead. *Fine*, he thought to himself. *I'll go clear across town if it means staying out of this house for a few minutes longer.*

"Are you going to write that down?" Harlow asked, looking skeptical.

"Why don't *you* write that down?" he mumbled beneath his breath.

"What was that?"

"Yes," he muttered, stalking across the living room in search of something to write with. "I'm writing it."

Harlow watched him for a moment, then disappeared back into the kitchen, apparently satisfied with Red's compliance. Because that was the only thing that satisfied her anymore—that and her boys. Never Red. Never him.

§

Drew wiped the sweat from his forehead with the back of his wrist and squinted against the sun. Two windows' worth of trim painted, he peered at the third. It was a fruitless job, obvious that there was no real reason to repaint the wood other than Red requesting it be done. The paint he was going over was flawless, looking like it had been refreshed not too long ago. For all he knew, he was using the same paint Red had used a few months back. But there he was, sweating in the heat, blinded by the virtuous white that blurred his vision, burning his corneas, lighting up his face like a spotlight.

Mickey's warnings about the Wards rattled inside his head. He had dismissed his housemate's opinion because it had come from an unreliable source—unreliable at least as far as Harlow was concerned. But the more he thought about it, the more it seemed like Mickey and the Wards had a bone to pick. Something about the way each side was trying to turn Drew against the other. Maybe Mickey had vandalized their property. Maybe Red had called the cops on something as trivial as a noise complaint. They were unlikely neighbors, and unlikely neighbors were the most likely to give each other trouble.

His sunburn was starting to sting despite the sunblock he'd slathered on himself that morning. He considered telling Red he'd finished painting when, in reality, he'd only done half the job. It wasn't as though Red would be able to tell the difference, and Drew would be out of this godforsaken heat. He was about to yank the bucket up and off the lawn, but the tinkle of ice against glass made him hesitate.

Harlow descended the back door steps, a tall glass of lemonade in one hand, a folded blanket draped across the other, a red-lipped smile pulled tight across her face.

"Whew," she said, "it's *hot* out here." Strutting across the lawn, she met Drew beside the window and handed him the glass. "Tomorrow, I'm telling Red 'no work outside.' This weather is too much. I'm betting money you forgot to put on sunscreen again."

"Nope," he said. "I was on top of it this morning."

"Thank goodness," she said, seeming pleased by his reply. "Let's take a rest," she suggested, motioning to a shady spot at the far end of the yard. "I'll open the umbrella."

They crossed the lawn together. Harlow handed him his glass, spread the blanket across the grass, and fumbled with a beach umbrella before the latch released and it sprang open. She yelped in surprise, then laughed it off, waving her hand at the thing before stabbing it into the grass, settling down next to Drew. "Stupid thing always scares me," she admitted. "Just like one of those snakes in a can."

Drew crossed his legs Indian-style and glanced at the stripes of color overhead. It reminded him of visiting the public pool when he was a kid, when the Morrisons were still a family. Scoring the pool loungers next to the outdoor umbrellas was a feat in and of itself. Every time they managed, Drew felt like king of the pool in his Speedo and arm floats.

"So, what's Red having you do today?" Harlow asked.

"Painting window trim," Drew replied. "Does he do that often?"

The question caught Harlow off guard.

"Often?"

"Paint the window trim; it looks perfect. It doesn't look like it needs another coat at all."

"Doesn't it?" Harlow looked back to the house with a disconcerted expression. "That's strange." Her reply was distant, oddly detached. "I don't think he's ever painted the window trim…" she mused, her words fading like the end of a song.

Her attention snapped back to Drew, her eyes set on his, her expression intense. "Are you happy here?" she asked, her tone carrying a renewed sense of purpose.

It was Drew's turn to be caught off guard. He blinked at the question, then took a small sip of his lemonade before cupping the glass between his palms.

"You mean here, as in…"

"On Magnolia Lane," Harlow finished.

Drew hesitated. His housing situation was less than ideal. Despite his efforts, the place was still a pit, and Mick had his eccentricities. They'd had their confrontation after Drew had woken to an open bedroom door; and then there was Mickey's insistence that Drew listen to crazy conspiracy theories about the Wards. But he didn't want to bring that stuff up. A woman like Harlow seemed less than inclined to understand the inner workings of a bachelor pad, or the tension that went with it. And while Drew could criticize every little detail, the fact of the matter was: Mickey was a guy, Andrew was a guy, and as guys they were both prone to dirty carpets and unkempt kitchens and occasional blowups that would probably resolve themselves in due time.

Was he happy?

"I guess so," he replied with a shrug.

"You *guess* so?" Judging by her tone, it wasn't the reply Harlow had hoped for. "Has that Mickey guy been giving you a hard time?"

There it was again: the Wards against Mickey. Drew frowned, wiping the condensation from his glass.

"Um." Drew paused, carefully considering his words before finally posing a question that had been nagging at him for some time. "Is there something going on between you guys?"

Harlow reeled back. "Going on?" Disgust crawled into the corners of her mouth. "Do I look like the type of woman who would…"

"I mean, why are you so against each other?" he added quickly. "I get that he has issues, but he's a decent guy. He doesn't seem to be hurting anyone."

"Where is this coming from?" she asked, her tone toeing the edge of irritation.

"You've told me to watch myself around him, and he's told me the same about you."

She blinked her eyes in rapid succession. "He what?" she asked, breathless.

"It just seems like you have a bone to pick, and I'm stuck in the middle of it. I only bring it up because I moved out here to get away from that sort of thing. Drama, I mean."

"I understand," Harlow replied, but she didn't look at him. Her words were distant, far away. "I'm sorry, you're right." Squaring her shoulders, she paused, then continued a moment later. "When we first moved here, Mickey would park that greasy old car along the curb, often in front of our house instead of his own. It leaked oil everywhere. Red confronted him about it, and ever since then we've had a bit of a feud. But you're right: you're stuck in the middle, and it isn't fair."

Sitting in the shade of a giant beach umbrella, sipping home-made lemonade, he thought Harlow's story was as plausible as a story could be.

"I couldn't help but to stay up worrying about you," Harlow told him, changing the subject. She kept her eyes on her hands. "You seemed so upset at dinner, and then Red…" She shook her head. "He's so stupid, bringing up your mother like that. It was completely out of line. I was horrified. I'm sorry."

"It's OK," Drew told her.

But Harlow wasn't having it. "He wasn't always like this," she confessed. "It's like I hardly know him anymore." She pressed a hand over her mouth. Drew blinked when he saw the shimmer of tears in her eyes.

"Hey, it really is OK," he reassured her, reaching out to touch her arm.

"It isn't just that," she whispered, running a finger beneath her bottom lashes, trying to keep the tears from streaking her makeup. "This house?" She motioned to Andrew's dream home with a wave of her hand. "It's a lie."

Drew chewed the inside of his cheek, his own gaze drifting back to the jewel of Creekside.

"It used to be perfect, but now it just looks the part," she said, her eyes still downcast. "Inside, it's a nightmare."

"What do you mean?" The question slipped past his lips before he could contain it. He didn't want to pry, but his curiosity was too great to contain.

Harlow pulled in a shaky breath, finally looking up at him with a weak smile.

"We fight. You know, that sort of thing. But you're young," she said with a nostalgic smile. "Too young to know how it feels to see something you love disintegrate."

Andrew frowned. It was his turn to look down. Harlow was wrong about that. He had watched his family fall apart. His father had been great, and then suddenly he was gone; just like Red had been great, and suddenly he was guilt-tripping Drew at the dinner table. He swallowed against the parallel. Perhaps the stars had aligned just right, and Drew had ended up on Magnolia Lane for more reasons than one. Maybe fate had a little something to do with it. Maybe he was supposed to be here to help Harlow through a situation Andrew had already lived through. Maybe he was here to hold her hand and tell her it would all be OK.

"Have you ever wanted to burn down your own home?" she asked him.

He blinked at her, shook his head as if to deny it, but he wasn't saying no; he was shaking his head because everything was shifting—his perception, his emotions, his loyalty.

"Every day," he told her.

"Me too," she whispered as her hand slithered across the blanket, her fingers creeping onto his knee.

And this time, the discomfort didn't come.

This time he didn't pull away.

CHAPTER TWELVE

Red and Harlow's wedding was small, but Harlow insisted on buying an extravagant dress anyway. She walked down the aisle in a fairy-tale gown billowing outward like Cinderella's dress, with a train nearly six feet long. It was then, seeing her for what felt like the first time, that Red Ward knew he was in over his head. Despite meeting her in the big city, Red was a country boy. He lived the simple life, didn't need much to be happy. Harlow was his polar opposite. She came from affluence, loved expensive things, and though she had never come out and said it, Red knew that she expected him to provide her with the perfect life.

Soon after they were married, Red found himself committed not only to his new wife, but to a baby on the way. Harlow had been over the moon about the unexpected news. She called their pregnancy a "happy accident" and spent hours in department stores, gazing at tiny pink dresses and bibs that read *Mommy's Little Girl.*

But a little girl hadn't come. Harlow named her baby Isaac Anthony—a strong biblical name—and tried to smile through her disappointment.

Red didn't notice his wife's disenchantment right away. With a young family to take care of, he didn't have time for anything but work—and waiting tables at the pizza joint wasn't going to cut it. He threw himself into supporting his wife and child, trading his apron and dishrag for a pair of slacks. He began selling insurance door-to-door, hating every second of it. Corporate life was his ultimate nightmare.

Despite her initial optimism, motherhood wasn't a good fit for Harlow either—at least, not when it came to raising a little boy. Depressed, she wept when Isaac wept. She abandoned him in his crib when he wouldn't sleep; cursed him when he needed to be changed. For the first year of little Isaac's life, Harlow was hard-pressed to admit she loved him, and the fact that Red loved their son dearly only seemed to make her resent Red as well. Like a king demanding a son to be an heir to the throne, Harlow was the queen who required a princess, the fairest in all the land.

When Harlow discovered that she was pregnant again, she was ecstatic. For the first time in Isaac's young life, he had a happy, spirited mother who took him to the park and showed him off to the women at church. She bought him all new outfits and even organized a birthday party when Isaac turned two, and Isaac was the happiest two-year-old in all of Kansas City.

But at the height of her optimism, the world came to a standstill.

On a clear summer morning, Harlow awoke with a head full of plans, but her day was stilted before it began. Pulling the sheets aside, she stared wide-eyed at a scene that wouldn't have fazed her had it not been her own blood. The sheets, her nightgown, her legs, even her arms, were streaked with gore redder than Danny Wilson's blood. She could hardly scream when she realized what it was.

The baby was gone.

It had been a girl.

§

For the first time in as long as he could remember, Mickey Fitch had insomnia. He glared at the glowing digital readout of the alarm clock as though it were to blame for his inability to dream. It wasn't even eight yet, and there he was, staring up at the ceiling, his eyes peeled wide open, his hair sweaty and plastered to his forehead.

He knew why he'd woken up so early, but he didn't want to admit it—not to himself, not to anyone. It pissed him off, because for all these years he hadn't taken much issue with his employment. He had been able to mentally distance himself from it all. He did it to preserve himself, did it to survive; but then Andrew Morrison showed up and the whole thing came apart. He'd spent years repressing his guilt, but now all of those ugly emotions were bubbling up to the surface. He had to ask himself: Was Drew really that different from the rest of the boys who had come and gone over the years? Did he deserve Mickey's interest more than any of the other ones did?

The answer was no, and that was what got to him most. Mickey remembered Drew as a scraggly little kid, an overeager child who was all arms and elbows. Those memories snagged on the edge of his sympathy. But his fond memories didn't make Drew's life any more valuable.

Mickey had allowed so many to fall into Harlow's hands, convincing himself that he couldn't do a damn thing about it because, the moment he tried, Harlow would turn him in. She still had that bag of cocaine, the one with his fingerprints all over it, the one that would indict him in Shawn Tennant's death. And while he knew that turning him in would lead the cops to Harlow, it didn't change the fact that he had been involved, a partner in crime, and if the courts didn't give him the death penalty, there was no denying that he'd get life in prison. It was something Mick had wondered about on more than a few occasions: If he were caught, which would be better—lethal injection, or day after day of solitary confinement?

Maybe if Drew hadn't scrubbed the grime out of the toilet bowl, if he hadn't played video games with Mickey or offered to pick him up a burrito; maybe if he had skipped doing all of those things, Mickey's ambivalence would be intact, memories or not. Yet there he was, unable to sleep, staring up at the ceiling, thinking about things like guilt and innocence, and whether hell smelled of burning hair and sizzling flesh—the scent of death by electric chair.

Sitting up, he shoved the sheet he was using as a makeshift window shade aside. There, in the sunshine, the Wards' house stood in all its glory. He knew Drew was over there, performing some menial job that had been done a hundred times before. He rubbed the back of his neck, considering his options. There was no way to stop her from doing what she was planning on doing. If he called the police, she'd call the police right back. He and Red would end up sharing a cell at the state penitentiary, spending their life sentences commiserating, trying to understand how Harlow Ward had turned them into the monsters they had become.

He shuddered, kicked his sheets away, took another peek out the window, and then wandered to the bathroom.

With hot water beating against his back, he had a moment of clarity: If Mickey weren't around anymore, she'd let Drew go. It would be too risky to cover up the crime herself. Mickey was part of the team now; without him, Harlow would be at a loss.

He had to disappear. It was Andrew's only chance.

§

Hearing the Cadillac pull into the garage, Harlow left Andrew in the backyard and reentered the house, her hands balled into fists.

Red was in his chair, reading the paper as usual, back from the store much sooner than she had expected. The mere sight of him sparked rage in the pit of her stomach. Not only had he nearly run Andrew off with his stupid comments, but he now appeared as relaxed as ever. It was as if the man were oblivious to what he had done.

Marching over to Red's chair, she snatched the newspaper out of his hands, leaned in, and hissed into his ear, "Did you see any articles in there about us, Red?"

Red first looked to his crumpled paper, then turned his head to face his wife.

"That stupid little shit of a junkie is sending up red flags," she told him. "He's putting Andy on edge, telling him he should watch himself around us, that he shouldn't be spending so much time around here."

Red opened his mouth to say something, but closed it soundlessly after a second of deliberation.

"Do you know what that means?" she asked, paper still crumpled in her right hand.

"It means you should get rid of him," Red replied flatly.

Harlow smirked as she looked out the bay window. Past the verdant lawn, the preened rosebushes, the whitewashed fence, was a perfectly acceptable house across the street. Harlow had wanted *that* house, not the one next door. But the tunnel would have been impossible to construct beneath the street, so Harlow had turned her attention to the pit next door. She bought the place for the sole purpose of housing a lowlife like Mickey Fitch, and now the lowlife was rattling his chains. The servant was defiant; the slave was taunting its master, and there was only one solution to stop that sort of behavior.

"Exactly," she snapped. "I want that worthless piece of garbage out of that house. He's no longer a piece of the puzzle."

Red cleared his throat as he leaned forward, adopting a more alert posture. She knew that when he suggested she "get rid of him," he had meant Andrew, not Mickey. But that wasn't anywhere near Harlow's plan.

"Wait." He paused.

"I'm talking about Fitch," Harlow clarified.

"So…" Red looked confused. "You want me to go next door and, what, slit his throat?"

Harlow exhaled a snort.

"You?" She rolled her eyes at him. "Please. I'd have a better chance of convincing Andy to do that than you." Red was squeamish. It was why Harlow had to hire Mickey in the first place. Had it been only her and Red, things would have been less complicated. But there had been no way. If she had relied on her husband, she may as well have done her killing on the police station steps.

But things were going to change. Red was going to buck up and be a man.

Pausing at the window, she gazed down the street toward Mickey's place. "I'm going to shoot him," she announced. "But once he's dead, I'll be down an employee, won't I?" She turned to look back at him, lifting an eyebrow, waiting for him to catch her drift.

Red tensed. He sat at the edge of his recliner, his fingers biting into the leather of the armrests.

"Congratulations," she told him. "You've been promoted."

"This is insane," Red blurted out, his words tinged with unfamiliar desperation.

She had never asked him to take part in her hobby because she knew he'd refuse, but this time he wouldn't be given the option. Mickey had become a nuisance, and she certainly wasn't going to waste her time searching for a fresh errand boy when she had a perfectly healthy man at her disposal.

"I told you no," Red insisted. "I'm not doing this."

"Oh, Red." Shimmying over to him, she slid onto his lap, pushing her fingers through his hair the way she used to. "Don't get upset." Leaning in, she pressed her lips to his cheek, a smile pulling at the corners of her lips. "You knew it would eventually come to this."

"Come to what?" he asked, his words choked with tension.

"This is your test," she confessed, leaning back to get a better look at him, her fingers gripping him firmly by his chin. "I've never asked you to prove your love for me, have I? Well, now's your chance."

Red sat mutely, his eyes wide, disbelieving.

"If I get rid of Mickey Fitch, I don't have anyone to fill his position, do I? I mean…" She chuckled. "You can't *possibly* expect me to put an ad in the paper. What's Mickey's title anyway, garbage man? Wheat field surveyor? Grave digger? If I get rid of him, you have to do his job."

"And if I won't?"

Harlow offered her husband a thoughtful smile, leaned forward, and pressed her mouth to his. He tensed beneath her as if allergic to her touch, but rather than discouraging her, it amused her instead.

"If you won't," she whispered against his lips, "then I'll find someone who will. And you, my darling, will simply have to go."

§

With a towel wrapped around his waist, Mickey made a beeline to his bedroom, shoved piles of clothes away from his closet door, and threw an old suitcase onto his bed. He was done. If there were any chance of helping Andrew, he'd have to save himself first.

He knew Harlow would come after him the moment she sensed that something was wrong. Even his mention of the Wards being "off" was enough to make her crazy with rage, her palms itching for blood, and if Drew trusted her as much as Mick suspected, it was likely that he had mentioned Mickey's misgivings about the Wards by now. He had to get out of the house, get out of Creekside, had to hole up in some roach motel until he could figure out what to do—*if* he could figure out what to do. All he knew for sure was that he had to vanish. If nothing else, it would buy Drew more time. Mick was confident that without him at Harlow's disposal, she'd stall on spilling Andrew's blood.

After his father had died, Mickey had insisted that he didn't want to move away from Cedar Street. Despite his inability to walk past the room where his dad had pulled the trigger, despite his sudden insomnia and heightened anxiety, he begged his mom to reconsider. When she had asked him why—why he would *possibly* want to continue to live in the nightmare that had become their life?—he had lied and said that he didn't want to change schools.

But Mickey hadn't given half a damn about his classmates. He hadn't wanted to move because it meant leaving Drew behind— scrawny little Andrew Morrison, all broken up about his pops disappearing; that kid didn't have two friends to rub together, and neither did Mick. Mickey had told Drew to scram more than a handful of times. Andrew could be a pest, always showing up after school, constantly asking about bands that Mickey listened to but Drew didn't know. He was more like a little brother than a friend, but Mickey liked it that way. It meant that no matter what, they'd always be close—because that was how brothers were. He didn't want to be the next person to disappear out of Andrew's life. And yet that was exactly what happened.

Now disappearing was exactly what Mick had to do to help him.

Grabbing arbitrary articles of clothing off the floor, he tossed them into the open suitcase. Clean or dirty, it made no difference. He'd find a Laundromat. He'd always wanted to visit one of those intensely bright places, shove a few quarters into a machine and sit in a plastic chair reading a magazine, waiting for the girl of his dreams to wander through the front door.

He flipped the top of the suitcase closed and looked around the room, considering what else to take. His eyes paused on the gun tacked to the wall. In that split second he imagined himself marching next door, that shotgun loaded, his intentions clear. He'd kick the Wards' door in and shoot Red square in the chest, and, as he lay dying, Mickey would trudge down to the basement where Harlow would be hiding. He always pictured her down there. It was the right place for her. She probably peeled that perfect exterior away every night before bed—flawless skin and bright red lips shed like a reptile, exposing a greasy troll beneath, teeth slick and black with blood.

He considered writing Drew a note, something dramatic like *Get out* or *Save yourself,* but decided against it. Telling Andrew to make a run for it was like telling him to jump off a bridge— he'd probably make it to the edge, but Harlow would give him the final push. No, it was safer to keep Drew in the dark. If she even suspected he wanted to run, she'd clip his wings and lock him away.

He dressed quickly. Clutching his suitcase, he jutted his arm into the bathroom and snatched his toothbrush off the sink on his way to the front door. He paused there, surprised at how hard his heart was beating. She would be watching. She was *always* watching. If the TransAm didn't start, if his bag tore open in the middle of the yard...these factors would decide whether Mickey got away or whether Red would tail him until the Pontiac ran out of gas. And if it did, she would put a bullet through his skull; a real-life Mexican standoff in the Kansas prairie, complete with wind and storm clouds and a lonely highway.

"You just gotta do it," he muttered, psyching himself up. "Just toss this shit in and jet." He took a deep breath, tore open the door, and bolted across the brittle grass.

§

Harlow nearly choked on her Tom Collins when she saw Mickey run across the front lawn carrying a suitcase. In a knee-jerk reaction, she called out to the only person she knew would help her.

"Red!" she squawked. "Get the car!"

Red scrambled out of his recliner, but stopped short of running for the door.

"What are you waiting for?" she asked, glaring at her motionless husband, her blood boiling beneath her skin.

Red shook his head, slowly at first, then with more fervor, alerting her that this wasn't going to happen, that he wasn't going to be part of her plan. "Get your boy to do it," he told her. "Let's see if *he* passes your test."

Stunned, she watched Mickey walk out of the house, across the front lawn, and down the tree-lined sidewalk, wondering whether he'd ever come back, wondering whether she'd ever see him again. She assured herself that she wouldn't care, that it would be better if he faded into the sunset—but she knew better. The idea of watching him bleed to death didn't shake her, but the idea of him walking out on her made her weak in the knees.

"You son of a bitch," she whispered into the empty air, reeling away from the window and to her purse upon the armoire. Drawing out her revolver, she narrowed her eyes at its weight in her hand.

That was when Harlow decided that Redmond Ward wouldn't be given the chance to come home, because she was going to march up behind him in broad daylight, press the barrel of the gun hard against his skull, and fire. And after he hit the ground with his brains spilling out of his skull, she'd shoot him again—shoot him until he resembled the pulp she had left in Danny Wilson's apartment.

She pivoted on the hard soles of her high-heeled shoes, her finger twitching against the trigger when she caught sight of Andrew out of the corner of her eye. He appeared at the far end of the yard, shielding his eyes from the sun. He was looking after

Red, looking in the direction Mickey had fled. Sweet, wonderful Andy—her darling, always so concerned for the well-being of everyone around him.

Squeezing her eyes shut, she took a breath, turned away from the door, and slid the gun back into her bag.

She wouldn't allow Red to ruin this for her.

Andrew was going to be hers, no matter how hard Red kicked and screamed.

§

From the side of the house, Drew watched the TransAm jump the curb and bounce into the road. Unable to contain his curiosity, he left his paint can and brush behind and wandered into the front yard, wondering what the hell had happened to make Mickey bolt the way he had. Half-expecting to find a cop parked on the street—red and blue lights whirling—he would have been less surprised to see Mickey in a standoff with the police than to see what he saw, which was a whole lot of nothing. Despite his abrupt departure, the house was still standing. There were no cops. No fire. Everything looked normal—just the way it had been since the day he arrived.

He nearly jumped when Red slammed the front door behind him and started to march, looking as though he were pursuing Mickey on foot. Drew opened his mouth to call out to him, to ask what was going on, but he stopped short of yelling Red's name. That man was no longer Andrew's friend. It was still unclear as to how it had happened—how Red had gone from gracious neighbor to reserved and reticent foe—but there was no denying that Drew was no longer in Red's good graces.

Turning away from the scene, he saw Harlow watching him through the front window. She offered him an odd sort of smile. It lacked her usual confidence—the kind of smile someone gave when they weren't sure whether they were in trouble or not. It was the smile Emily had given him the moment she knew he was staying in Kansas while she left for Illinois.

Harlow lifted her hand to expose her palm, a silent hello through a pane of glass. She eventually turned her back to him, pulling a knuckle across the apple of her cheek, her eyes glinting in the light. Just then, she looked like the ghost of his mother, standing at the window, waiting for her husband to return.

§

It was dark by the time Drew stepped into the garage. He stood at Red's basin sink, trying to wash as much paint out of the brush bristles as he could. Eventually, he wandered across the yard to announce that he was finished for the day, expecting Harlow to insist he stay for dinner, or just to talk. To his surprise, she met him on the front porch. She was lying in the hammock, puffing away on a skinny cigarette with the skirt of her dress folded in around her.

Andrew paused on the bottommost step when he saw her, taken off guard by the tendrils of smoke that curled from between her lips. She turned her head to regard him, but didn't make a move.

"Finished up?" she asked.

He nodded in reply, continuing up the steps, but stopped when she spoke again.

"We'll see you in the morning, then."

No invitation. No dinner. For a moment, Drew wasn't sure what was happening. He suddenly felt terrible, as though he'd done something unacceptably wrong. It was like déjà vu, but instead of his mother's detachment, it was Harlow. He pictured her beautiful golden hair fading to gray, imagined the smooth complexion of her skin growing sallow with grief. And that fairy-tale house—the flowers would die, the grass would sprout weeds, the front porch steps would sag with sadness.

"Are you OK?" he asked, but Harlow waved him away with the burning tip of her cigarette, smoke curling through the air.

"I want to be alone," she told him. "Off you go." She motioned toward the house next door, reminding him where he belonged.

Andrew frowned but did as he was told, stalking down the walkway toward the fence's gate. Halfway there he paused, turned back to her like a street urchin looking up at a rich debutante.

"Did I do something?"

Harlow didn't answer.

"Is it Red?"

She responded by getting up, crossing the porch, and slipping inside without a word.

Drew was left outside, surrounded by dusk, crickets chirping their sad song. He eventually turned toward Mickey's place, his shoulders slumped, his heart tight as a fist.

He was losing her. And it scared him half to death.

§

The house was hauntingly quiet without Mickey around. Somehow, even when he'd locked himself in his room, the place hadn't felt as empty as it did now. Drew sat on the couch, the silence humming in his ears, staring at his reflection in the convex curve of Mick's old TV. He wondered whether Mickey was going to come back, wondered whether his sudden departure was Drew's fault as well.

But the thing that unnerved him the most was Harlow's cold shoulder. It was completely unlike her. The flippant wave of her hand had been enough to crush him. She had told him he was a wonderful worker, a good person; they had made a connection. And yet there she was, unrelenting, motioning for him to go home like a cranky old woman shooing schoolkids off her lawn. It wasn't fair. He hadn't done anything but what she had asked him to do.

Staring at his hands, he considered calling home again. His mother had been happy for him the night before—and in less than twenty-four hours, everything had gone to shit. Mickey had taken off, Harlow had shoved him aside, Red had decided Drew wasn't worth his time. If Mickey didn't come back, who knew what would happen. His being gone meant not paying the rent, and not paying the rent meant that the bank would come knocking on the door. Drew would be out on his ass, right along with all of his crappy furniture and his stash of pudding cups.

Standing up, he looked around the room with his arms at his sides. His mother, Harlow, Mickey, Red: they were gone, and Emily was little more than a memory.

He was completely alone. Abandoned. And it made him want to scream.

CHAPTER THIRTEEN

Mickey Fitch sat at the edge of the bed in an old motel room that smelled faintly of mold—the kind of scent a room took on after it flooded, the odor of decay, spores colonizing between the carpet and the floor. It was hot, and the air conditioner that dangled from the window was broken, half in the room, half out; a lot like Mickey—balancing on the sill, not sure which way to tumble.

Harlow spent nearly all her time sitting in the front room of her house, staring out the bay window like a cat stalking birds. She had inevitably seen him toss a suitcase into his Pontiac before roaring into the sunset, tires squealing, smoke rising from the pavement. He'd gotten away, but it didn't mean he would go unfound, and it didn't mean he wouldn't end up going back on his own. Harlow kept a tight leash on the finances. Other than pizza and beer, she bought him his groceries, leaving them in the tunnel between 668 and 670 Magnolia Lane. He was like a child living off a meager allowance, forced to present receipts for anything above and beyond his normal expenses. Harlow was a hawk. She would find him. He didn't know how; he just knew she would.

His nostrils flared against the unnerving scent of mildew. He was on edge, waiting for Harlow to kick the door in with a pair of red pumps, to fling off her Jackie Os and slice his throat from ear to ear. She had assured him that if he ever took a misstep, if he so much as looked at her the wrong way, he was as good as dead. Sure, there had been times when Mickey had tried to convince himself that, even if she tried to blame him for her own crimes, the police would figure it out—they'd arrest them both. But there was always that shred of doubt. It scared him into submission every time.

And then there was Red.

Mickey had seen something unidentifiable in Red's eyes the first time he met him. It was the dead of night, a few weeks before Christmas, and it was his first glimpse of who the Wards really were. He stood in the doorway of an upstairs bedroom, one that looked more like a shrine than a room anyone was meant to live in. There on the bed was Trevor Thorne, the guy Mick had called his roommate for nearly a month. Trevor had been cool—strait-laced and friendly. He had escaped an abusive stepfather out in Oklahoma and hoped to eventually make it clear to New York City.

Had it not been for all the blood, Mickey's former housemate might well have been sleeping, dreaming of the Big Apple and endless opportunities.

Harlow watched from the hallway as Mick hesitated, his heart twisting in his chest. He had thought it weird when Trevor started going next door more and more often; odd when he started eating there on a regular basis. Trevor and Harlow had been a strange pairing, but Mick hadn't interfered. He hadn't stopped to consider that Trevor could possibly end up like Shawn Tennant. Somehow, he had convinced himself that Shawn was a fluke, a special case, something that would never happen again—not in his wildest dreams.

With Trevor's body wrapped in a sheet and tossed over his shoulder—nothing but an old friend helping a drunk comrade get back home—Red watched Mickey work from the base of the stairs. For a brief moment, they made eye contact, and Mick saw something dangerous in Red's eyes. It was envy, as though Mick's job of disposing of Harlow's prey elevated him in some way, making Red less important in the scheme of things. Red was seeing something he wanted to be a part of but didn't dare touch. That evening, Mick realized that Red was as wicked as his murderous wife. Because even if Red didn't get his hands dirty, he was just as ensnared in the game as Mick was. The difference between Mickey's involvement and Red's was that, at one point, Red had made a choice; he had embraced this lifestyle, while Mickey had been blackmailed into compliance.

Rather than dragging Trevor's body down the sidewalk, he stepped across the Wards' kitchen to the basement door. It was the first time he'd accessed the tunnel that connected the two houses together, the first time he'd set foot in the room inside his own home—stripped of carpeting, devoid of windows, hidden behind a locked door. There was a table bolted to the floor in the center of the room. Channels ran along its metal surface, gently sloping toward a drain that emptied onto the floor. Mickey lowered Trevor's body onto cold steel. That night he spent hours dismembering the body of his twenty-year-old roommate, tossing limbs into thick plastic bags between bouts of vomiting; tossing those bags into floor-standing freezers until he figured out what to do with them. He'd spend the next three months burying them in various parts of Kansas and Nebraska. Oklahoma had been an option, but Mick had driven a few hundred extra miles to avoid it as a dumping ground. Something about Trevor being buried in the state he had run from didn't sit right with him.

He felt like it was the least he could do.

§

When the alarm clock buzzed at six in the morning, Red swung his arm over the side of the bed and slapped the snooze bar. He hadn't slept a wink, but had faked it when he heard Harlow rise an hour before. She was downstairs, banging pots and pans against the kitchen counter the way she always did when she was mad. Red had spent most of yesterday sitting at a local park, plotting. She had refused to speak to him when he returned, which was just as well. He knew what he had to do, and though it would test his constitution, he was determined. Harlow thought he was useless, but he'd prove her wrong. He'd show her that he was just as able as Mickey Fitch; and once he was covered in blood, Harlow's heart would flutter at the sight of him—Red Ward, her husband, her one and only love.

He curled his toes against the cold floorboards, wandered to the bathroom, and executed his morning routine. He took extra time to shave his face, splashing aftershave onto his hands and patting his cheeks. Plucking stray eyebrows out with Harlow's tweezers, he leaned into the mirror and inspected himself. He felt good, looked even better. Today would be dedicated to his own personal renaissance: the first day of the rest of Red Ward's new, sadistic, bloodstained life.

Descending the stairs, he spotted Harlow standing in her usual spot in the front room, gazing out the window. If she heard him come down, she didn't let it show. With her back to her husband and her eyes on Andrew's bedroom window, her attention never wavered. Her obsession was growing by the day.

It was time to put an end to it, time to remind her where her loyalty truly lay.

After a solitary breakfast of grapefruit, granola, and a cup of coffee, Red climbed into the Cadillac and cruised into town. He had bought that Caddy in the summer of '83. Despite the contempt he held for his sales job, Red had earned himself a promotion. That day he walked out of his boss's office, climbed into his tan Volvo station wagon, and drove straight to the Cadillac dealership before ever coming home. Harlow had been dumb-struck when he pulled into the driveway. He had always asked her permission for everything, but this decision had been his alone.

Patting the steering wheel of his aged Caddy much like an owner would pat a trusty old dog, Red stopped by the barbershop and got a haircut.

Then, guiding that boat of a vehicle into the True Value parking lot, he reevaluated the shopping list he'd put to memory before casually walking inside.

Bill Jacobson greeted him with a wide smile once Red's shopping was complete.

"Hey there, Red," he said with a grin. "How's the wife?"

Bill and Red had known each other since the Wards had moved into town. There was no question as to Red's status as Bill's most valued customer; he had spent thousands over the years on renovation supplies. Every time Harlow had a new project—and a new boy to do them—Bill was the one who sold Red the required materials to keep his wife happy.

"Fine, fine," Red replied, angling his cart so he could unload his purchases onto the counter: one blue tarp, fifty feet of nylon rope, a roll of silver duct tape, and a pack of Wrigley's gum.

"What's the wife having you do now?" Bill asked as he rang up the items. "Kill somebody?"

"Wouldn't be surprised if she did." Red chuckled, and Bill laughed in return.

"Women," Bill quipped with a grin. "At least you've got your-self a looker, Red—pleasant to look at after a long day of home improvement, eh?"

"That's right," Red said, "at least there's that."

"Now, don't go showing up on the news," Bill teased, hand-ing Red his receipt. "Or I'll be halfway responsible, selling you all this."

"Oh, don't worry," Red said cheerfully. "I'll get away with it."

"I bet you will." Bill chuckled. If they had been buddies at a barbecue, Bill would have socked Red in the shoulder with a laugh.

§

Drew was reluctant to go to the Wards' that morning; he couldn't get the memory of Harlow waving him away out of his mind, though it had already gone fuzzy around the edges, like an old photograph, overexposed and blurry. But he made his way across the yard anyway, bound by what could only be described as allegiance.

There was something about her that comforted him, something that kept him coming back. He had been sick with worry over what he might or might not have done to make Harlow upset. He'd spent hours thinking about it, staring at the white picket fence, studying the rosebushes he'd pruned two days before. He wondered whether the grass would need cutting soon, considered whether the window trim looked brighter than it had before he had painted it, or whether it looked the same.

He wanted to please her, because there had never been any pleasing his mother. He wanted to win her over, because she was lost just like he was—because she was losing Red just like he had lost his father. He was sure that Harlow *wanted* to be pleased, that she was waiting for Andrew to prove himself. She had just had a particularly rough night. Her mood swing had nothing to do with him; at least, that was what he was desperate to believe.

As he crossed the yard that morning, he decided he was ready. He was going to show her that he was worth her time, that if there was a missing link in her life, he was it.

He put his knuckles to the door and knocked.

When Harlow answered, a cheerful smile spread across her face.

"Good," she said with a grin. "I'm making pancakes."

And just like that, everything felt right again.

§

Harlow made the best pancakes Drew had ever tasted—even better than his mom's. He burned through half a dozen before stopping to take a gulp of milk.

"They're your favorite," she told him, pleased with herself.

With a mouth full of breakfast, he was struck by her claim—as if she *knew* they would be his favorite even though it was the first time he'd eaten them. And yet they were so delicious he could hardly argue, so he nodded instead.

"They're amazing," he confessed. "The best."

The way Harlow's eyes lit up when he proclaimed his love for her cooking, Drew couldn't help but smile at her joy. At that very moment, he saw her not as a woman more than twice his age, but a girl, young and vibrant and heartbreakingly beautiful. He bet the entire world had been crazy for her when she was sixteen. The way she smiled at him just then, Drew understood why Red had fallen in love with her. Hell, he was halfway falling for her now.

"Where's Red?" he asked, taking another drink of milk. Drew had seen him come back home an hour after Harlow had waved him off her front porch steps. Waiting at the window, he had listened for signs of a struggle, ready to bolt across Mickey's crunchy lawn and leap over Harlow's picket fence to save the day. Red didn't seem like the violent type, but Drew didn't trust him anymore. With Red's swing from being Andrew's pal to being something altogether different, Drew wouldn't be surprised if the guy flipped a switch and went from being a perfect husband to being an abusive prick.

Harlow lifted a single shoulder in a dismissive shrug. She looked like she couldn't have cared less where her husband had run off to, and Drew suspected she wouldn't have cared if he didn't come back either. But rather than a simple "I don't know" or an understandable "Let's not talk about him," Harlow smiled and said, "We're alone."

Her answer roused a flurry of butterflies in Drew's stomach. Those two words made his skin tingle. It was the wrong answer, dizzying with its allure. His heart hitched inside his chest as she turned away from the sink, glancing over her shoulder at him with a ghost of a smile, her skirt swaying just below her knees.

"I know what I want to do," she said, and her face lit up as soon as the idea crossed her mind.

Drew forked another bite of pancakes into his mouth, trying to eat his nerves.

Her high heels went silent as she crossed the threshold into the living room, and within a matter of moments that silence was replaced by music—a song that Andrew recognized, a song that his Gamma used to love. Harlow stepped back into the kitchen, her expression almost as dreamy as Nat King Cole's voice.

"Dance with me?" she asked, an arm extended toward him.

Swallowing the wad of pancakes in his mouth, he shook his head in protest.

"Don't say you don't know how," she told him, plucking his hand up off the table, pulling him to his feet. "You know how," she said, stepping close.

"I don't," he said softly, but he let her position his hands anyway, his right hand holding her left, his left hand pressed to the small of her back. She rested her head on his shoulder as they swayed, back and forth, left and right. Taking a step backward, he led her into a twirl. She laughed as she spun beneath his arm, crashing into him with a wide smile.

"Don't know how?" she asked.

"Maybe a little." He grinned. His grandmother had been a hopeless romantic. As soon as Andrew had taken his first steps, she had him dancing to the likes of Ella Fitzgerald and Glenn Miller, twirling him around the living room like a top. His favorite had been Elvis. The King was Drew's introduction to a lifelong love of rock and roll.

They swayed until the song ended, Nat's final croon making way for a brassier number: Peggy Lee. *Chicks were born to give you fever, be it Fahrenheit or centigrade.* Harlow's mouth twitched up in a tempting smile. Drew took a step back as she swung her hips, her eyes fluttering shut. She danced for him, her hands drawing up her sides, sliding across her waist. Andrew's heart crawled up his esophagus, lodging itself in his throat. He blinked as she twirled around, shooting him a look over her shoulder. His head spun, unable to accurately assess the situation. Was she *trying* to turn him on, or were the thoughts he'd been trying to erase creeping back into his skull?

Harlow turned to face him, her smile giving her away. Drew felt about ready to fall over as she approached him, exhaling a sigh as she rested her cheek against Drew's shoulder again, her hand pressed to his chest. He was sure she could feel his heart thudding like a drum beneath her palm, sure that she understood why he was practically frozen where he stood, terrified to move or speak or breathe.

"I'm leaving Red," she whispered, and for a second he wasn't sure he had heard her right. "I'm tired of being unhappy. I deserve better." She lifted her head to look at him, her expression a question mark. "Don't you think?"

He couldn't bring himself to answer, afraid that any words that escaped him just then would be wrong. A part of him wanted to tell her that she was crazy, that she and Red were perfect for each other—everyone had their problems, they just had to give it time, sort things out. Another part of him—the part he'd been trying to suppress—whispered for him to wrap his arms around her, to pull her close and press his mouth against her ear, assure her that yes, she deserved to be happy, that he was going to give her everything she wanted, everything she deserved.

"Well?" she asked, surprised by his silence. "You think it's a stupid idea? I should just stay with him and hate myself?"

"No," he croaked. "Just..."

"Just that he's a man and you're a man and you're going to take his side?" Her hands slid down Drew's chest, falling to her sides in defeat.

"I'm not," Drew told her, feeling cornered. "It's just that...it's a big step, don't you think?"

"So was getting married," she muttered, turning away from him, retaking her spot at the sink.

He chewed his bottom lip, unsure of whether to follow or remain where he stood. Her sudden shift in mood was so disorienting, he considered bolting for the door, uncertain of whether to be excited or horrified, whether to feel dirty or captivated.

"Aren't you scared to do that?" he finally asked, forcing the words from his throat. His own voice sounded foreign, far away. He stepped toward the counter, his fingers gripping its edge, steadying him against the vertigo that was setting in.

"Leave him?"

Drew nodded, but he didn't look at her. Sick with nerves, he wondered whether this whole thing would result in him sprinting across the kitchen to the guest bathroom, his hands held firmly over his mouth.

"Why would I be scared?"

"Because you'll be alone," he said, forcing himself to glance her way. It was, after all, Andrew's worst fear. He had spent what felt like a lifetime on his own.

Harlow blinked at the boy in her kitchen, her eyes going glassy with tears.

"I see," she whispered, turning away. "I suppose I didn't think of it that way," she confessed. "I suppose I just assumed."

He didn't get it: Assumed what? That she *wouldn't* be alone after she sent Red packing? That Drew would keep her company?

His heart sputtered to a stop when he realized what she meant. He swallowed against the lump in his throat, shaking his head faintly, his expression pleading for her to explain it to him—to assure him that he was coming to the right conclusion.

"Was it wrong to assume?" she asked.

"I don't understand," he whispered. Drew would have been over the moon to keep her company, to come over every afternoon, do odd jobs, eat pancakes, and wash dishes after dinner. But that wasn't what the glimmer in her eye had been asking for. Had his own mother ever looked at him that way, he would have run out the front door screaming, unsure whether he'd ever come back.

But Harlow wasn't his mother.

That simple fact repeated itself over and over inside his head: she wasn't his mother, and this wasn't wrong. He cared about her. Her marriage was falling apart. She wanted him to stay with her. They were both lonely, both looking for a reprieve from what their lives had become: Drew from the guilt of leaving his mom behind, Harlow from the perfection she had built up around her like a wall—perfection that she had openly admitted was a lie. Why was he fighting his undeniable attraction, trying to bury her appeal? She was gorgeous. Amazing. Caring. Everything he had always wanted. Everything he missed.

"I'm not crazy," she said softly. "I know it would take time. I just thought..." Glancing over at him, she offered him an unsure smile. "Don't we like each other?"

A tremor skated down his limbs. He was suddenly back in the halls of Creekside High, trying to be casual next to Emily's locker while his stomach clenched and his head swam with anxiety. Staring at Harlow, he wondered how old he had to be to have a heart attack. If he denied her, she'd reject him forever. It would be all over. But if he accepted...

He felt his knees go weak.

"Andy?" She blinked, her eyes shimmering with saline, her hair shining like gold in the morning sun.

"Yes," he whispered, his confession inaudible beneath the whoosh of his pulse.

"And you like my pancakes?"

"I do," he said, those very pancakes rolling around inside his stomach, threatening to reappear. His grip on the counter tightened while Harlow's smile widened.

"I like your dancing," she told him, breaching the distance between them, the sweet vanilla scent of her perfume elevating his nausea to a new, blinding height. "And how thoughtful you are—how you worry about your mom, how you worry about me." She pressed her hand to his cheek. "You do worry about me, don't you?"

"I do?" he asked, his head swimming.

"You do," she confirmed, exhaling a laugh and wrapping her arms around him. But her expression went somber a second later.

"And if there are things about me that you don't like?" she asked, somehow turning this whole thing into Andrew's idea instead of her own.

"Secrets?" he asked, unable to focus.

"Everyone has them." Her tone was bashful—a schoolgirl thinking about the dirty things she wanted to do with her favorite heartthrob. She walked her fingers up his chest, hooking them onto the collar of his T-shirt.

What seemed like an oncoming confession was cut short by the slam of a door. Drew had been deafened by the pounding of his own pulse. He hadn't noticed the oncoming rumble of an engine, hadn't sensed the impending doom of being caught red-handed.

Red stood in the kitchen not more than a few yards away, his eyes fixed on his wife and the boy in her arms.

Drew's heart leapt into his throat for a second time, scrambling to leave his body forever. He reflexively retreated from

Harlow's embrace, taking a step backward as though doing so would somehow make the situation less horrifying than it was. Harlow blinked a few times, gave Red a look, and turned away from him completely.

Red's attention was steadfast on Andrew's panic.

"Scared?" he asked.

Petrified was more accurate, which was why Drew failed to respond.

"Good," Red muttered. "Because you're fired. Now get the hell out of my house, and don't you dare come back."

CHAPTER FOURTEEN

Long after the sun had set that evening, angry storm clouds crawled across the sky. Mickey parked his TransAm a block down Magnolia and killed the headlights. If he came any closer, there was a chance Harlow would recognize the rumble of his engine. Mick knew that his disappearance had forfeited his employment—but, more important, had forfeited the pact that kept him safe. The past few days had given him the opportunity to call the cops and give them an anonymous tip, but he hadn't. He should have made his move, but there he was, staring down a sleepy street, wondering what damage Harlow had done since he'd left. He assumed that Drew was still alive, but nothing was for sure.

Chewing on the pad of his thumb, he considered what he had to do: sneak along the street, hope he didn't wake the ceaselessly barking neighborhood dog, and creep inside the house. Mickey would tell him everything, help him pack his things and leave. But the more he thought about it, the more he didn't like the idea. If Drew was anything like the other boys, Harlow had already won him over. On top of the fact that Mickey had gone AWOL without a word, Drew had no reason to believe him; if he had been in Andrew's shoes, he would tell himself to go straight to hell. But there was one thing Mickey could do—something that made him shudder at the thought.

Creeping out of the car as quietly as he could, he cursed himself for being so habitually indifferent. If he had only asked for Andrew's cell phone number, he wouldn't be forced to pull this *Mission Impossible* move.

With the key to the house in hand, he inched along the sidewalk, his heart thudding with each step. He rushed across the lawn, pressed himself into the shadows next to the front door. His eyes were fixed on the Ward house; he waited for a light to come on, for the jig to be up. When nothing happened, he shoved the key in the lock and silently pushed the door open, sneaking into his own home.

The house was pitch black—darker than he remembered it ever being before—and the empty living room confirmed that Drew was asleep in his room. The wind pushed against the outer walls, making them snap and creak against the strain.

Tiptoeing through the house, Mickey held his breath. Every step was painfully slow. Halfway down the hall, his key ring jingled in his hand. He winced at the noise as he searched for the one that would unlock door number three, the mysterious door to that steel-walled room.

His plan was to leave it open for Drew to discover on his own. Mickey couldn't prove that Harlow was a murderer without a body, but the room would be enough to make Andrew run.

Leaning forward in a crouch, he brought himself to eye level with the doorknob, straining to see the lock in the dark. Just as he slid the key into the knob, a sickening realization settled over him: Andrew would find the dissecting room, but he'd just pin Mickey as the psycho. Hell, Drew might turn tail and run to Harlow for help. Crouched in the dark, Mick began to reconsider his plan when he felt a breath against his neck.

"I knew you'd be back," Harlow whispered against the shell of his ear.

Before Mickey could respond, something bit into the side of his throat.

And then he was gone.

§

There was no doubt in Drew's mind that he was out of a job, and of all the reasons to get canned, being caught with the boss's wife had never crossed his mind. His stomach was still twisted with anxiety; he was sure that Red would come banging on his door any second, determined to settle the score. But Red never showed up, and Andrew was thankful for that, because he needed to get the hell out of the house. He needed to clear his mind. He was still seriously weirded out by what had happened the day before; it had come out of nowhere and had left him feeling sick for the rest of the afternoon. But the longer he had to digest it, the less appalling the idea felt. Part of him was sure that after a few days, Harlow would realize just how crazy an idea it was for her and Drew to get together. She'd dismiss it, and they'd go back to the way things were.

But another part of him—the lonely, lovesick part—hoped that Harlow wouldn't come to that conclusion. She was the perfect woman. The only things that stood between them were Red and their age. It seemed that Red was stepping out of the picture voluntarily; and age, as they said, was but a number.

Tracking down the hall, Andrew paused beside Mickey's bedroom door. He thought he had heard Mick coming home the night before, but the emptiness of his roommate's bedroom proved that it had all been in Drew's head—probably nothing but the wind.

And that wind was getting worse. It whipped at his hair when he stepped out of the house. He turned to lock the door behind him—stopped short when he saw a notice taped to the door. The words "fumigation" and "pest control" stood out in bold letters. He plucked the paper from the door, the sheet trying to tear itself out of his hands as the wind howled behind him. It was dated three days earlier, but there was no way it had been taped to the door for that long. Drew had been in and out of the house almost constantly. No, this notice had arrived overnight, and it was telling Drew that he needed to vacate the premises by that morning.

He shook his head at the paper, looking for a number to call. There wasn't one, and it wouldn't have mattered if there had been. The wind snatched the sheet from his grasp and sent it whipping down the street.

He looked up, a dark sky hanging ominously overhead, but the growl wasn't thunder; it was an engine. He paused along the cracked walkway, holding his breath. Maybe Mick *had* returned. Maybe he had left early to pick up breakfast for them both—a meal to reconcile over while he explained his disappearance and the fact that they had to rent a motel room for a night or two.

But it wasn't Mickey.

A black van roared around the corner, veering so sharply toward the curb Drew was convinced the driver was aiming to hit him. The thing was a beast—one of those old-fashioned vans that looked like an oversize ice cream truck, nothing but sharp and awkward angles, no windows, ready to kidnap the neighborhood kids. It pulled up behind Drew's pickup, nearly ramming its flat front end into the back of the Chevy as the tires squealed to a halt. The weight of the van shifted to the front tires as its driver slammed on the brakes, then shifted backward with a violent shudder.

Drew stood dumbfounded as he watched a bearded guy slam the van into park. The logo on the side of the vehicle caught his attention: a giant red roach lay on its back, its legs pointed skyward above the name—*Big Chief Pest Control*.

The bearded driver ambled out of the van and stepped onto the sidewalk with a clipboard in hand. He adjusted his trucker cap, that same dead roach emblazoned across the front, and eyed Andrew for a second before approaching.

"You live here?" he asked, motioning to the house with a nod of his head.

"I do," Andrew replied, a frown creeping across his face. This couldn't possibly be happening. Not right now. Not after what had happened yesterday.

The driver scribbled something down on the paper fastened to the clipboard.

"This here fumigation is gonna take at least a couple a' days to clear out. Got an emergency call from the owner. I sent one of my guys to post a notice on your door."

"Yeah, *this morning*. I didn't see it until just now," Drew protested, hoping that this little detail would convince the guy to come back later—at least in a few hours, if not in a few days.

"Sorry, bud." He tapped his clipboard with his pen. "An emergency is an emergency. The owner should have let you know."

Drew couldn't help but to stare at the man in front of him. Mick had taken off without so much as a word as to where he was going or when he'd be back, and now this? "What a *dick*," he muttered under his breath.

The guy let his clipboard fall to his side with a disgruntled look. "You need to clear out, bub. Grab your stuff and go."

Drew frowned. He supposed he could stay with his mom, but even after their great phone conversation, the idea didn't sit well. Defiance would have kept him from going back before they had talked; now, it was more an issue of pride than anything else. She saw him as an independent young man for the first time in his life. He was scared to ruin that, scared that going back, even for a night or two, would have her reconsidering her words. But what other choice did he have?

With the exterminator showing no sign of compassion, Andrew did an about-face and marched back inside. This was fantastic. No job, now no place to stay. He grabbed his duffel bag and whipped it onto his mattress, started to pile a few days' worth of clothes inside. What the hell was he supposed to do now?

Dragging his feet across the lawn, he heard his name called before he could toss his bag into the bed of his Chevy. Harlow stood out on the porch, her arms folded across her chest, a kitchen apron cinched around her waist. She didn't look pleased.

Drew met her at the edge of Mickey's lawn, the picket fence separating them.

"What on earth is that?" she asked in a hushed whisper, motioning to the van.

Andrew peered at the van as though acknowledging its existence for the first time. It was real, and it wasn't going anywhere. The bearded driver seemed dead set on dousing the place with poison.

"Exterminator," Drew answered, his duffel bag feeling way too light for his liking. Standing at Harlow's fence, he realized that he didn't even have enough money for a roadside motel. He was scary short on cash, and the Wards hadn't paid him yet. Toeing the perimeter of Mick's dead grass, he figured now was as good a time as any to hold out his hand and ask to be compensated.

"Well, who called him?" she asked. "I thought that Mickey boy stormed off."

Drew opened his mouth to speak, but something hitched in his brain and his throat went dry. He hadn't told her Mickey had taken off, and even if he had, he certainly hadn't mentioned that he hadn't come back.

Then again, the TransAm wasn't parked in the driveway.

Drew sighed, shoving his fingers through his hair. He didn't know what to say.

"Well, this is ridiculous," Harlow said with a huff. "I'm going to go talk to that man." She motioned to the bearded driver with a small dish towel in her hand, like a Southern belle waving a handkerchief at a caller.

"It's fine. I'll just grab a room somewhere."

Just as Andrew was about to bring up the subject of money, Red filled the front doorway. Drew tensed immediately. Harlow noticed.

"Is he standing there?" she asked quietly. "He is, isn't he?"

Drew didn't reply, but she read his expression.

"I want you to stay with me," she whispered.

"What?"

"Stay with me," she repeated. "You can't leave me here with him."

Andrew blinked, shooting a look toward Red before taking a side step, repositioning himself so Harlow was directly between them.

"Are you kidding?" he asked her. "He'll kill me."

"He'll do no such thing," Harlow assured him. "He wants a divorce. We're over."

"Harlow…"

She gave him a desperate look.

"Andy, *please*. Don't fight me on this." She leaned forward half an inch, her teeth worrying the swell of her bottom lip. "I don't feel safe here," she murmured. "I need you."

So he had been right: Red *did* have a temper. He frowned at her admission. Now he couldn't leave her here.

"So come with me," he suggested, but she shot his idea down with a snort.

"What, to some nasty roadside motel? If anyone should be in a motel it's *him*." She shot a defiant glare at her husband, but Red was gone, having retreated into the house. "This is *my* house," she asserted. "*I* make the rules. I have a guest bedroom, and that's where you're going to stay."

Drew shook his head again. This was crazy. Red would be on him the second he set foot in that house, and why shouldn't he be? Drew could only imagine what it felt like, catching your wife with the next-door neighbor. It didn't matter that he hadn't had anything to do with it. That wasn't the point.

"Andy." She took his hand, pressing his palm to her cheek. He pulled away a moment later.

"This isn't right," he told her. "I can't. Imagine if you were me."

"If I were you, I'd do what I was asked," she told him. "If you told me that *you* were unhappy, I'd do whatever I could to fix it."

Andrew wasn't convinced. He couldn't bring himself to do it. If there was anything that felt truly wrong, of all the things that had felt off or strange so far, this was it.

"He's leaving *me*," she told him, which was odd, because from what Harlow had said the day before, she was ready to leave him. But it seemed probable, especially after Red saw Harlow hanging off Drew like a coat on a hanger in the middle of his kitchen. "I'll be alone," she pleaded.

That all-too-familiar nausea washed over him, reminiscent of the day before. She was putting him in an impossible position. Again. He exhaled a breath, jabbing his fingers into his hair again.

"Jesus, Harlow—"

"Fine," she said, cutting him off midsentence. "I'll just tell him to get out. Done is done. He has to go."

"What?"

"I'm kicking him out."

"Just like that?"

A laugh tumbled past her lips. "Just like what?" she asked. "This is how divorce works. Bring your things inside."

"Now?" He blinked in disbelief. What the hell was happening? He shook his head, ready to refuse taking part in any of it. But the moment he opened his mouth to say no, he remembered her stopping him at her front door after that awkward dinner; he remembered her wrapping her arms around him in the warmest embrace he'd felt in years. He recalled the plates of cookies, the card tucked into his wallet behind his driver's license, the fact that he'd positioned his bed beside the window so he could stare at the Wards' house, secretly yearning to live within those walls. This was his chance, and he was contemplating turning down the opportunity?

Harlow looked over her shoulder, blinking at him. "Well?" she asked.

Drew took a steadying breath, momentarily closed his eyes, and murmured, "Fuck it," before falling into step.

Harlow gave him a smile.

"I'm excited," she said, then shimmied up the walkway to give Red the bad news.

§

While Drew sat on the porch, not wanting to enter the Wards' house while Red was still inside, Harlow stood in the doorway of Isaac's old room. It would have to do, at least until Andrew was comfortable enough to share the master bedroom. This wasn't Harlow's typical routine. The boys who stayed in this room were nothing but toys—empty-headed children she took pleasure in seducing, then disemboweling on that very bed. But Andy was different. He had, by some miracle, enchanted her with his boyish charm. Andrew Morrison would take Red Ward's place in her life. It was high time for Red to be exiled to the old house next door; he would be demoted from husband to butcher whether he liked it or not, living out the rest of his days watching Harlow laugh with Andrew on her arm. And if he refused, she'd take care of it. But she was confident that Red wouldn't refuse. He wasn't *that* stupid.

She closed the door to Isaac's room and crossed the hall to the master bedroom. Red was there, packing a suitcase without a word.

"I warned you for years," she told him.

He flipped the hard shell of his luggage closed and clasped it shut, giving his wife a look that could kill.

"You've underestimated me for far too long."

CHAPTER FIFTEEN

The room gave Drew the creeps. He sat at the edge of the bed, listening to the branches of a tree scrape against the glass in the wind, feeling like he wasn't actually allowed to touch anything. Everything was strategically placed, from the books on the bookshelf to the trinkets on the shelf above the bed. If he moved anything, Harlow would know. He was already anxious, and the museum-like quality of the guest room made him even more so. Harlow's extreme organization hadn't bothered him before, but now that his choice of staying or going had been taken away, it was like an itch he couldn't scratch.

But that wasn't what disturbed him most.

The thing that got to him was the room itself. It wasn't the typical guest room that most households had—nicely decorated but lacking personality: neutral colors, not too girly, not too masculine. This room felt like it had belonged to someone. The books were all novels he had read in school: *A Brave New World* and *Lord of the Flies*, held in place by a makeshift bookend—a golden baseball trophy, the pitcher's arm pulled back to make the winning throw. There were a couple of spiral notebooks stacked on the top shelf of the bookcase, perfectly aligned; bits of paper were held captive between the twisted metal binding, a telltale sign of pages being torn away. There was an outdated stereo on top of the dresser, though no CDs that Drew could see from where he sat. And if he opened the closet, he was almost sure to see someone's forgotten wardrobe hanging there, clean and pressed, ready to wear. He felt like he was trespassing by just sitting there, his duffel bag at his feet.

Harlow called up to him from the base of the stairs. She wanted to celebrate her newfound freedom by letting someone else cook dinner for a change. Drew didn't much feel like going out, but he didn't have the heart to deny her.

Peering at his hands as he sat there, he leaned down to unzip his bag with a sobering awareness: his packing job had been little more than a random grab at various T-shirts and a few pairs of jeans, leaving him completely unprepared to accompany Harlow to whatever restaurant she chose. Undeniably, it would be some fancy place where he could hardly read the menu—if places like that existed in Creekside at all.

"Goddamn it," he muttered, regretting not having spent more time deciding what to take with him on this unannounced hiatus. He sat there for a long while, his elbows pressed to his knees, his head in his hands, the duffel bag peeled open like an in-process autopsy.

When he finally dragged himself down the stairs, he found Harlow sitting in Red's recliner. She stood when she saw him, smoothing down the front of a little black dress with the palms of her hands. But her smile was quick to fade when Drew held out his arms like Jesus on the cross, wordlessly showing her the sorry state of his clothes.

Her fingers toyed with the pearls around her neck as she surveyed the situation. But rather than showing disappointment, she cracked a girlish smile and gave Andrew a helpless shrug.

"Oh, forget it," she told him with a laugh. She pulled her high heels off her feet and dashed up the stairs, coming down a minute later in an ensemble he hadn't seen before—an outfit that made his heart flutter like a butterfly in a net. Standing on the bottom step, she wore an old Kansas State T-shirt tucked into a pair of jeans. An outfit that would have made anyone else look careless and disheveled made Harlow Ward look elegantly casual. She flashed him a girlish smile, pushing a strand of flaxen blond hair away from her forehead.

They piled into his pickup and rambled into town, Drew's stereo—the newest addition to that Chevy—playing an old INXS CD on repeat. Harlow rolled down the window, letting the storm-cooled wind whip through the cabin, her right arm sticking outward, grabbing at the air.

She directed Drew to Creekside's one and only drive-in. It was an old place, one that he assumed had been there almost as long as Creekside had. Despite being run-down, it still held an air of nostalgia, of the glory days it surely must have seen—candy-colored hot rods pulling up with greasers behind the wheel and Pink Ladies in the passenger seat.

A roller-skating girl twirled just outside Drew's open window, delivering their burgers and shakes on a bright red tray. While nobody had officially called their outing a date, Drew paid the bill out of what little cash he had left. He wouldn't have felt right otherwise.

He watched Harlow struggle with the giant sandwich.

"My goodness," she said, trying to keep the wrapper in place, sizing up the quarter-pound burger as if searching for the best place to bite.

He laughed as a glob of ketchup ran down Harlow's slender wrist, and she blushed when she managed to get the entire thing into her mouth, chasing it down with too-salty fries.

"I ate nothing but burgers when I was in college," she told him. "Completely addicted."

Andrew shook his head at her, smiling around a mouthful of shake. Her confession would have had him raising his eyebrows a few days before, but now, seeing her so casual in her jeans and sneakers, he couldn't help but be delighted by the idea of her having been a normal kid, just like him.

"My daddy loved hamburgers," she said. "He was like that fat little cartoon character on *Popeye*. What was his name?"

"Wimpy?"

Harlow threw her head back and laughed, the name spurring some hilarious memory Andrew wished he could share with her; he wished he had memories of his own dad that he could contribute. But rather than dampening the conversation by bringing Rick up, he stuffed a few fries into his mouth and smiled instead.

Drew couldn't help being surprised, not by her appetite but by how casual Harlow could be. It was like seeing a snapshot of the girl she had once been—someone he'd never met before. He wondered whether Red had once had the pleasure of meeting this girl, or if Harlow had always been the perfect picture of the atomic age. Her head lolled atop her shoulders when she turned to look at him, her eyes glittering with lazy contentment.

"I love this," she told him, motioning with a flick of her wrist to the interior of the truck, the drive-in just beyond the windshield, the red tray hanging outside Drew's window, the ketchup-and mustard-smeared burger wrappers crumpled between them. "I love this truck," she mused, her fingers sliding across the blanket that covered the bench seat's imperfections. She smiled at him, her expression growing wistful. Drew furrowed his eyebrows as he watched her grow pensive, a sad sense of longing wafting off her like a pheromone.

He didn't say anything; he just reached out to touch her hand, reassuring her that everything was going to be OK. She looked down, his hand on top of hers, her bottom lip trembling for the half second it took to compose herself.

"I'll miss him," she said softly, looking out the window across a dark expanse of wheat. "But it's time to move on. *You* did."

Drew nodded faintly. He supposed she was right. Leaving his mother behind had been the hardest thing he'd done since letting Emily go. He imagined that Harlow letting Red go was a lot like that. Turning her hand palm up, she closed her fingers over his.

Andrew stared at their hands for a long while. It was all still so strange, being here with her like this. He was hesitant to let his guard down, but the longer they sat together, the cabin of the truck redolent of pickles and french fries, the more relaxed he became. Harlow had dropped the act. Beneath the pretty dresses and frilly aprons she was a real person, just as vulnerable as he was. The fact that she trusted him enough to show him that side of her meant a lot.

Exhaling a sigh, she looked back to Drew and offered him a weary smile.

"Let's go home," she said.

And so they did.

§

Harlow couldn't help but think of Danny Wilson and his baseball trophy, that little pitcher caked in Danny's blood. But rather than goring Andrew when they returned, she led him up the stairs instead, heady with the memory of dates with other boys, her heartbeat thumping in her throat as she'd lean in and whisper, telling them what she wanted, asking them to be rough. She felt Andrew resist when she turned toward the master bedroom. Glancing over her shoulder, Andrew looked more like a kid than he ever had—nervous, uncertain. She turned to face him fully, closing the distance between them. Her fingers swept across his forehead, brushing his hair aside.

"Are you afraid of me?" she asked, her eyes fixed on the design on his T-shirt. She could hear him breathing, his chest rising and falling beneath the palm of her hand. It was funny;

all the others had been so easy to lure. And yet the one she truly wanted was standing before her, wavering.

Silent, Drew shook his head no.

"You know what they say," she said, looking up at him. "You only regret the things you didn't do."

"Do you think that's true?" he asked, his words thick with anxiety.

Harlow lifted a single shoulder in a lopsided shrug, letting it drop a moment later.

"I don't know," she confessed. "I always do what I want."

"And you don't regret anything?"

She considered his question, her mind spiraling back to Isaac, and then to Danny, to all the boys she'd ended with a wink and a kiss. She thought about Mickey and all the things she'd made him do; Red, and all the things he'd endured. And then she looked back to Andrew, the boy before her so painfully child-like that it twisted her heart, so vulnerable that it made her skin tingle with desire.

"No," she told him, her fingers curling beneath the neckline of his shirt, pulling him just a little closer. She leaned in, her lips brushing along his jawline, his pulse jackhammering in the hollow of his throat. Stepping backward toward the master bedroom, she pulled him with her. "I don't regret any of it," she whispered. "Not a single goddamn thing."

§

After Harlow lost the baby, she pulled into herself. She hardly spoke, and she most certainly didn't play with her little boy. Isaac spent his time watching *Sesame Street* and playing with his toys, as silent as any toddler could be. With the death of Harlow's unborn baby girl, Isaac was destined to be an isolated child, left to fend for himself while Harlow slept and his father worked.

When Isaac was old enough to go to school, Harlow became even edgier. She'd fly into a rage when he'd leave his shoes out, when he'd leave the living room littered with toys. One morning he made the mistake of leaving a box of Lucky Charms on the kitchen counter. Livid, Harlow snatched him up from his Saturday cartoons and marched him over to the stove.

"What's this?" she demanded, shoving his chest against the counter's edge. "You want to leave your cereal out so we'll get ants?" Pushing him aside, she snatched the box up. "I'll show you how to catch ants. Are you watching?"

"Momma, no," Isaac whined, reaching his scrawny arm out for his cereal while she tore open the top flap. She yanked the bag from inside the box, took it in both hands, and pulled. Lucky Charms exploded like a Fourth of July firework, the sweet smell of sugared oats and marshmallows filling the space around them. Isaac's eyes went wide as purple horseshoes and lucky clovers bounced onto the kitchen floor.

"There," she said with a sneer, dropping the torn bag onto the floor. "Now it'll attract ants for sure." Her high heels ground cereal into the tile as she caught him by the shoulder, shoving him onto the floor. "Now clean it up."

Isaac had been six years old.

And the older that boy got, the more infuriated Harlow became. At ten, he wanted nothing more than to play baseball. Red thought it was a great idea: baseball was his favorite game. It was a win-win for them both; Isaac would be able to get out of the house, and Red could take him to see the playoffs. Neither of them stopped to consider that Harlow hated sports, and that their little pastime would leave her home alone. But Red refused to relent, and after weeks of smooth talk Harlow agreed to Little League.

It was all for nothing.

Isaac returned from his first practice with a soiled uniform—knees and elbows bright green, the front of his shirt streaked with dirt from sliding into third. Harlow took one look at him and flipped. She tore the uniform off him in a frenzy, grabbed the scissors, and began hacking away while Isaac bawled. By the time she was finished, the uniform was a collection of dishrags. Isaac spent all afternoon trying to Scotch tape his uniform back together, eventually approaching his mother with a tearful apology. He was sorry. He'd never slide during a game again, even if it meant being tagged out. Harlow wasn't interested. She sent him to his room. Isaac wasn't allowed to participate in sports again.

But Isaac's love for his mother was undeniable, just like Red's, and she knew it. Listening in while Red comforted a whimpering Isaac in his room, Red excused Harlow's outbursts, explaining to his son that his mommy had bad memories, that they haunted her; and for that very reason, Isaac had to be as good as he could possibly be. Harlow was given a free pass, having convinced Red that his unconditional acceptance was what was keeping his wife from leaving them behind. Isaac fell in line as well, because kids were gullible. They'd do anything to win a parent's love. Harlow knew that from experience.

Harlow's past—the trauma and pain—was what kept Red's mouth shut throughout their marriage. Even when she was caught sneaking out of Isaac's bedroom in the middle of the night; even when she repeated history. Harlow knew Isaac never complained to his father about her climbing into bed with him. She had convinced him that it was the only way she knew how to show him she loved him. And so the cycle continued. Rather than being saved from her madness, Harlow slipped farther beneath its surface.

§

That night Andrew lay in a bed that wasn't his. He stared up at the ceiling of the master bedroom, Harlow's head on his chest, hardly able to believe that he'd gone along with it—that he had let her seduce him.

It hadn't taken much. The idea of losing someone who actually understood him, someone who represented everything he had always wanted—it was too much to risk. He had followed her into the master bedroom, seeing her as someone broken, someone as used up as he was. And yet after all had been said and done, the sickening churn of his stomach refused to let him deny it: what he'd done was wrong. The restraints; the things she had asked him to whisper into her ear. It had freaked him out.

But he'd done it anyway.

Unable to get back to sleep, he carefully slid out from beneath her, sneaked out of the room, and stepped across the hall to the room he was meant to occupy. He stopped by the window, his attention paused on Mickey's fixer-upper—the house that still held most of his things. The trees bent and swayed in the unrelenting wind. It was strange looking toward that house instead of away from it. He'd spent so many nights looking at the Wards' perfect home, wondering what it would be like to stay there rather than where he had been, but now that he was there, he gazed back toward where he'd come from. It was true what they said—the grass was always greener. The grass on the other side of this particular fence was dead and brown, but he wanted to be back there.

Something crossed behind one of the curtains, but he dismissed it as a trick of the light, nothing but shadows and paranoia—the storm throwing gloom like a magician throwing smoke. But the longer he stared, the more convinced he was that Mick's house wasn't empty, that there was someone in there.

He crawled into the guest bed, pulled the sheet up to his chin, and squeezed his eyes shut in an attempt to sleep, but he couldn't breathe. It was as though a demon had crawled out of the darkness to perch on his chest, its weight pressing heavy against his diaphragm—Fuseli's painting come to life. He sat up, trying to swallow, but his esophagus refused to cooperate. With his heart pounding hard in his throat, he pulled his knees up to his chest and pressed the heels of his palms against his eyes. *It's just anxiety*, he told himself. He was losing his grip, losing himself. Harlow had proved one thing, whether she had meant to or not: she was in charge. She'd pulled him into her bed, and Drew had done what she wanted.

He shook his head as he took a deep breath, trying to calm himself. Overwhelmed with the need for a drink, he shot back to his feet. He had seen a liquor cabinet downstairs.

In spite of his runaway heart, he tried to be as silent as possible. Creeping into the hall, he didn't want to wake the owner of the house. Something about going downstairs without her knowing felt forbidden. Harlow had never demanded Drew stay upstairs, but he felt as though she expected him to stay in his room until the sun came up, waiting to hear the June Cleaver clatter of dishes in the kitchen. This, however, was no June Cleaver moment. This was *A Nightmare on Magnolia Lane*.

He wondered if Red had tailed them to the drive-in, wondered if he had followed them back to the house. Perched up in one of the trees that flanked the street, he could have easily seen everything that had transpired in the hallway just hours before. He would have seen Andrew following Harlow into Red's old bedroom. And if she had been anything the way she had been with Red, Red would know exactly what had happened behind closed doors.

Harlow hadn't had time to call somebody to change the locks, and that meant Red still had a key. He could have been hiding in the shadows at that very second, waiting to grab him, to wrap his hands around Drew's throat, to swing an ax high over his head and embed it in Andrew's skull. His heart thumped inside of his chest like a boxer punching a speed bag.

He tiptoed past Harlow's door even though walking normally would have looked far less suspicious. He stopped at the top of the stairs, took a deep breath, and crept down the steps. Outside, the wind roared.

Stopping in the dining room, he tugged on the liquor cabinet door. Naturally, it was locked. He closed his eyes, exhaling a steady breath of defeat. Rather than searching the place for the key, he settled on the kitchen instead.

Squinting against the brightness of the fridge, he pushed the milk aside to reach farther into its confines, fishing out a hidden carton of orange juice. He shook it, popped it open, and poured himself a glass—and was thrown into blindness as the door swung closed. Groping for the door handle, he pulled it open again, illuminating the kitchen in a cold white glow, nearly choking on his juice when his eyes found a silhouette standing at the base of the stairs, watching him from afar.

His mind reeled; he was sure it was Red, come to settle the score. Every horror flick he'd ever watched came rushing back to him, ready to flatten him with all the slasher scenes he'd seen, the thousands of gallons of fake blood, the terrified screams and the pitiful begging: *Please, don't kill me.* If he ran, he'd hardly move at all. It would be nothing but one continuous shot—a dolly-zoom effect, woozy and claustrophobic.

"Andy?"

Drew's heart flip-flopped. It was Harlow.

"Oh God," he murmured, nearly squeaking out the words. "Did I wake you up?"

"I was still awake." She took a few steps forward. "Are you OK?"

"Yeah, why?" he replied, but he knew what she meant. What had happened upstairs, combined with looking as though he'd just seen a ghost, very likely made him look ready to run for his life.

"I just don't want things to be awkward," she told him.

"I'm OK. Just thirsty." He lifted his half-drained glass of orange juice.

Harlow nodded and turned to go back up the stairs.

When she finally disappeared, he stood there, staring at his glass of OJ, wondering how the hell he'd gotten himself into this situation.

§

Even in exile, Harlow had a hold on Red. While she and Andrew romped around Creekside before rolling between the sheets, Red had spent hours on a metal-legged stool, staring at a motionless Mickey Fitch.

He imagined this was what Mickey had done before his first time—sat, stared, prayed to hear the distant buzz of an alarm clock growing louder, louder, loud enough to rouse him from this nightmare.

But Mickey wasn't dead.

Red looked down to his hands for the thousandth time. A twenty-milliliter ampoule of propofol rested in his right palm. Though he had never administered the stuff himself, he had seen the effects firsthand. Harlow called it "milk"; it was one of her favorite drugs because it kept the object of her hobby quiet—a surprised gasp when the needle pricked the skin, but that was all. Years before, Harlow had complained about how difficult it was to obtain. But that was the magic of the Internet, and Harlow knew where to look.

Turning his attention from the emulsion in his hand to the man on the autopsy table, he watched Mickey's chest rise and fall with shallow breaths. He had no idea how long the guy had been lying on the table, no clue when Harlow had shot him full of anesthetic. If he administered another dose too soon, the result would be grim. Death by cardiac arrest wasn't nearly as grue-some as dismemberment, but it was forbidding enough to keep Red where he was, sitting atop that stool, wondering what the hell to do.

If Mickey had been the guy who was sleeping in his house, sleeping with his wife, he wouldn't have given two shits about taking a bone saw to the bastard's throat. But Mickey had just been doing his job.

Andrew was the problem.

He eventually left the safety of his chair to wander the perimeter of the room. Before now, he'd never actually set foot in this room. Harlow's determination to purchase two homes rather than one had bewildered him until men in hard hats descended his basement stairs. She told them she was lilapsophobic, and tornado anxiety wasn't exactly conducive to Kansas living. The house next door would be occupied by their only son, she said. The tunnel would serve as a storm shelter as well as an underground bridge linking the two properties together. If the workers had still been skeptical, their suspicions were tossed aside when she paid them in cash, tax-free, no strings attached.

That room was lined with stand-alone freezers—twenty-nine cubic feet of storage space per unit; plenty of room for an intact body in each one, big enough for a duo if they were torn apart. Three of those freezers were lined up end-to-end. Harlow liked to overplan. She had enough room for half a dozen bodies, just in case Mickey couldn't toss them into the trunk of his TransAm and drive them out to wherever he took them fast enough.

Red stopped at the freezer closest to him and pulled its top open. Cold air rolled over the open top, spilling over the side of the chest like dry ice in a witch's cauldron. It was bare. The second freezer matched the first: vacant, hardly used. Hesitating in front of the third icebox, he had to wonder why he was looking inside them at all. This wasn't his pastime. He wasn't interested in discovering the body of a kid who'd mowed his lawn and painted his window trim. But much like driving by a freeway accident, he had to look, and there it was: A red streak decorated the back interior wall, as though a limb had tumbled out of a bag and made a wide, gory sweep—a calligraphy brush with flesh for bristles. A single bag sat inside the icy, frigid vastness—black plastic hiding its contents from the world.

Seeing it, Red suddenly understood why he'd gone from freezer to freezer—this bag was his ticket out of this mess. He'd paid the True Value a visit with full intention of laying Andrew out, gutting him like a fish not only to remove him from the equation, but to show Harlow that he could do it. But this was better.

He let the door slip from his grasp. It slammed shut loudly enough to incite a wince. Red's eyes darted to the autopsy table. His wife's former employee took a deep breath, fighting against the haze of anesthesia, trying to claw his way back into consciousness. Red stepped across the room, grabbing for the syringe on the counter—he had found it there when he had arrived, unable to decide whether to chalk it up to Mickey's mess, or whether Harlow had set it out for him, anticipating this very moment. The syringe skittered across the surface in his haste, tumbling to the floor and rolling out of view.

"Goddamn it," he hissed, crouching down, trying to locate it, but it was gone. Exhaling a frustrated sigh, he threw open the cabinet doors. But despite the freezers being mostly clean, Mickey's shortcomings were housed within those drawers; chronic disorganization that Red was now forced to dig through at the most inopportune time.

If Mickey had been able to peel his eyes open and bear witness to the scene, Red was sure he would have roared with laughter. Each second that ticked away was a second closer to waking up, a second closer to Mickey's saving himself from poetic justice. If he roused before Red found what he was looking for, he'd be saved by his own mess, delivered from a premature grave by chaos rather than kindness. This was irony at its best.

While Mickey tried to surface, Red flung the contents of each drawer onto the floor by the handful. He would have marveled at the senselessness of the stuff he was pawing through if his pulse weren't rattling his brain—fast-food coupons and Starbucks receipts, loose music CDs and a copy of *American Psycho*. For the first time in his life, he could hardly see through his own dread. As careful as Harlow was in constructing this steel trap of a room, she hadn't splurged on restraints. There was no point. All the boys who ended up here were already dead; and if Mickey Fitch came to, Red was as good as dead too. There would be no plea bargain, no leniency for his case. If Mickey Fitch woke up, he'd grab Red by both sides of his head and twist. The last thing Red would hear would be the breaking of his own neck.

Naturally, the last place Red checked was the place he should have looked first: a one-hundred-count box of syringes sat at the bottom of the cabinet that housed Harlow's endless supply of "milk"—the same cabinet that had been at his elbow the entire time he was sitting there, watching Mickey sleep.

"Son of a bitch!" he barked, snatching the box up, tearing at its cardboard lid. It wriggled its way out of his grasp, the contents spilling out, detonating like a faulty bottle rocket, exploding against the ground. He scrambled to grab one in midair, feeling like Wile E. Coyote just before that dim cartoon canine plunged off a desert cliff.

Mickey's arm twitched, sending Red headlong into a fit of panic. Snatching one of the syringes off the floor, he grabbed for an ampoule of anesthetic, uncapped the needle with his teeth, and stabbed the needle through the plastic vial before pulling back the plunger. Ready to stab the needle into Mickey's neck, he stopped himself, remembering all the medical shows he'd watched over the years. Taking a steadying breath, he tapped the syringe and pushed the air bubbles out.

And in his hesitation, at that very moment, Mickey Fitch opened his eyes to the world.

CHAPTER SIXTEEN

By his seventeenth year, Isaac Ward's unconditional love had run out, and Harlow knew it. He had pulled away from her years before—a growing distance Red blamed on adolescence and rebellion. But Isaac's eyes told a different story. He'd endured a life of secrets, just like his mother had, and he hated her for putting him in that position. The way he looked at her made Harlow wither: his gaze accusatory, heavy with condemnation. She had defiled him, and he had no intention of forgiving her.

At first, Harlow tried to ignore his glares, but Isaac's eyes were deep. They pulled her under, threatening to drown her in an ocean of guilt. His critical glances reached beyond the scope of his own abuse—and reached into Harlow's past, pointing out all of her indiscretions. His biting gaze, along with the way he turned away from her when she came close, it caught her by the ears and rubbed her nose in her sins. Suddenly, she could hardly look at her only child, because she didn't see Isaac anymore. She saw herself, her own anger toward her father. She saw a broken life—one that had left a hole in her heart.

She was disgusting. A sinner. A wicked, wretched, horrible woman who was bound for hell. And that infuriated her, because it wasn't her fault. Reggie Beaumont was to blame.

Everyone had admired him as he beamed the word of God into living rooms; he was the white knight of televangelism. But the world forgot that knights wore armor, and beneath that armor there was sinning flesh and lecherous blood. Reggie Beaumont hid behind a veil of faith, and his daughter was the only one who knew his secret.

She had denied it for years, blaming fuzzy memories on bad dreams. The dream was always the same: a bedroom door opening in the dead of night, a pink ruffled comforter being pulled aside, Daddy whispering into her ear that Jesus loved her while her skull knocked against the headboard.

It was Danny Wilson's fault too, the boy who had been nothing but a gentleman—until he got Harlow back to his apartment. It was the fault of the highwayman who'd left her mother along the road for dead, and now it was Isaac himself, with his unrelenting gaze. *They* had turned her into a monster. If she could only erase them all, she'd be free of the guilt; she could shrug off the stigma and finally go on with her life.

The problem was, Reggie Beaumont was dead, burned to death while he slept. Harlow had watched the flames lick up the sides of her childhood home before turning away, only a week from her wedding day. Danny Wilson was dead, pummeled to death with his prized baseball trophy. The man who'd killed her mother had never been apprehended. Harlow could only hope he had left this world with Bridget Beaumont's screams reverberating inside his skull.

Isaac was the only one left.

She hadn't been fancy with it, and maybe that was the problem. Walking in on him while he brushed his teeth, she grabbed him by the back of the neck and jammed his toothbrush down his throat. Startled, he stumbled backward in bare feet, his hands desperately groping at his neck when he should have been shoving his fingers into his mouth. He gasped for air, his face contorting in ways she'd never seen before—a mixture of pain and surprise, terror and disbelief. When the bathroom rug curled beneath his feet, Isaac lost his balance.

Watching him tumble with bated anticipation, she thought his fall was oddly graceful; he twisted in midair like Mikhail Baryshnikov, coming to an abrupt stop when his temple met the corner of the tub.

Isaac's blood trickled from the corner of his mouth, his nose, his ears, pooling along the joints of the bathroom tile, crosshatching the stark-white floor with crimson veins. The delicacy of that pattern was almost artistic—bloody filigree curling across an unspoiled canvas. When Danny had fallen at her feet, a weight had been lifted from her shoulders. She killed, and for a second, the pain was gone. But now she felt nothing. No release. No absolution. Nothing but more emptiness, an emptiness that went on forever.

Harlow took a seat on the edge of the tub while Isaac bled onto the bathroom floor. Chewing on the pad of her thumb, she wasn't thinking about what she'd done; she wasn't thinking about her father or her son. She was thinking about the hollowness she felt, and how she must have done it wrong.

She had to get another boy. She had to try again.

She had to try over and over again until she got it right.

§

Drew considered jumping in his truck and taking off, but he didn't want to give Harlow the wrong impression. He felt hideous after what had transpired in the master bedroom the night before—but that was his fault, not Harlow's. He should have never let it go as far as it had. Harlow was lonely. He could hardly hold her responsible for what had happened.

But that didn't change the fact that he desperately wanted out, wanted to fly away with the wind like Dorothy. He didn't want to sit at Harlow's kitchen table, and he didn't want to listen to Frank Sinatra. If he had to listen to one more Rat Pack tune, he was going to lose his fucking mind.

And so, needing escape but not wanting to run away like his own father had, Andrew settled for the next best thing: the front yard. He slipped into the garage and prepped Red's push mower for another morning of work. The wind was bad, but he couldn't stay inside for another second. Watching Harlow flit about the kitchen didn't feel the same anymore. The idea of having ruined something amazing turned his stomach. He was afraid the fairy tale was over, that he had destroyed it by getting too close.

The garage on Cedar had been a wreck, full of cobwebs and old tools that Rick had left behind. It had been a disaster before he disappeared; a virtual cacophony of random instruments— piles of chrome-plated wrenches and pliers, screwdrivers and mismatched sockets. As a kid, Drew would sit on a padded stool and watch his dad work on the Chevy, but he always got bored and left before he could learn anything: Rick spent more time hunting for the right tools than he did using them.

Red's garage was in an entirely different hemisphere, one that Andrew had previously marveled at, but now, for whatever reason, it gave him the chills. The place was meticulous—not a single screw out of place or a single tool left on the workbench. Even the floor was spotless, coated with a gray oil-repelling sealant. If Red did anything besides read the paper and mow the lawn, it was keeping the garage as pristine as a showroom. And what struck Drew as odd was that Red didn't seem the garage-lurking type. Andrew thought back to Harlow's confession—that the house was a lie. Maybe Red was a lie as well.

He crossed the length of the garage to the mower propped neatly against the wall. If anything, he could spend half the day in the wind, waiting for the inevitable tornado to suck him up into the sky. He couldn't get his thoughts out of his head, imagining what his mother would say if she found out about Harlow, wondering what Emily would do if she knew he had slept with someone so much older—that he'd tied her down like some twisted rapist and still managed to be turned on.

"You're fucking pathetic," he muttered to himself, rubbing the palms of his hands against the front of his shirt, trying to cleanse himself of what he'd done.

He shuddered, pulled the mower from its spot, and rolled it out of the garage and down the driveway to the side of the picket fence. Its wheels sank into grass that didn't need cutting, but he'd be damned if he wasn't going to cut it anyway. Narrowing his eyes against the wind, he was determined, convinced that completing this task would turn him back into the guy he used to be.

"Andy?" Harlow peeked out the front door. "Jesus, what are you doing out here?" Her soft curls flew into her eyes, blinding her. She fought them, pushing them out of her face.

Her voice put him on edge. He wanted to face her head-on and scream for her to stop talking, just don't say anything, just please don't talk anymore. But he didn't scream; he turned and answered instead.

"The lawn needs mowing."

"What?" She stared at him. "Are you crazy? It absolutely does *not* need cutting," Harlow protested. "You can't stay out here. Get back inside."

"It needs it," he insisted, and he began to push the mower along.

Harlow hovered in front of the door for a long while before disappearing inside, and the relief he felt when she was out of view was so overwhelming it actually disturbed him.

But he knew Harlow well enough to know she wasn't going to give up. A moment later, she stepped onto the patio for the second time, poised herself on the bottom step of the porch stairs, and crossed her arms over her chest, bracing herself against the inevitable tornado that would be born of the clouds overhead.

"What's this about?" she asked, her expression nonplussed, annoyance peppering her tone.

"This?" Drew asked.

"This." She motioned to the yard. "Don't play dumb. I read men like you read comic books."

"It's my job," he reminded her, backpedaling to a relationship they both knew was gone.

"It was," she agreed, "but it isn't anymore."

Andrew opened his mouth to both question and protest, but she cut him off before he could get a word out.

"You heard Red; you're fired. Now put that thing away and come inside before the storm takes you with it."

Drew furrowed his eyebrows at the mower. His attention slowly shifted to Mick's place. Gazing at it, he felt weak with longing. He wanted to be back there in that mess, in the dusty darkness that smelled of stale sheets. Amid the dirty carpet and the makeshift curtains, there had been freedom—gritty and muddled perhaps, but freedom all the same.

"Andrew."

Harlow's voice slithered around him from behind, curling around his neck like a noose.

"I'm waiting."

This wasn't the woman who brought him cookies when he first moved in; nor was it the woman he had burgers with the night before; it wasn't the person who had begged him to stay with her while a black van loomed in the distance. This was someone different, a third personality: not motherly and loving, not vulnerable and girlish, but demanding, secretly deviant. He turned to look at her, disquiet accentuating his features like a punctuation mark.

"We'll get someone else to do it," she told him. "Some kid. Later."

Pivoting on the hard soles of her shoes, she stepped back inside, leaving Drew feeling vacant, as though every last bit of insight into the situation had poured out of him onto the lawn, swept away by the storm. Because she *had* hired some kid to do it, and that kid had been him.

Which left the question, who the hell was he now?

§

Mickey's eyes were wide, wild, and feral. Red backed away from him, stumbling until the backs of his calves hit the row of cabinets behind him. The syringe dangled there, stabbed into the meat of Mickey's neck. Red had pushed the plunger down, shooting his wife's former employee full of propofol, and Mick had dropped instantly, but instead of passing out again—peaceful and quiet—he bucked on top of the table. His arms and legs went rigor mortis stiff. The cords of his neck stuck out like ropes pulled tight beneath the skin. He seized, convulsing so violently that his thrashing threatened to toss him onto the floor—and all Red could do was watch while Mickey Fitch bit through the flesh of his tongue.

"Oh God," Red groaned. Why, oh fucking *why* had he used an entire vial of anesthetic? It had been an accident—but it was precisely what Harlow had wanted.

Mickey foamed at the mouth, the bubbles of his spit tinged a brutal crimson. The syringe swung side to side like a metronome before coming loose and falling to the floor. Mick was dancing with the Reaper; there was no doubt in Red's mind that the kid was dying. Scrambling back onto his stool, he waited for it to be over, pressing a hand over his eyes, trying to ignore the sound of Mickey's shoes banging against the metal as he thrashed. But he couldn't ignore the choking. Mickey coughed as he shook, asphyxiating on a mouthful of blood. It boiled over his lips, spitting up like a sloppy volcano. There was something about the arcs of crimson that leapt from Mickey's mouth, something that threw Red into motion—a pang of guilt, a sense of responsibility, a genuine need to not let Harlow win.

Bolting to the table in the center of the room, Red's hands clamped down on Mickey's arm and threw it forward. It took all his strength to roll Mick onto his side as he continued to convulse, making it impossible for Red to get a firm grip. So Red did the only thing he could: he took a step back, extended his arms in front of him, and lunged forward. Mickey careened off the table and hit the floor with a slap, rolling onto his stomach. The force of impact steadied the involuntary jerking of his body until he was still, a small lake of blood gathering around his mouth. Red dropped to his knees, shaking him by the shoulder as if shaking were the antidote to a lethal overdose.

"Wake up," he said, his fingers biting into Mickey's shoulder. "Wake up, you son of a bitch!"

He realized the impossibility of his request as the words tumbled out of his throat, knowing Mickey wouldn't wake up because he couldn't; knowing that if he could, he'd kill Red first and wonder what the hell happened later. Pulling his hand away, he stared at the bleeding man before him, unnerved. *At least if he dies now, you know you tried to help him*, he thought. *At least if he dies, you can say you did your best.*

If Mickey died, Harlow would think Red did it for her. He was supposed to cut Mickey up and bury the evidence all over Kansas—this was to be his act of devotion to her. But if he was going to become the monster Harlow wanted him to be, he'd be damned if Mickey Fitch was going to be his first victim. The rope, the tarp...those were for someone else—someone who truly deserved it.

§

Drew spent the rest of the day on the Wards' couch, staring at the television, trying to make himself as small as possible. After his attempt at mowing the lawn had been derailed, he had climbed the stairs to retrieve his truck keys. He wouldn't deny that it was dangerous outside, but the truck would keep him safe enough. But the moment she spotted him descending the stairs, she plucked those keys out of his hand and dropped them into the pocket of her apron. Harlow had made herself clear: she wanted Drew inside.

Andrew didn't want to do anything to draw attention to himself. He didn't want her coming over to talk, didn't want to feel her hand on his leg or see her teeth when her mouth pulled back in a smile. He needed space, and he thought he was being pretty obvious about it.

But Harlow was either missing all his signals or ignoring them altogether. She spent the morning making apple pancakes. In the afternoon, she made a pile of tea sandwiches with the crusts cut off. By the time dinner rolled around, he wanted to bury himself in the backyard, but coq au vin was already on the table, complete with a bottle of red wine and a basket of Harlow's home-baked bread.

It wasn't that he didn't enjoy being spoiled; after a decade of eating nothing but fast food and boxed mac and cheese, Drew thought Harlow's gourmet cooking was like water in the Mojave. But it was terrifying to see her acting the way she was.

And that horror was magnified when Harlow sauntered over, placed a hand on his shoulder, and whispered into his ear, "Why don't you sit over there?" She nodded toward Red's empty recliner. "That's your place now. Go on. Give it a spin."

By the time he sat down at the dining room table, his stomach was a ball of anxiety. He was on the verge of screaming, ready to jump up like a man on fire—jump up and run the hell away. But he couldn't bring himself to do it. Rick Morrison lurked at the back of his mind.

He had mixed feelings toward his father—love, hate, disappointment, sadness; he missed him but never wanted to see him again; he loved him but couldn't stand the sound of his name. There were days when he couldn't bring himself to crawl into that pickup truck, days where he couldn't look his mother in the eye because although she was looking right at him, he knew the reflection in her eyes wasn't his. At the end of the day, Rick Morrison had destroyed their family. He had walked out on them both, taking hope and happiness with him—the same hope and happiness Drew had once seen on Harlow's front doorstep, in the carefully cared-for flowers along the picket fence. The joy that his mother had lost danced at the corners of Harlow's mouth; the passion she had lived in Harlow's laugh, in the way she threw her head back and smiled toward the sky. It was what had broken him—that need, that yearning to get it all back, to have what he'd been missing for so long. He wished Harlow weren't who she was. If she could only be split into two—his mother, the happy housewife; his girl, so beautiful it hurt to look at her.

After a few minutes of chewing around Tony Bennett's vocals, Harlow put down her fork, squared her shoulders, and swirled her wine as she gazed across the table.

"I found a few boys," she said, lifting the glass to her lips.

Putting his fork down, Andrew stared at his plate.

"To work around the house," she clarified, "since you won't be doing it anymore."

The wind rattled the windows. He couldn't remember a storm that had ever lasted this long.

"Andy?" There was concern in her voice. She didn't like his silence.

Drew hesitated, eventually forcing the words from his throat.

"What am *I* supposed to do?"

Harlow shook her head, not understanding the question. He furrowed his eyebrows, still not meeting her gaze.

"Andy." She chuckled. "What are you saying? That you *want* to do menial work? You want to cut grass for a living?" She lifted her glass to toast him. "You're better than that, baby. You're better than that and you know it."

"I wasn't better than that a few days ago," Drew said softly.

"Things change."

"I can't just sit around," he protested. "I need the cash."

Harlow leaned forward, her elbows pressed atop the table. She smiled as she swirled her glass, but there was a spark of defiance in her eyes.

"Do you?" she asked. "What for?"

He swallowed against the lump in his throat, daring to look up at her.

"Rent," he said, his insides lurching with what he knew was to come.

"You can't go back there."

Panic flared within the center of his chest.

"It's poisonous," she said. "Those chemicals never *really* go away. And besides..." She shrugged a shoulder. "That place is a pit. You're better than *that*, honey."

"I can't just not go back. I made a deal."

"With who? Mickey Fitch?" She snorted, throwing the rest of her wine down her throat.

Drew blinked when she spit out Mick's last name. He'd always just been "that Mickey boy" until now. He felt his suspicion start to spiral out of control. "I can't just walk out on him."

"What are you, *loyal* to him?" Harlow asked, a hint of envy coloring her words.

When Drew didn't answer her question, she pushed her chair away from the table and stood.

"It doesn't matter," she told him, catching the wine bottle by its neck, pouring herself another glass. "You don't need to pay rent. That Mickey kid is probably gone for good anyway. And he quite obviously doesn't care about you, calling that exterminator without so much as a warning. Well." She swirled her wine, then took another sip. "We both know that wasn't the truth, now, don't we?"

Drew blinked at her. He opened his mouth to speak, to protest or ask what she meant about Mickey not coming back. He *had* to come back. All his stuff was there. And Drew refused to believe Mick would just up and take off without so much as a good-bye. But Harlow lifted her hand and waved away whatever he was about to say, just as she'd waved him away the night Red had stormed down the sidewalk.

"The boys I called will be here bright and early," she said. "I found them on that Craigslist site, so they're probably felons, but they'll do. They'll bring your things over—at least, whatever things are salvageable. The furniture can't come, obviously. I won't have any thrift store trash in my house."

Drew could do nothing but stare at her. "We'll move you in first, and they'll do whatever yard work there is to be done afterward. We'll find steady help later, when I can put an ad in the paper. Who knows, maybe Mickey will come back and they'll settle in next door."

He couldn't put her words together; they were all mixed up, nonsensical, dancing through the air like cartoon music notes.

"Wait." It was the only word he managed to croak out before she was at his elbow, angling his chair away from the table so that she had enough room to slide onto his lap.

She pushed his unfinished plate of food away, replacing it with her glass.

He tensed. Wanted to scream. Wanted to push her off him. Because he didn't understand what was happening. He couldn't comprehend this sudden spiral into madness.

"Andy," she said, sliding her fingers through his hair. "This isn't open for discussion. You're already here."

The wind howled.

§

That evening, the neighborhood dog, with its inconsolable barking, decided to lose its mind again. He barked and yowled, sounding afraid—perhaps trying to warn all of Creekside that the end was near.

Harlow had led Drew by the hand to the master bedroom for the second time, but relented when he ended up bolting for her bathroom, vomiting a stomach full of food into her sparkling toilet. She wrapped her arms around him and rubbed his back, voicing her worries about his sudden bout of indigestion, but he could see a lingering hint of disgust in her eyes. He hadn't only robbed her of another night of romance, but he'd fouled up her bathroom in the process.

Drew couldn't sleep. He rolled out of the guest room bed and dragged his feet across the carpet, heavy with queasiness, his nerves completely shot.

It was clear to him now that it was time to go home. What had started out as a fantasy had turned into a nightmare. Mick was gone, as was the dusty comfort of his rental house. Harlow had transformed right before his eyes—perfection gone crazy, her apparent fear of being alone twisting her into something unrecognizable, something that scared him more than his own phobia of turning into his father.

He stopped in front of the window, his heart prickling with nerves as he squinted into the night. He had listened to her walk up and down the hall for over an hour—no doubt scrubbing the toilet at half past midnight, but she was outside now, her bathrobe whipping in the Kansas wind, her matching slippers making her look her age. She stood along the curb, staring at her hands. When she turned, a black smear stood out against clean terry cloth like Hester Prynne's scarlet letter.

Despite the distance between them and the darkness and the wind, Andrew knew what it was. His gaze wavered, pausing on his truck, and while it looked untouched, he knew: Tomorrow, when the moving guys came, if he managed to steal his keys back from her, his Chevy wouldn't start. He would be stuck.

Twisting away from the window, he had seen enough. His first thought was to call his mom, but what could she possibly do to help? She was as stuck as he was, imprisoned by something completely out of her control. Help would have to come in the form of cops. But rather than dialing 911, he was left to stare at the top of the dresser from across the room. He had left his phone there just before dinner, and now it was gone.

Scenario after worst-case scenario spiraled through his brain, assuring him that the whole situation was insane. The kind of stuff you saw on TV. He played it out in his head—the feeling of being watched the moment he had pulled up to the curb; the way Harlow had shown up asking for help when she didn't need it; the way the truck—which had always been reliable—suddenly refused to start, and how Red fixed it—a magic trick, like pulling a coin out from behind his ear. His skin crawled as the pieces fell into place, but not everything made sense.

Mickey had driven off into the sunset without a word. Harlow had kicked Red out—and unless Red was up for an Academy Award, the resentment Drew saw in his eyes had been real. The rage that boiled beneath the surface of Red's skin was undeniably sincere—as genuine as Harlow's tears when she confessed she was unhappy; as heartfelt as her laughter had been as they drove toward the drive-in for burgers and shakes.

If it had all been an act, Harlow had known exactly how to claw her way into his heart.

Dread bloomed beneath his diaphragm, creeping up his throat, threatening to suffocate him with awareness. He was an idiot—accepting job offers from strangers, messing around with a married woman, an *older* woman. He should have run the moment Harlow had danced in the kitchen, shooting him a look over her shoulder; he should have run like hell until he was too far to reach.

But instead, he had run in the wrong direction—right into her arms.

"Fuck." He hissed the word into the silence of the room. "Fuck!"

On the brink of a meltdown, he blinked against an idea—a last grasp at escape: He'd go to Red for help. Drew would tell him everything; that his wife was crazy, a fucking *loon*. He'd tell Red that Harlow was moving him in against his will, that Andrew wanted nothing to do with it, wanted nothing to do with *her*, that this was all a huge mistake, that what Red had seen in the kitchen—the slow dancing—it had all been her idea. He didn't even know how to dance. And Red would fix it, because he'd literally run Drew out of town. Red was the answer. The guy had to come back sooner or later, at least to grab a couple of shirts or a suitcase for the final move.

"He'll come back," Drew whispered. "And when he does he'll end this whole thing."

Determined to stay up and watch the street for signs of Mickey or Red, exhaustion pulled at Drew's eyelashes. He fought against sleep by walking around, doing his damnedest to stay alert. But he'd hardly slept the night before, and despite his attempt, fatigue was a powerful thing. Sitting on the windowsill, he let his head loll forward enough to press his forehead against the cool glass. He shut his eyes, assuring himself that it would only be for five minutes—just five, to give himself a boost of energy.

He saw himself at the foot of the front steps, the old house on Cedar towering over him like a monolith. It was twice as big as he remembered, its windows slightly off center, the door skewed, inducing vertigo. Each step up to the wraparound porch groaned under his weight. The front door swung open, unassisted, inviting him inside. He hesitated, stopping just beyond the door, inspecting the house he'd left behind. It was all the same—peeling wallpaper, wooden floors scuffed and dirty.

He approached the living room.

The television flickered in a smoky haze, blue light casting garish shadows across the walls. The mess Andrew had made before he left stood silent, illuminated. He stared at it, knowing his mother had cleaned up, but there it was again, haunting him, reminding him of a reaction he had grown to regret. Toeing one of her empty bottles with the tip of his sneaker, he drew near the table, ready to set it upright in its original position.

But his attention was jarred in a different direction. A picture frame slid off the far wall and crashed to the floor. Glass exploded. It tipped forward, falling onto its face, hiding the photograph of his mother, smiling and pretty before his father had left.

Stepping across the room, he squatted next to the frame. A silver key winked at him, taped to its back like a secret. He pulled it away from the frame's backing, held it in the palm of his hand. It shone in the murk, shimmering like a speck of gold in dark water. A creak echoed in the silence—an old kitchen door swinging open, revealing an outline of sunshine: irresistible, beautiful.

In the diffused light of the kitchen, flecks of dust hung suspended like stars. A vase of white daisies sat on a kitchen table, smiling toward the sun. His eyes locked on a woman standing at the counter, a basket of fruit at her elbow, a butcher knife hitting a cutting board with a metronome-like whack. She wore a polka-dotted red dress; the same dress his mother wore to church when he was a boy; the dress that reminded him of cherry sours and trips to the candy shop. She lifted her arm—a slow-motion movement that streaked the air—then brought the knife down, each chop more jarring than the last.

Drew's heart accompanied its repetitive thud.

He took a backward step.

The woman jerked her head up.

Andrew exhaled a gasp.

Her skin was a sickly blue-gray, her eyes and cheeks sunken, her lips peeled away from her gums. She looked as though she had been buried for months, rotting six feet beneath the earth, but he recognized her just the same. And she recognized him too.

His mother canted her head to the side, that knife held upright in her hand, looking at him like a dog inspecting an unfamiliar face, ready to strike.

Her voice came—but those rotten lips did not move. "Andrew. My darling…"

She turned to face him in a series of stops and jerks. Hobbling on invisible strings, she dragged her feet, the knife glinting in her grasp.

"You left me," she wept, mouth still unmoving. "You left me here to die."

Drew backed up, his heart knocking against his ribs. Backed against a wall, he couldn't run, but she continued to drag herself forward, knife held high. He shot a look toward the door. All he had to do was run through it. Run out of the house. Run into the street. Run as fast as he could. Run hard, until his lungs threatened to explode.

She saw his eyes shift, and before he knew it she was sprinting toward him, a ragged, putrescent mouth gaping wide, greasy black hair flying around her skeletal face. Andrew tried to scream, struggled to find his breath.

But it didn't matter.

That knife plunged deep into his chest.

His eyes went wide. He fought for air, gasping like a waterless fish.

"You left me," she said, her eyes wide, her mouth hanging open. "You left me here to die."

He couldn't breathe. Anxiety clutched at his throat. He clawed at his neck, desperate to pull in a breath, screaming inside his head, flailing like a kid being held underwater.

Air finally came with consciousness. His lungs burned; his heart throbbed. Scrambling to his feet, he was determined to get out of there. But the shadow that lurked just beneath the closed bedroom door assured him that Harlow was in the hall, guarding it, playing sentry. He twisted back toward the window instead. Screw waiting; he'd crawl down the side of the house if he had to. But when he threw the curtains aside, he was hit by another fit of panic. The window didn't have a latch. Someone had sealed it up—as though whoever had lived in this room at one point in time had been a prisoner as well.

That was when he lost his grip.

He broke down and wept. He wept for his mother, wept for the past, wept for the fact that somehow, under this roof, nightmares weren't something you could wake up from.

Here, under this roof, the nightmares were real.

CHAPTER SEVENTEEN

Red stood over Mickey's body like a mourner over the dead. A flower of gore had blossomed around Mickey's head, growing like a virus despite his stillness. Mickey Fitch had bitten through his tongue, and if Red hadn't shoved him off the autopsy table, he would have choked on his own blood. Red was as motionless as the body at his feet, unable to tear his eyes away from the damage inflicted at his own hands.

He had done this—but it had been an accident.

He approached the third freezer along the wall, shoved the door open, and stared at the bag inside. Jabbing his arm into the swirling cold, he gave it a yank, momentarily stumbling, surprised at how heavy it was. For all he knew, there was an entire person beneath that plastic sheeting—an entire human being chopped into perfect cubes.

Giving it a stern pull, the bag cleared the lip of the freezer and fell to his feet with a rock-solid thump. He pulled it across the room toward the door that led to Harlow's bunker—the one that connected both properties beneath the tranquility of Magnolia Lane.

He had never been in the tunnel before. At one point, he'd convinced himself that it hadn't actually been built, that the construction workers were building something else—anything but a passageway that would allow his wife to kill with ultimate ease. That illusion was shattered the first time he watched Mickey drag a sheet-wrapped body through their kitchen and down the basement stairs.

Fumbling with the latch on the door with cold fingers, he eventually got it open, only to stare into the darkness that swallowed what lay beyond it. Patting down each cinder-block wall in search of a light switch, he came to a sickening realization: the construction workers had built the tunnel, but they hadn't wired it. But Mickey certainly didn't stumble through the darkness with dead bodies tossed over his shoulder. There had to be a way.

Turning away from the mouth of the passageway—a damp, earthy smell wafting up from it like a scourge—his gaze fell on the orange plastic of a lightbulb safety cage. It hung from beneath one of the counters, a snake of black cord coiled beneath it. There was no way it ran the length of the entire tunnel, but Red was out of options. Unhooking it from its holder, he flipped the thing on, grabbed hold of the plastic bag, and stepped through the door.

§

Andrew rubbed at his eyes as the soft tones of Rosemary Clooney drifted up the staircase and beneath the door. For half a second he couldn't remember how he had gotten into the Wards' guest bedroom; he completely forgot the panic that had seized him the night before. The trumpets, the Cuban vibe, the butter-smooth tone of Clooney's voice—he pictured Harlow downstairs, swaying her hips around the kitchen, twirling across the tile, the skirt of her dress fanning out like the petals of a flower.

In that fleeting moment, he swore that nothing strange had happened here. Everything was fine. Perfect as always.

And then he looked out the window and noticed the sky, thick with clouds, black with rain. The tornado hadn't come, and neither had the answers Drew was desperate for. There was no bolt of inspiration, no affirmation or understanding. He remained lost, and while there wasn't a lock on the outside of the bedroom door, he felt as trapped as ever.

But he had to move. Urged forward by his nerves, he didn't care where that movement took him. He had to get the hell out of there, and he'd bowl Harlow over to do it if he had to.

Still wearing his clothes from the day before, he shoved his bare feet into his sneakers and escaped the room. He took the stairs two by two, but rather than bolting for the door the way he had planned, he hesitated at the base of the staircase.

His gaze immediately moved to the kitchen, Harlow's usual haunt. But the kitchen was empty. Music played—but Harlow wasn't there.

The emptiness was so unexpected that it drew him forward, as if he needed to make sure that his isolation was real.

He turned away, blinking, confused by his sense of disappointment despite his desire to run. He wanted to believe that the hours they had spent apart had brought her to her senses, that she'd come to the realization that what they were doing was insane. He yearned to see apologetic embarrassment drift across the delicate curves of her still-youthful face, longed to hear her confess that she had been wrong, that this was all a silly mistake. He wanted to see the morning sun shine through her hair.

"This is nuts," he whispered. Just a minute ago all he wanted was to find his keys, for his Chevy to rumble to life, but there he was searching for his captor, wondering where she was, worried about where she'd gone.

The light shifted in the living room, as though someone had moved.

Red was sitting in his old recliner.

"Red." The name came out as a croak. "Thank God."

Raising an eyebrow at Andrew's greeting, Red crossed his legs, nudging a black plastic bag behind the far side of his chair with his heel.

"I need your help," Drew told him, each word cracking with dryness. "I…Harlow, she's…"

"Crazy?"

A slow smile spread across Red's mouth, a smile that confirmed that Harlow's insanity wasn't anything new to her husband.

And yet that smile failed to reassure him. Andrew felt a dull throb of dread pulse at the base of his throat.

"She's making me move in. She's having guys come by." His tone was desperate, nearly pleading for Red to save him.

"She's *making* you?" Red smirked, unconvinced. "Like she made you dance with her?"

Drew opened his mouth to protest.

"Like she made you sleep with her? Like she made you tie her up?"

He snapped it closed with a sickening chomp of teeth.

Red squared his shoulders, pushing himself out of his recliner.

"You think I'm stupid? That I haven't noticed the way she stands next to you?" He exhaled an emotionless laugh. "Fat fucking chance, my friend."

"I swear, Red…" The panic was crawling up Drew's throat. "You've got to believe me."

"Oh, I believe you," Red replied. "She's a mystery, isn't she? A heartbreakingly beautiful mystery. But guess what?"

Drew shook his head without reply.

"She's mine. Till death do us part."

Red took a step forward as if to make a move. Andrew lifted his hands in surrender.

"Hey," he said, trying to keep Red at a distance. "I don't want to take her from you, I swear. I want to get *out* of here. Hell, I was going to go look for you. To help me."

"To help you," Red repeated, bemused. "You want to get out of here?" He motioned to the door. "Leave."

Drew stared at the door, unable to help the questions that were clawing at the inside of his skull: Where was Harlow? Was she hurt? Had he tied her up somewhere?

"But you won't," Red said, snapping Drew back to the present. "Because you like it here. Let me guess…" He looked around the living room as if seeing it for the first time—the crisp curtains, the pristine carpeting, the dustless furniture. "It fills some sort of void, right?"

Drew swallowed. His mouth was dry.

"I get it," Red murmured. "I do; seen it a hundred times."

"But I don't want to be—"

"It doesn't matter."

Red took another step forward, his fingers sliding into the pocket of his pants.

"What matters is that *she* wants you here. And that's the problem."

"I'll just leave," Drew told him. "Seriously, I'll just go. Right now."

"But will that take her desire for you away?"

"She was just upset." The words tumbled from Drew's mouth. He struggled for something to say, something to interject some hope into their conversation. "She loves you."

"Does she?"

"She does," he insisted. "She told me so."

Red cracked a smile—and Andrew knew right then that he'd been caught. "That was nice," he said. "I appreciate your attempt to spare my feelings, but it makes me feel a little guilty."

Again, Andrew shook his head as if to say he didn't understand.

"Guilty because I'm not going to spare yours."

Another forward step.

"I don't…really know what—"

"I don't expect you to understand," Red told him. "It's complicated. And it would be pointless anyway."

"Pointless," Drew echoed.

Red's fingers curled around something in his pocket while Andrew stared back at him, wide-eyed.

Time stood still as the blood drained from Drew's face. He could feel it happening—heavy with gravity, failing to travel upward because his heart ceased to beat. The room went horrifyingly silent. The music faded. The wail of the wind fell away. There was nothing but the sound of his own breathing in his ears. He was an astronaut. This wasn't Earth.

He saw the muscles in Red's arm twitch. Somewhere, in the distance, he heard a siren wail. At first, he was sure it was all in his mind—a figment of his imagination, conjured up by his fear—but it was too familiar. It was a sound he'd grown up with, a warning that danger was ahead. Somewhere in Creekside, the clouds had swirled into a cyclone. The tornado had arrived. It was time to take cover.

His gaze snagged on the safety scalpel in Red's hand.

He blinked as Red slid the blade out of its plastic cover, unable to process what he was seeing. This wasn't real. He was dreaming again, asleep on the windowsill. That was why Harlow wasn't here.

"What is that?" he asked, knowing full well what it was—a weapon, something Red was going to use to do something unspeakable to his wife.

"What, this?" Red lifted the scalpel as if to inspect it for himself. "Just something I found next door."

Andrew shook his head. What the hell would Mickey do with a scalpel, and how would Red have been inside Mick's place anyway? Red must have meant another neighbor. Maybe that was where he'd been staying, getting up the courage to come back and get his stuff—or to do what he was doing now, which Drew still couldn't put together. His mind was rebelling against what it knew was true.

"I don't know where Harlow is," Drew confessed. "But you can't do this."

Red canted his head to the side, apparently listening to Drew try to reason his way out of the situation.

"She didn't mean anything," he continued. "Just…don't hurt her."

Red stared ahead blankly. And then he burst into laughter.

Andrew blanched with realization.

That scalpel wasn't meant for Harlow. It was meant for him.

His nerves hissed and snapped. He made his move.

He lurched forward, dodging Red as he ran for the front door. His sockless feet felt loose in his shoes, as though his feet had shrunk by two sizes. His hands flew out in front of him like frightened birds, slamming against the front door. He fought with the lock, but in his panic, it wouldn't open.

Veering around with his back to the door, he stared at the man before him.

"I just want you to know that I'm sorry," Red told him, a strange sincerity crossing his face. "I've never done this before. But a man's gotta do what a man's—"

"—gotta do," Drew whispered.

Red vaulted forward. Andrew swerved to the right, but Red guessed correctly and the blade bit into Drew's shoulder. Stumbling away from the door, Andrew pressed the palm of his hand to his wound, the blood warm against his skin. He blinked in disbelief, perplexed that Red had actually gone through with it, that he actually cut him, that this was real. Instead of running, he stared at the man who had so cheerfully given him a job.

And then the needle on the record skipped. Rosemary's voice began to warble, the storm siren wailed outside—and reality finally hit him.

Andrew watched blood flow down the length of his arm, detour into his palm, and drip in time with the record's skip— the first drop devastating the perfection of the room, the second ravaging the idea of the wonderful life he wanted so badly to be a part of.

How could they do this to him? They were supposed to be flawless—amid the flat Kansas landscape, this was supposed to be Oz.

Red hesitated, as though considering his own treachery. For half a second, Andrew wondered whether he would change his mind, whether he'd realize that he was out of control. Red wasn't genuinely intending to kill him, was he? No. That was impossible.

But Red lurched forward again, and Drew was forced into motion. As he turned to run, his shin caught the edge of the coffee table. He tumbled, spilling Harlow's candlescape onto the floor, taking a couple of issues of *Good Housekeeping* and the remote control with him. He groped at the rug with bloodied hands as Red bolted toward him. Frantic, Andrew searched for something to throw. Catching hold of one of the candles, he reeled back, ready to defend himself with little more than a pillar of scented wax, but it was startled from his hand when a deafening crack rang in his ears.

Red froze in place, staring forward, before extending his arms as if in apology. And then, just as Andrew realized what that crack had been—a gunshot, a fucking *gunshot*—he was shoved aside from behind, and Harlow hurtled toward her dazed husband with a guttural scream.

§

The gunshot made him twitch—an involuntary spasm of muscles before the pain set in. He rolled onto his stomach and exhaled an animal groan; strands of white hair tinged a gruesome scarlet; his nose, mouth, and chin coated in gore.

Mickey Fitch had woken up, looking like he had eaten his captor alive.

§

Harlow watched Andrew scurry toward the kitchen as she lunged ahead. Grabbing a metal candlestick off the mantel, she marched toward her bleeding husband, Red's hand pressed over the bullet wound that had pierced his chest. Red was doing the same thing Drew was—using his legs to push himself away, his free hand keeping him upright, his expression a peculiar mix of terror and expectation. But there was no surprise on his face. She had warned him. He had to have known it would come to this.

"So this is it?" Red asked, breathless. "After all this time, you just replace me? With *him*, Harlow? A kid?"

Seeing the corner of the plastic bag peeking out from behind Red's recliner, Harlow hesitated.

"You think he'll understand you the way I do?" Red asked her.

But Harlow was distracted. Could it have been? Had Red really dismembered their long-faithful servant the way she'd asked? Her heart swelled at the thought of it. She pressed a palm to her chest.

"Oh, *Red*," she whispered, turning her eyes back to her husband. "Why didn't you tell me?" she asked with a shake of the head, her soft hair bobbing around her cheeks. "If you had just *told* me." She would have shot him anyway. But it was nice to think that Red had a change of heart, that he had done away with Mickey to keep her secret safe.

But the tenderness between them was fleeting, cut short by Andrew wobbling to his feet on the other side of the room. The sight of her injured beau pushed the affection for her husband from her heart, replacing it with a pang of indignation, of purest pitched hate.

"Were you looking for extra credit, Red?"

Despite his shortness of breath, he forced a smile.

"Gold star, baby." He closed his eyes, swaying where he sat.

§

Andrew's eyes went wide as the candlestick streaked through the air above Harlow's head. It arced downward, its corner meeting the ridge of Red's brow, sinking into the hollow of his eye socket, soft tissue muffling its strike. An elegant fan of blood sprayed outward, misting the carpet, the closest wall, and the woman who stood over him.

And then, to Drew's horror, she pried that candlestick out of the pulp and pulled back again. The wet thud of Red's death rang in his ears. Too terrified to move, he watched Harlow demolish her husband's skull, collapsing onto her knees as she hammered away, each swing accompanied by a strangled cry.

§

Mickey's shoulder hit the wall as he tried to gain his balance. His head throbbed like a pulsating star, each palpitation rattling his teeth, each beat assuring him that his brain was about to explode. He stumbled through the dim hallway, caught himself on the frame of Drew's bedroom door, left a bloody handprint on the wall before pushing forward, stumbling headlong toward his room.

§

Caked in blood and bits of flesh, the candlestick fell from Harlow's hands and thumped against the carpet. Bent over the wreckage that was Red's body, she wept into her hands. Her shoulders shook with each sob, each cry creeping closer to hysteria, each weep a veritable scream—her cries mimicking the screaming inside Andrew's head.

Drew turned away from the sight of her, the sight of *him*, laid out like some highway accident. He rushed into the kitchen, covering his mouth with a hand to keep himself from scream-ing, from vomiting, from exhaling a devastated wail. He nearly tripped over a spilled paper bag of groceries. Fruits and vege-tables were scattered across the floor next to Harlow's purse, a shopping list lying on the ground next to the gun she'd shot Red with. He blinked at the list, Harlow's perfect script etched into the paper; her confidence that Andrew wasn't planning to leave her, that they had a bright future together, was written out in careful loops.

His eyes darted across the kitchen to the door leading into the garage. All he had to do was make a run for it. He'd bolt into the street and scream for help; he'd stumble onto the side-walk before running as fast as he could, run until he was back on Cedar Street, standing in front of his disheveled childhood home—not perfect, but better than this.

He stepped forward, grabbed the gun off the floor—and nearly screamed when Harlow caught him by the wrist, her bloodstained fingers slick on his skin. Reeling backward, he tore his arm from her grasp, tripping over his own feet as he stumbled along the cabinets, desperate to put distance between them.

Harlow's expression seesawed between devastation and resentment. And when he pointed the gun at her with a shaky hand, resentment bloomed into full-blown heartbreak.

Harlow couldn't believe it. The two of them had made a connec-tion; Drew knew what she was going through. And yet there he stood, pointing her own gun at her, scared out of his mind. She had wanted him because they were both broken. He made her happy, made her feel like the girl she used to be. But the moment he saw how broken she really was, he turned on her. The boy she was sure she could love, who could potentially fix her, if only for a little while, was trembling in front of her like a leaf in the wind, utterly terrified.

"Are you going to shoot me?" she asked, her words unsteady with emotion. "*Me*, Andy? You're going to kill me?"

She looked back to the living room, her eyes glistening with tears. She had made a mistake. Red *had* been the one, and she'd killed him.

Everything was ruined. Andrew had turned her against her husband. He had manipulated her. He had pretended he cared, won her heart, and tricked her into pushing Red away. And now, at the moment of reckoning, the moment he should have stepped up to the plate and taken her hand in understanding, he was going to shoot her instead.

She narrowed her eyes at the kitchen counter, remembering all the meals she'd made for him, how sweet she'd been. He would have been dead days ago if she had wanted him to be, but she'd kept the little shit alive—and for what? He was just like Isaac. Spoiled. Unappreciative. Selfish. Her fingers wrapped around the hilt of a carving knife, pulling it from its block.

When the stormy light gleamed off the knife blade, Andrew's heart came to a stop. Harlow's white dress was spattered with red, like polka dots—the gory opposite of his mother's church dress. Harlow's typically buoyant hair hung limp around her face, wet and slick with crimson. The knife winked in the filtered sunlight, and in his panic, Drew could see specks of dust through the air like tiny stars. His dream had all but predicted this scene; all that was left was for that knife blade to plunge into his chest.

She lunged at him.

He exhaled a tortured yell, pulling the trigger. He felt a metallic click beneath the pressure of his grip, but there was no ear-splitting gunshot. He pulled again, Harlow nearly on him now, but it didn't shoot. The damn thing was empty. She had used the last bullet to save Andrew's life—only to kill him herself.

Drew scrambled backward, tripping over his feet. The gun slid across the floor while Harlow hovered over him, that knife held high over her head.

And then, the sound of a shotgun being cocked.

Mickey Fitch stood in the doorway leading to the basement.

Andrew's eyes widened. Mickey looked as though he'd torn out someone's jugular with his teeth—a vampire rising from the basement of a house he didn't belong in.

Harlow veered around. "Mickey," she said, Drew's stomach turning at the relief in her tone. "Get busy. It's time to work."

She dropped the knife in the sink and stepped to the side, exposing Andrew to the barrel of Mickey's gun. Mick narrowed his eyes at the boy on the floor while Drew's heart thudded in his throat.

Andrew's head spun. So that was it, then—they worked together. That was how Harlow had known so much; that was why Mickey didn't seem to have a day job. Because he housed Harlow's victims. He held on to them for her until she was ready to strike.

"Don't," Drew said. "Mick, please."

"Shut up," Harlow snapped, looking back to her employee. "What are you waiting for?"

Mickey aimed the gun and fired.

Drew threw his hands over his head, a garbled scream erupting from his throat. He waited for the pain, for the blood, for death to grasp him by the throat and choke the last breath from his body. But when the buckshot failed to bite into his flesh, he opened his eyes.

Harlow swayed where she stood, staring at Mickey's bloodied face, the tremor of the gunshot gently rocking her back and forth. Her eyes were wide, her expression dazzled.

"You," she said, her mouth curling up in a ghostly smile. "Don't forget who your boss is."

She tipped forward, didn't extend her arms—and hit the ground.

Mickey stepped over her body with an unsteady stride. He extended a hand to Andrew, but Drew scrambled away, terrified by the monster that stood before him. He jumped to his feet, backing away from this perversion of his childhood friend.

He opened his mouth to say something, *anything*, but there were no words.

Mickey attempted to speak, but all he managed to do was expel a river of blood down his already gory chin.

"Oh God, Mick," he said. "Oh Jesus, what…?"

Mickey mutely shook his head, motioning for Drew to get out of there.

"But you need help," Drew insisted. "I can't—"

Mickey cut him off midsentence by cocking his gun and pointing it square at Andrew's chest. He nodded to the door, and this time Drew didn't hesitate. He backed up, his palms out in surrender, staring at his bloodied roommate for a second longer before turning around and running.

Running straight for home as hard as he could.

He didn't stop, even when he heard the third gunshot explode behind him.

§

He ran into the rain for an eternity, but the house on Cedar Street was finally in front of him. The steps sagged, the mailbox sat crookedly in the ground; the curtains on the front windows hung as limp as they ever did. Collapsing onto his hands and knees, Andrew wanted to weep grateful tears at its disarray. It was still there. It hadn't disappeared, hadn't been swallowed by a tornado the way he'd hoped so many times.

Staggering up the front steps, he shoved the front door open and stepped into its murky dimness. The television flickered in hues of blue. The coffee table he'd overturned before he had left was clear—nothing but a couple of mugs dotting its otherwise pristine surface—but the uncharacteristic cleanliness of the living room hardly registered. His mother's bare feet hung over the edge of the sofa, and for a moment he was sure she was dead.

"Mom." The word cracked the silence of the room as he lurched toward the couch. "Mom, I'm home."

His bloodied hands hit the arm of the sofa as he leaned forward, dizzy from his run, numbed by the gory images stamped onto his memory, weak with fear.

Julie Morrison sat up with a start when her son crawled over the arm of the couch and into her arms. As soon as she moved, he curled into her the way he used to as a child, clinging to her as he hid his face against her shoulder.

"My God," she said, "Drew." She pushed him away to get a better look at him. "Oh my God, Drew!" she repeated, seeing the wound on his shoulder. "What happened?" she asked, jumping to her feet.

"Nothing," he told her, only coming to realize that he was crying when his breath hitched in his throat.

"What do you— *Nothing?* You need to go to the hospital."

Looking up at her from the couch, he saw nothing but deliverance. Her hair was disheveled, her cheek crosshatched with an impression of the sofa's upholstery—but this was his mother: broken but perfect.

He reached out to her, but she turned away. His heart sank, sobs tearing themselves free from the depths of his soul. She was rejecting him; she didn't want him back.

"Andrew." Her voice sounded far away. His shoulder stung when she shook him. He blinked past his tears, her slippered feet planted on the floor in front of him, the hem of a coat brushing the ankles of her sweats. "We have to go," she said, catching him by the arm.

"What?" He stumbled to his feet, confused.

"We have to go," she repeated. "You need help."

Guiding him to the front door, she hesitated as he wobbled onto the porch. He looked back at her, still unable to comprehend what was happening. Was she kicking him out? But rather than slamming the door in his face, Julie Morrison took a steadying breath and stepped over the threshold of her front door.

He watched her push past her fear, astonished by the sight.

"Everything is going to be OK," she reassured him, catching his hand in hers.

He didn't know how true that was, but it didn't matter. He nodded anyway. Following her down the porch steps, she looked back at him, bewildered.

"Where's your truck?"

"I don't—I left it…"

But rather than going back inside, she squeezed his hand and pulled him toward the sidewalk, leading the way.

This was an emergency.

The neighbors would help.

ACKNOWLEDGMENTS

As usual, many thanks go out to an army of people, without whom *The Neighbors* wouldn't have been possible. To the folks at Amazon, you're all amazing. Without you and your constant reassurance, I'd probably have died of a heart attack by now. To my agent, David, thanks for reading my novel-length e-mails, for holding my hand in the streets of Manhattan, for introducing me to "the big boys," and for making me feel like your favorite author and only client. I'm determined to overstep my nemesis and win *all* of your gushing shortly. To Tiffany, my superstar content editor, you've ruined me. Your direct uplink into my brain is a scary thing. How did I ever live without you? To my friends and family, thank you for the constant encouragement and unwavering confidence that this crazy writing thing is going to work out. To my husband, Will, without you, I would have never made it this far. I love you. And finally, to the readers who have cheered me on since the early days of *Seed*, you guys are awesome. Stories are nothing if they aren't read and loved. Thank you for giving life to my work.

ABOUT THE AUTHOR

Photo by Ania Ahlborn

Born in Ciechanów, Poland, Ania Ahlborn is also the author of the supernatural thriller *Seed*, and is currently working on her third novel. She earned a bachelor's degree in English from the University of New Mexico, enjoys gourmet cooking, baking, drawing, traveling, movies, and exploring the darkest depths of the human (and sometimes inhuman) condition. She lives in Albuquerque, New Mexico, with her husband and two dogs.